~ Junia ~

By Mercedes Prunty

Hope you enjoy x

Junia

Copyright ©: Mercedes Prunty

Published: 7th March 2017

Publisher: Mercedes Prunty

Other titles by Mercedes Prunty:

In the Alone series:

*Alone

*Lone

* The Keeper of the Key

* Junia

Why not check out Mercedes Prunty on:

Facebook : Mercedes Prunty Author

Twitter : @MercedesPrunty

Blog: www.mercedespruntyauthor.wordpress.com

For everyone who believes that
Magic is real. .x.x.x.x.

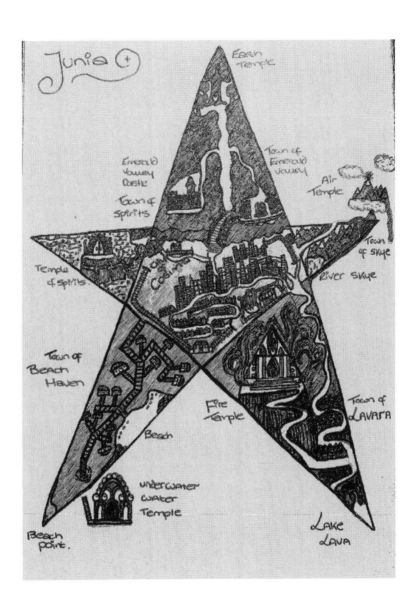

Junia

Earth Temple

Emerald Valley Castle
Town of Spirits
Temple of Spirits

Town of Emerald Valley
Air Temple
Town of Skye
River Skye

Town of Beach Haven
Beach
Fire Temple
Town of Lavara

Underwater Water Temple
Beach Point.
Lake Lava

~ Dark Paradise ~

The palace was alive with noise, a steady thumping and crashing sound which vibrated through all the walls and echoed achingly through my bones, strangling my throat so I couldn't make a sound. I made my way through the crumbling building that I was so familiar with, my heart hammering through my chest as I made a dash for it trying to get to my own private security chamber, which was located on the same floor as my personal bed chamber but this one was reinforced, it was a panic room that I could run to when things went wrong and tonight things had gone extremely wrong.

The noise had awoken me about an hour ago but through fear and I suppose stupidity I froze, hidden under my bed until I hoped help would arrive, one of the palace guards in emergency situations were meant to come and escort me to my security chamber hidden within the palace but no one had come, too busy fighting off whatever was happening on the outside and sounding like it had also made its way inside.

A while in time had passed me by and I knew I had to do something, I felt enough courage to crawl out from under my bed like a frightened little mouse and ran to the wardrobe door grabbing my dressing gown to cover my cold bare shoulders, I didn't want to be caught by heathens in my nightgown. I had walked to my door with sweaty palms followed by sharp shallow breaths as I had no idea what to expect, my toes wriggled on the bouncy soft carpet that flowed through out my room and I had to resist the urge to run back under my four poster bed and cry.

"Pull yourself together", I told myself scrunching my hands into fists and digging my nails into my hot damp palms, I knew I might draw blood but it helped stable my nerves, enough to make me grasp the handle of my door and turn it, slowly pulling the door open and peering out. My face lost in the dusty gloom of the grand hallway that was normally filled with light and laughter, I felt lost and so small and a bit like a sitting duck just waiting for someone or something to jump out of the gloom.

Taking a small step out of my comfort zone I nearly screamed out loud as a voice wheezed through the dust, "Lady Mira? Why are you not in your security chamber?"

The voice belonged to one of the guards and by the way his voice rasped breathlessly and how the dust clung to his uniform which was gelled with blood I knew he was in a bad way, "Mr Sampson what's happened, your hurt?"

He coughed before answering, "Someone's attacking the palace, we can't hold them off…You need to get to safety Lady Mira".

I nodded, "Ok, I'll go but not without you", I leant down and tried to lift him up my hands shaking feverishly.

"What are you doing?" he asked me shocked.

"You need help, there will be supplies in my chamber that can help you", I told him but he shrugged me off.

"No Lady Mira you must go alone I will only hold you back…" he was cut off by a howl that turned my blood cold, it sounded animal not like the human invasion I thought was happening, humans don't have that sound to their throats, "Go Lady Mira go now!" He lifted his palace issue pistol and aimed it the direction the howl had come from, I watched as his eyes widened, "Run now".

I done as he said and took off down the corridor away from the howling thing behind me, I heard the gun go off twice before it all fell silent. I didn't look but I just kept running, my bare feet slapping on the marble floor, occasionally a bit of gravel or dirt would stab into my sole but I had to keep moving, that noise scared the hell out of me and I wasn't about to stop to see what it was.

Finally I made it to my private chamber, the only way in was to put my hand over a security panel so it knew it was me, the seconds ticked by like hours as the device scanned my prints. Another howl ripped through the air and I cried out for it to hurry, *these seconds shouldn't take this long.* A bleeping sound indicated I had passed the security check and the secret door flew open, it was disguised by a huge oil painting of one my ancestors, *what would they think of me now? Running away in terror.* Rushing inside I turned to shut the door and let out a small scream, a beast was running towards my open door, its eyes were blood red and it had the longest fangs I had ever seen, it ran like a hound but howled like a blood thirsty creature. Crying out I shoved the door as hard as I could my feet slipping on the marble floor, the beast gaining on me every second, my heart screaming in my chest, "COME ON!" I screamed and gave a final push and the door slammed shut locking out the beast.

I leant back on the door sobbing and slid down it, I could hear the thing outside scratching and howling to get inside but the door was sealed and it would be for the next twelve hours. I had twelve hours to wait to see if someone would come to my rescue or whether I would die down here on my own, a frightened little girl.

~

"Lady Mira is that you?"

A lone woman's voice asked waking me from my troubled slumber, looking up I felt happiness erupt through my whole body, it was Freya my personal maid. She looked tired and filthy her clothes torn and covered in dust and grime, big black bags sat under her eyes and her hair was so dishevelled she looked like a tramp who had just walked in off the streets.

"Lady Mira thank Junia you are ok", she smiled running to me and holding me tight, I held her back and snuggled into her shoulder.

"What happened Freya?" I asked her, her eyes gave everything away, she had bad news.

"Something terrible happened last night Lady Mira, we were attacked, many say by the Anti-Religious group the *Junia Rebellion* but I don't think they done this, this was different and powerful. They only stand to prove a point they don't kill but people died last night and I feared you were one of them", she shook as she spoke remembering all of the events she had witnessed, I placed my hand on her shoulder to comfort her but I knew it wasn't doing much, my hand was as of much comfort as a fluffy kittens.

Suddenly a thought occurred to me, "There was a guard outside of my room, I heard shots is he ok?"

Freya shook her head, "No Mr Sampson is one of the dead, his soul has moved on with the others to *Spirit* now".

"Oh, I'm sorry to hear that, he was a nice guy, saved my life", I felt a little numb inside, he had died to save me.

She nodded, "That is what they are trained for my lady".

Her words hit me making me feel a huge sense of guilt, the guards that had died done so to save myself and my parents, the royal family of Junia. They were trained to protect us but where not permitted to protect themselves, they had sworn an oath that in the event of danger our lives where the ones that mattered not theirs. It made me feel sick.

"What of my parents? Are they safe in their private chamber?"

Freya once again shook her head, "They have been taken".

"Taken? By whom may I ask?" Panic was rising inside me now, who could have taken them?

The maid before me shrugged, "No one knows, most believe the rebellion is behind it but they of course disagree, I for one do not believe they would do such a drastic and horrific thing but I assure you my lady the palace guards are on the case, they will find whomever did this hideous crime", she held my shoulder now as if to reassure me, I felt the hot bubble of emotions rise to the surface and the tears began to fall uncontrollably from my eyes, rolling down my cheeks like the open flood gates of Beach Haven.

"So what now?" I sobbed.

"We need to get you dressed to address the nation, as the only royal family member left I'm afraid that duty is left to you".

"I can't talk to the people without my parents here, I'm fifteen I cannot be a stand in Queen", I sounded horrified and I was even by my standards which were pretty low as everything scared me but going on live telly and addressing all the people of my kingdom? *This was something I definitely couldn't do.*

"Yes ma'am you are only fifteen but teenager or not the nation needs a voice and yours is the one they need to hear. We need to tell them what has happened here and what we as the palace plan to do about it. Now come on we need to get you dressed you cannot address your people in your grubby night clothes now can you?"

An hour later I sat shaking in my personal bedroom which too had been destroyed to a certain degree, the large windows that gave me a sweeping view of Cosima had been obliterated, glass and bits of rubble sat where my four poster bed had been last night, which I had at one point been hiding underneath but all that was left of it now were a few chunks of the dark wood which it had been hand crafted from. Freya was adding the last few final touches to me before we were to be called to the throne room which the staff were desperately trying to clean up so things didn't look so bad to the audience I was about to address.

Freya had dressed me up in one of my mother's dresses which was of course Royal Red which matched my Royal Red hair, in the centre between my collar bone and my waist embroidered in gold was the emblem of Cosima which would stand out to the people. White frills decorated the top of the dress around the neckline and around the sleeves of the arms which were long and trailed down to my wrists flaring out around my pale shaking hands. The dress fell well past my feet and a long flowing train flowed out behind me but she had assured me that once sitting on the throne it would look every bit as regal as it should. She had set my hair up into pin curls tying the back up with pins and letting a few loose strands curl their way down my neck, lastly came my mother's ruby set tiara which she lay perfectly in place on my hair. My makeup was minimal but made me look older than what I was, Freya told me that it would settle people's doubts about me and their nerves if they thought I was older and more mature especially if my parents didn't return and I had to take over the role of Queen.

I had of course been trained my whole life for the point when I would become Queen, in the hope that the transition would be easy, *but what was easy about becoming the next Queen of Cosima and the whole of*

Junia? And never once did I think when I was fifteen I would have to sit on my mother's throne in her place, the throne was a big deal, it was forbidden for anyone but the Queen and King to sit on them but here I was about to go and plop my young butt on it and try and look and act like someone I wasn't.

I had imagined my life would go smoothly like my mother's had before me, I had known I would go to the *'College of Fine Arts'* and study hard and come away with a degree that I would never use but would give me some form of realism that I could achieve something, that the future Queen wasn't just a dosser but a hard worker too. I had imagined making friends at the College and to party, those friends like my mother had previously done before me would become my own ladies in waiting if they accepted the invitation and that invitation was not to be sniffed at, they got their own rooms, money to spend and all they had to do was be my friend and keep me entertained when needed but more importantly they would become the people I could trust the most. I had looked forward to that, that had been the only thing keeping me sane within these large cold stone walls, for the life of the princess of Junia was a grand but lonely one, I had no real friends other than my parents and Freya, I was not allowed out to venture around the kingdom I would one day rule over, it wasn't safe for the princess to be out of the palace without a large entourage of soldiers due to the Junia Rebellion group and then that gave a hard impression for people to want to get friendly with me.

"We are ready", a dark haired maid said appearing from beside my broken door, I looked behind her to where

Mr Sampson had laid the night before his blood still clung to the stonework and the dust that filled the marbled floor. My heart bled for him and all the people who lost their lives, *why did it happen?*

Freya helped me up and lifted the train of the dress so as to not dirty it on the way to the throne room, my shoes luckily where flats just in the royal red which Cosima associated with the royal household but it also meant I would be able to walk without breaking my neck. As I entered the throne room the place fell silent, a few gasps left the maids mouths and the guards all bowed out of habit, I looked around at the room which luckily hadn't taken too much of a hit, a few cracks in the walls and some rubble scooped into one corner but mostly not too broken. Freya led me to the throne which loomed in on me, I felt my mouth go dry and my palms clamed up with sweat.

"Just relax Lady Mira", Freya soothed as she helped me take the seat, she fiddled with my dress so it framed me perfectly but it couldn't hide how much I was shaking, "Take deep breathes and let them out slowly".

I done as she said and tried to take control of my breathing but my nerves still screamed wildly at me, soon a camera was pointed in my face and Mr Philippe Goole the palace camera man and interviewer was talking me through all what I needed to say, how I needed to act. "Hold your head high, show no fear, you can pretend to the nation that all is fine, all is in control. You can do this!" He also whispered to me that if I didn't the whole kingdom could go into a panic and a frenzy of riots could manifest. I needed to crack this first time round which made my nerves spike up to a whole new level of fear. He soon began to count me down, "5, 4, 3, 2, 1 and you're on".

The royal anthem that usually played on special occasions when one of my parents were giving a speech sounded out around the room along with Mr Philippe speaking into a microphone to announce that it was me and that I was about to address them all, "Her majesty the grand Princess of Cosima Lady Mira".

I took a deep breath and looked at Freya who smiled and gently flowed her hands out to make me remember to let go of my breath, I then turned to the camera lens and hoped that I didn't muck this up, "Hello to my people of Junia, it is my duty to tell you all of the events that have unfolded at the palace". *Breathe!* "Late last night we were attacked by an unknown force and I'm afraid to tell you that the King and Queen, my beloved parents have been kidnapped. We ask you not to panic and to stay vigilant if you see or hear of anything please contact your local guard. We are doing our best here to find out what has happened and as soon as I know I will report to you. We will find our dear King and Queen and they will soon be back where they belong, here with me…"

Suddenly a strange flapping noise erupted through the room and I spotted a screen at the other end which the guards were watching the nations address on showing my confused face and then breaking up and coming back to a flickering, smoky image.

"Hello dear citizens of Junia, I am the one who has your precious King and Queen", the voice belonged to a woman and sounded like velvet as it rippled through the sound system around me, the woman stood there smiling at the screen like she had just won the Junia money pot, she wore her hair thick, long and dark trailing down her back, her face was pale and dazzled the screen as if it was made of diamonds, she wore a strange get up of feathers but she looked mean and the glint in her dark eyes told me that she was evil. *I wanted to cry, to run up to the screen and demand she give me my parents back but what would that achieve? Nothing.* I had to play this cool like I had been taught, I had to show her no fear. Then she spoke again, "I am the grand dark witch Andromeda and I am going to be keeping hold of your royal chess pieces until I get what I desire".

I bit my lip and felt a tremble shiver through my body but luckily the camera was on her but my voice needed to sound strong, I needed to sound brave, "And what is it you desire, Andromeda? My parents are not simple game pieces, we wish for their safe return."

"Ah Princess Mira missing mummy and daddy are we?" she taunted me but I tried to keep my cool.

"What is it you desire?" I repeated.

She laughed a deep and spine tingling cackle, "I desire all the elements of the countries so I can unlock the final element soul".

"I'm sorry I don't understand?" I said back to the screen.

"Oh dear people of Junia did you hear that? Your soon to be Queen doesn't know of the element souls and what they can do, does she even know about the religion of Junia which our beloved world was born with?", she taunted me, showing me up on how naïve I was, how I hadn't been taught about the religion because the royal household and the capital city of Cosima didn't believe in the religion, we banned it from our country a hundred or so years ago during the great war.

"I know of the religion of Junia but as the new age royal family we do not practice it and no longer support the religion due to the difficulties of the past war", I replied, I knew a little about what had happened all those years ago, how the people of Cosima demolished the religion of Junia from its streets due to Cosima not having its own magical element so they didn't feel the need to be a part of the religion, they wanted to be free from prayer and stepped away which caused conflict in the temples and a war between the religious countries and Cosima broke out. Thousands died on both sides but eventually the temples backed off and left Cosima to it, left us to worship our nothingness. I had to admit I had heard of the element souls once before, my mother had said something about them but didn't repeat it when I asked what they were. So I had no real clue as to what they were.

"Difficulties of the past war? Do you even know what you are saying little girl? All the countries in your kingdom still worship the religion of Junia all except Cosima, the difficulty is the royal family, the difficulty is Cosima and the difficulty is people like you. And with the final element soul I wish to restore what is lost to Cosima and dispose of the people who try to force the so called modern hand", She said strongly.

"Restore what is lost? Dispose of the people? Are my parents even still alive?" I asked.

She howled with laughter which made me less scared and more angry, I could feel it bubble up inside but I held my tongue, I didn't want to say something that might push her to hurt them if they were still alive, "They are for now but I can't tell you how long for, especially if I do not get what I want".

"Then why should I give you what you want if you will kill them anyway?"

"Because you don't know what will happen. You will give me what I want because there is the hope that they are still well and alive. You couldn't possibly not do it, not if there is that chance", she chuckled, she swung her camera sideways and I could see two blurry shapes in the background, I could make them out anywhere and anytime, they were indeed my parents but I knew the nation would struggle to see who it was, "I want all the element souls by the setting sun on the day before the eclipse in two weeks' time or I'm afraid you will not see them again, dead or alive". And she blinked out, the screen came back to my dumbstruck face.

For a moment I sat there not knowing what to say or do, I could see Freya's hands urging me to say something, then it came out, "You heard her people, she wants to scare us and force a further divide between the royal family and those of you who practice the religion, do not let her words force your hand. Do not hand over the element souls to her you do not know what it is she wishes to use them for, we will find the King and Queen and we will become a United Kingdom once again", I said trying to sound believable.

With that Mr Philippe pulled the plug and the screen went blank, I took a deep long breath and let it out, my whole body trembled with adrenaline.

Freya smiled and came over with some water for me to sip, "You did very well my lady".

"Yes you did brilliantly, other than the whole united kingdom thing that will never happen but I'm sure the people who watched won't have noticed that", Mr Philippe added, "Now all we have to do is wait and see if any information will come in", he wondered off and began talking to some of the guards.

I just stayed where I was and stared at Freya and she knew what was coming, "My lady we do not practice the religion here in Cosima you know that and it would be treason against the King and Queen if I was to discuss anything about it or how to find out about it with you".

"I don't want to know about the religion as such Freya, just the element souls, I need to know what they are if I am to be able to have any chance to find my parents and bring them back", I replied.

"I cannot discuss them with you either, I could risk execution if I tell you anything that might cause you to revert to the religion", she told me and she look worried just telling me this simple answer of no.

"There must be someone who can and will be willing to tell me, I need to know what they are and why she wants them. I am after all acting Queen in my parent's absence so I can take it as my responsibility so they would understand".

"Sorry Lady Mira but there is no one in the palace I know of who would be willing to risk their life to tell you of the religion", her tone sounded flat and I knew she was lying but she walked off anyway knowing staying with me would mean I would only keep badgering her, "There has to be someone", I whispered.

I sulked off out the throne room on my own and started to wonder the palace taking it all in, my mind whirred with hundreds of questions none of which could be answered because the people who needed to answer them were not here. Racking my brains I tried desperately to think of something and then an idea struck me, the palace library, there were thousands of books in there and even a restricted section I was not allowed in alone but with the palace in the state it was in would there be any guards on duty? *Only one way to find out I suppose.* I thought to myself.

The library was deathly quiet and like I had hoped not a guard was in sight, the library was a mess just like the rest of the palace, bullet holes had torn down whole sections of shelves shredding them to tissue paper, blasts from something I could not explain had burnt holes into the heavy duty stonework and claw marks lined the marble floor. I stepped carefully over the piles of books which littered my path to the restricted section. I passed a broken atlas ball which showed the whole of Junia, the pentacle star shape which held all the countries of our world together looked strange going round an orb shape, most maps I studied were flat and I didn't get much of a glimpse of anything other than Cosima itself, most of the other countries had been written off. I knew that the other countries still had access in parts to Cosima to gain entry to the other countries but no outsiders ever stayed here.

The restricted section was dark, a dusty gloom had settled over everything and even the chain that showed where I could normally access up to was snapped and in a pile on the floor. I stepped over it carefully checking behind me every so often in case a guard or maid passed by and noticed me rummaging where I shouldn't be.

I traced my finger over the spines of many books as I made my way further into the gloom, my eyes slowly adjusted and I could make out the gold lettering of the names of the leather bound books none of which caught my eye or threatened to tell me anything, that was until I made it to the second to last book on the middle shelf, *'Junia: The magic of the elements and their history'*, I swallowed hard and noticed how dry my mouth had become walking around in here, partly due to the dust residue and partly down to my nerves which were causing me to shake, this was so irresponsible of me to be in here but I needed to know.

Opening the first page I scanned a few lines but nothing made any sense until I turned to chapter three and a picture jumped out at me, it was of a strange bird like beast covered in flames and the caption *'Fire Element Soul'* sat below it. I scanned the page opposite and began to fall into the book, the words jumping out at me like the picture had.

'The Elemental Souls are the BE all and END all of each element, each element has a soul, FIRE, WATER, AIR, EARTH and SPIRIT. These souls are made from hundreds of souls and they contain all the POWER to keep their chosen COUNTRIES alive with power, their power flows through Cosima giving it energy and life through ancient fault lines. For instance the Elemental Soul of Fire resides in LAVARA hidden deep in its depths and it keeps the flames and lava alive so the people have granite and coal

to mine, the FIRE element burns through into COSIMA giving it heat but it also flows through to the other countries either DIRECTLY or INDIRECTLY...'.

I paused thinking, so all the countries had an Elemental Soul except for Cosima which I had known in a way as we had no magic of our own to wield but it now really become more of a truth as I read it. Cosima had no power of its own to use we had to channel power from each of the other countries, so now I knew there were powerful fault lines that ran under the city joining together at each country but also as I read on there were a few manmade fault lines which connected in the middle and I knew in the middle of Cosima was the power station which fuelled everything we needed from hover cars, to trains and electric and heat for our buildings. *But why didn't we have an Element soul of our own? And why was it such a problem to the people of Cosima back in the day? And why are the other countries still allowing us to take power from them if they hated us so much and we hate them?* I still had more questions and no answers, I needed to find out more, looking down I went to read on but a shadow loomed over me. I gulped and slowly turned to see a guard standing behind me.

"Hey look I'm only here to try and find out information, I need to help my parents!" I stated but he ignored me.

"Come with me", was all he said and he walked off out of the library.

"Hey wait", I ran after him keeping hold of the book, "Wait look I know I was in the restricted section but you should understand that..."

He put his hand over my mouth, "Do you want to get me killed?"

I shook my head confused.

His cool blue eyes glared into mine, "Then keep it shut I'm trying to help you, Freya sent me".

"Freya…"

He lifted his finger to his lips to stop me talking then he turned on his heel and headed off down the corridor, his uniform was dirtied from the night before and his thick ash blond hair was hung down by the weight of the dust and grime. He turned a corner and headed up a flight of stairs and I tried my best in my mother's long flowing gown to keep up. He reached the entrance to my own security chamber and ushered me to unlock the door with my royal hand.

"Um won't we be trapped in here for twelve hours?" I asked him doing as he said and then looking wearily inside.

He shook his head, "I know of another way out".

"Another way out but how it's a dead end?"

But he ignored me and rushed inside, I had no choice but to follow him, I rushed in and jumped as he closed the door behind me and flooded the room in darkness. He switched on a torch and led me over to where my bed sat, lifting it up and moving it across the room we found a rather grubby looking rug which when he lifted it revealed a tired looking trap door. Lifting the huge knocker which opened it I peered down to see a stone staircase.

"Where does this lead to?" I asked.

"Just come with me I know someone who will talk to you about what you need to know".

"Under the palace?"

He huffed exasperated and started off down on his own, not wanting to be left in the dark I followed closely behind. Without warning he turned off his torch and I let out a yip but I needn't have panicked as within second's torches on the walls burst into flames showing us a light to lead the way.

"How did they do that?" I asked mesmerised by the strange happening, they weren't like the palace lamps which ran on electricity they were old style torches with wood and a funny burnt orange stone in the centre.

"You will find out soon enough", he replied not looking nearly as bemused by the self-lighting torches as myself.

The stone staircase was cold and void of anything other than torches, I had no idea how deep down under the palace we were going, I also had no idea how many of these strange secret tunnels lay under my home, yet here I was the so called future Queen of Cosima and I was completely clueless about everything around me. *How could my parents not have wanted to teach me anything about the world I was going to rule over?* I sighed.

The staircase came to an end with a large stone archway which towered overhead above me, just past it through a rather narrow hallway and many cobwebs with a creature or two scurrying over them was a rusty iron hinged and splintered wooden door which was a smaller version of the archway. The guard approached it and tapped on it six times, at the end of the sixth one the door slowly opened with a heart scrunching groan which sounded like the whole palace above us might hear. Inside was yet another stone room which was completely empty other than a large silver framed mirror which lay up against the far wall, torches beamed to life as we walked further in giving a weird and eerie soft purple glow off the glimmering object. The guard closed the door behind us and I heard it click locked shut, I suddenly felt very alone with him, I hadn't told anyone where I was going and what if it turned out he was working for the Andromeda witch? Staring at him he just motioned for me to look in the mirror.

"Where are we?"

"We are in a chamber even more private than yours, it's a soul chamber".

"A soul chamber?"

He nodded in response but said no more instead he walked over to the large mirror and wiped off the fine layer of dust which was covering it, "She's here", he said to the mirror and bowed, then he stood back up and walked to the door and stood with his back to me and the mirror.

I studied the mirror for a moment taking in all the intricate detailing, I had seen this before or one like it in my mother's personal chamber which my father was not allowed into but then she wasn't allowed into his either, I remember as a child staring into the mirror, when I had been lonely I would talk to myself in the mirror and pretend I had a friend, a friend who was always happy to see me, a friend who was always there to listen to me, but it was just…me.

"What shall I do?" I asked feeling strange about this whole situation but I got no reply, turning around I found the guard had disappeared. "Oh no", I cried out and ran to the door and pulled on the handle but it wouldn't budge, it didn't even give off a little creak of noise it was locked tight. That's it I had walked straight into a trap and now I was going to die down here and no one knew I was even down here.

"Mira, don't panic", a familiar voice said from behind me.

Spinning on my heel and nearly tripping over the long train of my mother's dress I looked for the owner of the voice but no one was there, "Hello?"

"Come to the mirror Mira", the voice commanded but in a soft friendly way, like it always used to.

I walked up to the mirror and looked in and at first all I could see was my own reflection which made me giggle, I felt so stupid, my mind was obviously playing tricks on me making me think I could talk to myself like I used to but I wasn't that child anymore. As I stared at myself harder I noticed my eyes were different and not like my own, mine were normally dark brown with a hint of light brown tones in them but the ones that stared back at me were hazel coloured and male. As I got even closer my image swished and changed like a breeze had flushed through and blown my image away replacing it with that of a guy around my own age, he wore an old guards uniform not the style of today but from a century or so ago, his eyes smiled at me and it grew as his mouth upturned into a big grin, he had chocolate brown hair which was cut short and feathered with layers.

"Thane?" I asked not believing my own eyes.

He smiled and nodded, "Yes it's me Mira".

"But how? You're just my imaginary friend", I laughed nervously.

"I'm your soul guardian".

"My what now?" I said confused.

"Your soul guardian, I have been with you since the day you were born, stuck in your mother's mirror but I knew you would find me and you did, as a child you were forever lonely and hiding in your mother's chamber", he told me.

"So this is my mother's mirror? I thought I recognised it. What's it doing here?"

"When she realised that you were talking to me she panicked as she didn't want you punished as magic and elements were banned from Cosima, so she took the mirror down and had it hidden down here in the hope that you would never find it, not until the time was right".

"The right time, for what? How come that guard knew you were down here?" I asked.

"He was the guard that brought me down here by your mother's orders, on that day I told him all about who I was and that one day you would need me and that when that day arose he was to bring you here".

"But why?"

"Because Mira, your destiny is set for something great, powerful and dangerous and Andromeda has set those wheels in motion".

"So why do I have a soul guardian I've never heard of one before?" I asked him.

He grinned a rather boyish cheeky smile that showed off his full set of white teeth, "Everyone has one but most people don't see theirs, we act as a sort of muse for most people guiding them through life trying to help them make the right choices. But we are not around forever…" This made his smile dampen.

"What do you mean?"

He lifted up his hand a presented me with an orb, "This is my soul orb, once it is filled with light I can move on to the otherworld, to the heavens, to Spirit and beyond".

"And how does it fill with light?"

"We help the people we are assigned to and once we have helped them to the point their destiny is fulfilled it fills up with light and we use that as our guide to the heavens".

"I thought the country of Spirit was heaven?"

He laughed, "No Spirit is something else altogether, Spirit is the place between Junia and the final heaven, a half way plane. For most souls if their life was not fulfilled as it should have been the Soul Converter at Spirit assigns you to a living person who you must help, then once you have fulfilled that assigned then you can move on but if you had a life fulfilled with goodness and greatness then you're soul orb will already be full and you can move straight on.".

"So you used to be a real person?"

His smile widened, "Of course".

"And you were a palace guard judging by your uniform".

He nodded, "Yes".

"So why wasn't your soul orb already full?"

He sighed, "Back when your ancestors started the great war of Junia, myself and my men were patrolling when a group of religious rebels attacked us, we fought and unfortunately I was killed."

"I didn't think the rebels attacked or killed people?"

"Not anymore, they are more peaceful now a days, more protesting than fighting but back then they were fuelled by new hate and anger fighting was the norm. That day it was a fight that got out of hand and..."

"My family got you killed and here you are trying to help me?"

He smiled again but this time it didn't reach his eyes, "Your destiny is meant to be different to those of your ancestors, you are meant to do something great but you need help on your journey".

"Journey?"

"Come with me there are things I need to show you", and he pushed his hand out of the mirror, I swallowed hard and took it half expecting my hand to go through his but it was soft and warm and whole. Closing my eyes I felt him pull me inside the mirror, I felt like I was floating in cool air which whipped past my hair and face, then as I opened them I saw that I was floating in the air, in the skies over Junia looking down over the kingdom.

~ The Birth of Junia ~

The air thrust past me as we moved through it with almost supersonic speed, I thought I should feel scared at the strange turn my life was steering towards but I didn't really feel much of that, more excitement and a longing to know what it was Thane, my long lost imaginary friend was going to show me.

He spoke, his voice soft but telling, I could tell by his tone that these were all things I needed to know, "Junia your kingdom and home, full of secrets and lies but what we want to tell you is the truth, when the world of Junia was born so was the religion of Junia, the Elemental Souls are the gods which created our home and they wish for you to know what your family kept from you". His eyes looked deep into mine and I nodded, showing him I wanted to be shown.

"I thought each country had their own religion, or at least that's what I heard", I said shyly feeling even now with him that I shouldn't know anything about this.

"The countries do each have their own gods, a different element that they worship and pray to but all together the religion is the same…Worship the elements as the elements are what power our countries, our homes and our lives. To have forgotten this…is".

"Wrong", I sighed, "It should be criminal not the other way around".

"I was going to say it is a shame…To not know about the magical world that someone who doesn't know does truly live in".

"Oh", I blushed.

"So Mira, do you truly wish to learn?"

"I do".

Thane swiped his hand out over the world and then began to rewind time, taking me all the way back to the birth of Junia itself, a small star appeared in the universe and with it a boom of particles, then the planet of Junia created its own orbit and began to pull itself together. From inside the small star planet appeared six brightly coloured lights shooting out into the heavens above Junia, they swirled in the skies above the newly born planet and bestowed great powers upon it. The first light a burning flame of reds and crisp oranges flickered and zoomed down to the planet forming itself neatly over one section of the star, a huge volcano exploded up and erupted causing masses of lava to flow down and set hard as granite, as it did the country of Lavara was born.

The second light was of fresh blue hues and golden yellows it poured down over another section of the star planet and flooded the lands creating an ocean so pure and calm and beaches so sandy and soft, hence the country of Beach Haven was born.

The third light was of a white and cloudy grey illusion, it fluttered down over the land where hurricanes blew and massive mountains erupted out from the section of star it landed on, clouds hung heavily in the skies and therefore the country of Skye was born.

The fourth set of lights were a bright dazzling Emerald green which burst into seed and littered the section of the star with thousands of them, out of the ground burst up trees and plant life so lush and glorious, then the country of Emerald Valley was born.

The fifth and sixth set of lights flickered and danced together swaying and dancing until one lost control and plummeted to the ground into the very heart and centre of the star planet and fizzling out. The last one stayed alight with the sparkles of light purples, light blues and greys all swirling together and raining over the last section of the star, out from the lights came all the souls of everyone that would one day inhabit the very world the lights had created and lastly the country of Spirit was born, set into the five pointed star pentacle that was the world of Junia. In the centre of the star came the country of Cosima but its light had faded out and nothing became of it until thousands of years later when people ventured over the lands and built their homes on it.

The world of Junia had been formed and was alive with magic and souls to live on it, a heaven on a planet of earth, air, water, fire and spirit, where souls could wonder freely, a paradise, a world like no other.

The countries all lit up and fuelled by their own element soul they thrived, with temples being built in each country to represent their elemental soul other than Cosima who had no elemental soul and the people found themselves at loss with which god to pray to. Wanting something to worship and celebrate the royal family were born out of two pure blooded families both of which had been born solely in the Cosiman threshold and not one of the other counties, they became the heirs to Cosima. Over the years Cosima grew more powerful with the fault lines that ran underneath the country each and every other country unwillingly powering the capital with their elements. Cosima grew rich which angered the gods and the people who prayed to them as Cosima had become selfish and kept the riches for itself. Around one hundred years ago the great war erupted over the lands which ended in the royal family banishing the religion, magic and the people from the other countries from the whole of Cosima, the people of Cosima became outcasts and looked to the royal family for guidance and for many years this stayed the same until riots broke out as the other countries wanted access to each other through Cosima and with the threat of the fault lines being destroyed and with it Cosima's power source the royal family then agreed to let the countries come and go between Cosima but any worship of their religions would result in prison or execution. The people of Cosima didn't want to travel mostly due to the fear of the unknown with the religions and the hatred from the other countries towards them and the brainwashing from the palace about what the royal guard were allowed to do to anyone connected with treason, so they stayed put in their beloved country but soon lost all knowledge about the religions and the power from the Elemental Souls. I watched as Thane swiped an orb out of the sky and crushed it in his hand, instantly we were thrown into a memory of some sort, it showed me the guards at the palace burning history books with all knowledge of the element souls, the magic and the religions. The elders who refused to forget the time of magic and religion where taken to the palace and sentence under trial with treason and then shot, their knowledge too being banished from the lands. Those who were left that knew simply closed their mouths and never spoke of it again, the fear the palace created kept the religion at bay.

I felt my heart fall at the sight below me once upon a time Junia had been whole, it had been joined and a fully happy place to live in but now the divide was so wide no one knew much of each other, I had to change this. I saw it with my own eyes we were meant to have our own element soul but for some reason it hadn't made it, it didn't survive the fall from the heavens. *Did that mean we should have accepted all the other element souls in its place and worshipped them all, like a multi religious world instead of a broken and angered one?*

"I don't understand why they kept it from me?"

Thane looked at me his hand still holding mine tightly, "Your parents believed it was what was right as that's what they had been taught to believe. Your family are not bad people Mira just a little, misguided by their ancestors but you can help that".

"How?"

"You are the only royal family member that is around at the moment, you could take it upon yourself to go on a journey of rediscovery and bring back the knowledge of the religions back to Cosima. You could collect all the Element souls and defeat Andromeda, you could use the final soul not her and you could stop her from destroying Junia".

"What is the Final Element Soul?"

"It's all the elements summoned together, they become the ultimate force and can destroy either that darkest of evils or the greatest of goods depending on whose hands they are in", he told me.

"So I need to make sure Andromeda doesn't get them?"

He nodded, "If she gets them Junia will be no more, it will be a place of darkness, a place of magic but only the darkest of magic…Junia will become the evil form of itself".

"But I'm just still a child what can I do to stop her? I know of the element souls now but I don't know how to summon them".

"You don't have to. Their soul keepers otherwise known as soul converters will do that for you. In each country is a temple and residing in each temple is a person who can control the element of their home, they are the converter and only they can summon the element soul. Once all the converters and element souls are together the final element soul can be called upon but it's you who must bring them all together, without you they will simply stay in their temples and wait for Andromeda to do the job herself and collect them", he said looking deeply into my eyes, trying to read into my own soul, to show me this was my destiny and my path.

"Converters? Temples?"

"I know it's a lot to take in all at once but I needed to show you so you could make your own decision. What will it be?"

"My decision? This is all down to me whether Junia survives or not!"

"You won't be alone, not anymore Mira", he smiled at me, so warm and friendly, his eyes pulling me in.

"When can we leave?" I said trying to sound stronger than I felt, "I need to help my parents and if it helps all the people of Junia in the process then I'm all in".

He grinned at me with such awe in his eyes, I remembered him so well from my childhood, I had missed our conversations, I had missed telling him all my secrets and fears and I missed having who I had thought of as my only friend. Looking at him now and knowing he was kind of real made my head feel a little fuzzy, I had just thought he was some imaginary person I had created to cure my loneliness but no…He was real, "Are you ready for the journey of a lifetime Mira?"

I nodded, "Yes".

"Then we leave NOW!" and he shoved me so hard I flew back out the mirror and into the hands of the royal guard.

~ The Country of Lavara ~

I had been marched to the throne room where Mr Philippe and Freya were waiting, there was also the head guardsman by the name of Mr Gorgio, he was a stern man and took his job all too seriously. He had two of his guards holding me tightly while another searched me and took the book that I had found at the library.

"Princess Mira there have been reports that you were seen near the restricted section of the library. This book proves to us that you have been, you know the rules you cannot go there not unless the King or Queen commands it!" Mr Gorgio said angrily.

"But I am acting Queen whilst my parents are not here so if I wish to read from the restricted section then I will, I will have you banished for trying to stop me".

He laughed, "Dear little Mira you are merely a child, you are not acting Queen you are simply the face of Cosima in a time of need. We are in charge until your parents return".

"So what happens now?" I asked him, I had to admit I was scared I had no idea what they would do with me without my parents here to tell them otherwise, I also had this feeling of complete and utter anger inside me and I wanted to let it out but I held my tongue as Mr Gorgio spoke again.

"Bring him in".

The doors opened and in came the guard who showed me how to get to the secret hidden chamber where I found Thane, he was cuffed and had been beaten, his dirty ash blond hair covered in small amounts of his own blood.

"What happened to him?" I said leaping forward but the guards held me tightly.

"He was found to be feeding you information on the religion, it is penalty by execution", Mr Gorgio hissed.

"I forbid you to execute him!"

"I'm afraid it is law Lady Mira".

"Can you not imprison him until my parents return and let them decide?" I asked.

Mr Gorgio turned to me and sighed, "It is law…"

"But surely under the circumstances it would be wise to wait till their return Mr Gorgio", Mr Phillipe said from the other side of the room, Freya's face was covered with tears as she stood beside him, "There is no harm, we have room in the palace cells. He can be held there until the Royal family make a decision".

I looked at the guard who bowed his head at me, his eyes trained fully on Freya. *Were they a couple?*

"I'm afraid law is law Mr Phillipe whether the royal family are here or not".

There had to be something I could do, I had to stop this.

"Take him to the dungeons, we will execute him tomorrow", Mr Gorgio said and the guards holding the man's shackles escorted him away, "I have much to do tonight".

"This is wrong", I spat, "He didn't actually do anything wrong, he hasn't told me a single thing about the religions".

"He might not have said anything but he took you to someone who could and would", and everyone turned to look at Thane who also was cuffed and had been forced to the floor, his face kissing the marble.

How was Thane even there? He had been in the mirror! "But they haven't done anything wrong, all they have done is tell me the truth, which as future Queen I should know", I said feeling so furious and I let it flow right out of my mouth in the tone of my voice.

Mr Gorgio stepped in front of me and came right up to my face, "You are not out the woods either missy, you went into the restricted section and willingly followed a man who swore to tell you about the religion…Take her to her private chamber and do not let her leave, she will be under palace arrest until I see fit".

"I might be the only one who can safe guard my parents return and bring the King and Queen back to their rightful place. You arrest me I cannot save them", I hissed.

"The palace guard will take care of them".

"What do you mean?"

"We will find them and deal with them", he snarled.

"No, I will find them and I will with their help" and I pointed to the guard and Thane.

He ignored me and nodded to the guards who took hold of me and began to drag me out of the throne room, "If this is not stopped then when my parents return I will have you executed!" I hissed at him.

Mr Gorgio came to me, a dark glint of something evil in his eye, "I don't believe they will ever come back, do you?" he whispered it so only I could hear, "Andromeda will make sure of that.

Anger boiled inside me as the guards dragged me kicking and screaming all the way to my safe chamber closing and locking the door behind me. *How could he betray my parents like this, his King and Queen?* As I stood there kicking and punching the door something dawned on me, it must have been him who let Andromeda and her people into the palace. I began my tirade at the guard again, screaming at them to let me out but it was to no avail, they weren't listening. I ran over to the trap door only to find it had been nailed shut, kicking it in anger I screamed and threw myself onto the bed, I cried for a while before deciding that too was no use to me.

I had to grow up, I had to find a way to save them all, Thane, the guard and my parents, this room housed one trap door, *maybe it housed another?* I began searching the room, throwing bookcases down on the floor, pushing against the walls to see if any loose bricks or stones were buttons that would open a hidden doorway, I even tried in the small bathroom area looking under the bath by ripping the panel off and shoving my hand behind the toilet to check but nothing. I felt like giving up when I heard a small squeaking noise coming from the trap door. Going over to it I listened, it sounded like quiet banging, like someone was hitting the nails, just as I thought it a nail flew out from the trap door, then another and another until all of them were out. I lifted the trap door to find Freya the other side, her cheeks were red from crying but she looked determined and angry.

"Freya!" I exclaimed in whisper not wanting to alert the guards outside.

"We need to move quickly once they notice I am not in my room they will come looking here".

Nodding I followed her down the staircase and down through to the soul chamber where Thane had been residing, "It's a dead end".

Freya shook her head, "How do you think I got down here?"

I looked around but the only thing I could see was the mirror, surely that wasn't the way out? She took my hand and smiled at me reassuringly, "Follow me".

She pulled me into the mirror with her, I felt the strange breeze that flowed all around me like before but the mirror was different to when Thane had pulled me in, this time it was a circuit of tunnels that all looked like those of the palace but they were dark and ominous, they were gloomy and inky and held no signs of life. I felt a chill run down my spine as Freya led me through them turning at certain junctions and occasionally losing her bearings and taking me back a few tunnels before being back on track. We soon came to a wall which was a dead end and I thought we had made a wrong turn again but Freya tapped on the wall six times in certain places and it shimmered out revealing the dungeons, we stepped out cautiously surveying the room around us for any threats or guards that might be standing keeping guard. Looking back around I spotted that the wall we had come out from was in fact a mirror, not as fancy or as decorative as the other one but it was a mirror none the less. *Did this mean all the mirrors in the palace led to other places and chambers?*

Freya tapped my shoulder and I looked to see she was pointing to two dark shapes that moved in the moonlight, there were bars across the windows and there was a cold and damp atmosphere down here. We stood still for a moment and watched them but they didn't move again, *were they guards?* We silently crawled through the room, all the cages made with their tough iron bars and cold stone flooring made this place frightening.

"Over there", she whispered pointing again to two more shapes that moved but these two were knelt down and in a cell, "It's them", she breathed.

I looked back over at the two shadows that had moved before and noticed they had moved again and were clearer to see by the moonlight, they were guards but they were too busy dozing off then watching their prisoners.

"How do we get them out?" I breathed.

"I'll show you", she smiled and took out a small branch like stick, it was pointed at one end and blunt at the other.

"What is it?" but she didn't reply she crawled over to the lock on the cell door and pointed into it. A small burst of light shot out and a small clink echoed through the cells. The two shadows in the cell came alive and crawled over to us, I saw Thanes cheeky grin smile at me and Freya opened the door and cradled the other guard in her arms.

"We need to take out the two guards", Freya said to her man and he nodded in response.

"Leave it to us".

He crawled out from the cell and kept to the shadows, one then the other he took them both down. Then he rushed back to us showing of some rather shiny keys and two palace issue rifles.

"Lady Mira, we need to get you out of the palace", Freya said.

I nodded, "Yes but how? And where do I go? I have a feeling I will be an outcast in my own kingdom? That Mr Gorgio is a traitor to the crown".

"I do believe that Mr Gorgio is under a spell of some sort although he is normally a rather detest-full man", Freya smiled placing her hands around my face cupping them, "And you will never be an outcast my dear, from the first day I became your maid I knew you would be the one to free Cosima and Junia and you would be the one to reunite them".

"But how can I free Cosima and reunite Junia? I'm just a child".

"You are not just a child Mira, you have the heart and bravery of an adult, I can see it in you, I always have, you strive to know the truth and you will find it".

"But how?"

"With my help", Thane said from beside me, "I have always been here for you, you just wasn't allowed to know it".

I nodded feeling a little stronger knowing I had people to support me, "So where to?"

"We go to Lavara and then work our way through to the other temples from there, but we must go carefully we cannot let the palace guards capture you or you will not be able to go on with your journey", Thane said.

"Are you coming with me to?" I said to Freya and the guard.

She shook her head, "No we need to split up, we will head off to another country and make sure we are seen then after we will head to Lavara in the hope it will keep them off your trail".

"Oh".

"Don't worry Mira, Thane will look after you and we will see you again", she said hugging me, "Also once you're in Lavara get yourself some new clothes your royal attire will only give you away".

"Ok", I smiled, then I looked back down at the strange pointed stick she had in her hand, "Um Freya what is that?"

She looked down at her hand and smiled, "I'm originally from Emerald Valley, my element is Earth, which means when I use twigs that have been crafted into wands I can tap into some of the elements power".

"That is so…Cool".

"It is and I wish Cosima was more…Free…So people could be free to use their element power".

"Why did you come here? Away from Emerald Valley?" I asked.

"All these questions and we have no time", Freya smiled hugging me, "Soon I will answer them but for now you need to get to safety".

I hugged her back, maybe a little too hard but she cradled me, tears rolling down her cheeks, "Do us proud Mira, go and fight on", Then in a heartbeat they both left, running off into the night and out of sight and I was left with my imaginary friend.

Thane took my hand and we made our way out of the dungeons, luckily for us most of the other guards were at the palace hoping to keep me safe and locked in they didn't think to watch the dungeons more closely. The door was right in view of the main watch tower to the palace and I could see guards patrolling and manning the main gate, this was not going to be easy.

We ran out across the main courtyard which was full of seasonal flowers and a large water fountain that normally spurted out the purest, bluest water in all of Cosima but today it was dry due to the gaping hole in one side from the attack, broken rubble was scattered over the main pathway. We used the fountain as a quick place to take cover behind, Thane looked at all the possible routes finally deciding on one of the fences which had been blown apart and although the necessary precautions of blocking it up had been met Thane said he could see a weakness to get us out. Using the darkness and the shadows as our friend we snuck all the way to the wall keeping low to the ground hoping we wouldn't be found. We reached it panting and me sweating with the anxiety of being caught, my palms were so hot and damp I took to wiping them down my mother's dress.

WHOOP! WHOOP! WHOOP!

An alarm sounded in the courtyard and the guards all flurried into motion, we stayed still for a moment to see if it was because they had seen us but to our amazement and luck they were all scrambling inside other than a few that remained at their designated posts, maybe they had finally noticed I was missing which meant we had to move now. Thane took my now not so sweaty hand and with his other sent out a surge of something powerful and some of the crumbling wall collapsed away, he then pulled me through a small gap in the wall, we raced down the road as the sirens grew louder from the palace and lights began to blaze all around us, the palace search lights began to scan the streets not just the palace grounds and I felt my heart escape into my throat.

"Thane we're gonna get caught".

"No we won't", and he motioned to movement up ahead which I spotted to be Freya, she pointed away from her position and Thane turned, forcing us into a run up the main street. BANG! Gunshots sounded around us and I had to bite my tongue to stop myself from screaming out loud, briefly turning I saw the bullets were being fired at Freya who managed to dodge them and run the other way. My blood ran cold as a realisation hit me, *the guards were using bullets and they knew I had escaped did that mean the bullets were meant for me or just the others?*

Thane pursued on with the getaway and charged turning down an alleyway that squeezed between two large blocks of offices and then hit a small housing community, we kept running until my legs could take it no more, I pleaded to stop but Thane urged me to carry on until finally he began to slow down.

"The border gate to Lavara is only a few miles from here, I think we should keep going", he said.

"I'm tired and my legs hurt so badly", I said.

"I know but we need to keep going, they will send out a wider search party soon enough and we need to be out of the hot zone before that".

Feeling like I had no choice we continued on walking until finally the sun began to rise in the morning sky. We had reached a metal electronic gate, it was skyscraper high and held a force field around it which shot up into the sky.

The gate to Lavara was not very well guarded from a guard point of view but there were camera's scanning all around it which would pick us up and soon the palace guard would know of our whereabouts but before I could think of anything to say Thane sent out a strange flurry of grey energy which swam in front of the cameras lenses, circling around blocking the view, shoving me past them Thane got us through the gate and closed it before taking back the energy.

"What was that?" I said looking at him funny.

"I'm a soul guardian which means I have been to Spirit, when you have been there as a soul and become a guardian you then can perform soul magic, I cast an illusion over the camera's so they wouldn't notice us and hopefully Freya will have been seen somewhere else".

"Wow, soul magic".

"It's not as glamourous as it sounds, I am basically using recycled souls in my power", he said looking saddened.

"Recycled souls?" I said, "I thought we all moved on to a better place?"

"We do but these souls are bad souls that cannot go to the heavens but the heavens have given them to the magic of Spirit to repent for their sins", he told me, "Once they have been recycled enough to be classed as pure they then can move on".

"That's a plus side I suppose", I smiled and he smiled back, his warm eyes glowing into mine and I felt so safe here with him, with my old friend.

"Come on, we have much to do and not a lot of time on our side", he said and we headed off into the country of Lavara.

As I took in all my surroundings I felt awed at how different Lavara really was to Cosima, this place was hot and I mean swelteringly hot, the sweat dripped down my back within minutes of walking away from the gate, the heat that swarmed all around us was unbearable but we had a mission to do and no time to ponder on the uncomfortable heat. The countryside of Lavara was odd, it was all dark and burnt to a crisp, there were what used to be trees that lined the charcoaled fields but they were merely fossils of plant life, their twisted and blackened arms reaching out to each other. The atmosphere in the sky was not the blue skies I would have seen in Cosima it was stale and hot, burnt oranges and flame reds littered the heavens with an unmoving array of clouds which I soon found to be smoke from a huge volcano which was like a smouldering giant in the distance.

"That's where the temple of fire is", Thane told me watching as my eyes darted over the volcano trying to spot it.

"This place is amazing and strange".

"It's hot", he grinned.

Not wanting to waste energy talking as we soon found ourselves thirsty we hurried on down the blackened hillside which was all part of the great volcano. After many miles of wondering down we came across the first hint that a town was nearby, a few lone houses sat embedded into the hard rock, at first I thought they had been carved from the granite itself but then I saw that the rock face had been mined first and houses built in its place, all of them cleverly protected from flying debris from any eruptions but they were all as black and as sooty as the mountainous hillside behind and around them. A spiralling road showed us the rest of the way down and we followed it, soon enough we hit the heart of the town which was literally just rows and rows of soot covered houses all built like the others we had seen up the top, shops adorned the adjacent side to the houses and I felt thankful to see that they sold water and other things like food and clothing.

Heading straight over I then encountered a problem, I had no money on me! Turning to Thane he sensed something was amiss, "What's wrong?"

"I have no money to buy things", this was suddenly a whole new worry for me, I had been brought up around money not being a problem and now I had none.

He smiled and pulled a pouch from his pocket, "I do, not a lot mind you but enough for water, food and a new outfit, hopefully we can score some money on the way round the other countries for anything else".

Breathing a sigh of relief I ran to the shop grabbing a bottle of water and guzzling the whole contents of it down whilst Thane just laughed and paid the rather angry looking shop keeper that I had taken the water from in his shop. We stocked up on a few supplies, mainly bottles of water and a few food sources before moving onto the next shop, another new experience for me, a clothes shop.

The door chimed cheerfully as we strolled in and a small petite woman of around fifty looked up, her skin was almost as dark as the soot outside and her eyes glowed at me cheerily, her hair was greying and crispy on the ends, "Hello welcome to Annalise's fashions how can I help you?" Her voice was playing and charming and I couldn't help but be taken in by her.

"I need something a little less…"

"Hot", the woman suggested.

I nodded, "Yes please".

"We are on an extremely tight budget", Thane added and the woman chuckled.

"We will find something, I always do", she headed out into the back of the store and brought out a rather beaten up cardboard box, "This is my old stock that I normally take to the local orphanage but I guess for a small fee towards the orphanage you can look".

"That would be very much appreciated", I smiled and took to the box, inside the clothes were not something I would normally have chosen, mostly because most of my outfits were chosen for me and because as a princess most of my outfits were frilly ball gowns but rummaging through it showed me how nice it might be to dress down for once. I placed some to one side as a maybe pile and some into a no pile until I came across the perfect dress, it was cropped at the top with no sleeves or straps and would come up to the top of my breast plate just under my collar bone, it trailed down and was slightly fitted in at the waist with a golden belt and small satchel which was attached to it, the dress ended before the knees, sloping longer on one leg and shorter on the other, it was set in a flame red with pretty golden stitching around the hem at the bottom and at the top, all matching the belt and bag. Trying it on I knew instantly this was the one I wanted, it fitted well and was easy enough for me to move around in for travelling. The woman came over with a pair of knee high boots, they were black leather and a little worn and used but I couldn't be too choosy now could I plus they had pretty gold laces that had been threaded through them giving them a hint of style. She let me put all the clothes on in a changing room, as I was in there alone I also decided to change my hair style a little, I tied my hair up into a messy ponytail and braided a few small sections to give it some youth style and I was set.

"You look amazing young lady", the woman smiled and turned to Thane for the donation for the orphanage, once done she bowed to us, "I take it you are travellers from one of the cooler countries?"

Thane nodded to her question, "We sure are".

"And have you ever been here before?"

"No we haven't".

"Then you simply must see the Fire Queen's performance this evening, she is amazing and the most enchanting performer there is. I have two tickets you can purchase for cheap?"

Thane sighed, "How much?"

"Ten Junians", she stated.

Flinching a little over the price he brought them and when we left the shop I asked him why, "Because she said the Fire Queen is performing, there's a good chance that she will be the fire converter that we need to see and befriend and what better way than to see her performance and tell her how great she is", he smiled.

Liking his logic partly because I really wanted to see a show that wasn't a few magicians in the palace doing card tricks and a few doves or rabbits appearing out of a hat but a real magical thing but also because he seemed to know his way to a girls soul, compliment them and tell them how great they are, win, win in my book.

By looking over the tickets we found out that the show was going to be held in a small area called Lake Lava, this so called lake was meant to be the one place the Fire Queen could really show of her skills according to a woman who was gushing with excitement just outside the shop with a few friends.

Thane followed a group of people that were already heading down to the lake to reserve some good seats. As we walked down a crumbling road which once looked to be lava which had dried and set I spotted a group of men all covered in soot, dirt and grime. Every single one of them had the same colour skin as the woman in the shop but theirs was darker due to the extra layer of soot, as we passed they all chanted and cheered, "Fire Queen, Fire Queen", "Junia worship the flame". The men were all standing near to what I presumed to be a mine shaft, a large wooden train like device was sat atop some rails with crates full of coal and other fuels inside them, some men were heaving the crates around like they weighed nothing, their muscles flexing in the heat with sweat dripping down them. Made me think how lucky I really was in my cosy palace, I didn't have to lug heavy, dirty stuff like that around but these people all looked happy doing their job, all chatting and laughing together, I wanted that, I wanted a friendship so that I could gossip and laugh too, this made me feel selfish that I wanted that for me when I had life so easy, so I shook the thought away and followed Thane.

Passing the men we continued on down the road which soon ventured into a burnt forest, the same looking trees I spotted when we first arrived also had grown on this patch of land and then had burnt and died leaving behind their skeletons, the air around them was thick with dust and I hadn't seen a small animal or critter since our arrival. The lava gave the trees an eerie red glow along with some puddles of lava that bubbled away between the roots. Finally we made it to Lake Lava and I felt my mouth open in awe, this really was a lake full to the brim with lava, red bubbles popped and hissed sending out sparks and ashes. The lake went on for what looked like miles but only a few hundred feet in was a large granite type platform, *surely that could not be the stage for the Fire Queen?* She would be burnt to a cinder making her way to it. Taking a closer look a bubbling lava flare bubbled up and burst making me yip out loud, Thane had my arm and immediately pulled me away, "Please be careful", the look of pure worry in his eyes for my safety was genuine and it made me sad he felt like that, I guess he was like another guard to keep me safe, like so many…That had lost their lives keeping us safe…Like Thane already had before.

"What you thinking?" he asked looking at me so intently.

"Just how you died saving my family before and now you will do it in a heartbeat again for me, I just feel…Guilty".

"Don't, this is my path to the heavens. I will be able to move on to a happier and better place, somewhere I can rest. Helping you will make that happen, keeping you safe makes me happy too, it always has".

"Why?"

"I can see how lonely you are and always were, I knew I was the only friend you really had and…I liked that…Because you were my only friend too. Being in that mirror wasn't too good for my social life", he smiled.

"How did you get out of the mirror?"

"When you agreed to go on the journey with me it released me from it, right into the arms of the guard but I was out so I'm not complaining. Plus the guard couldn't really kill me, I'm already dead", he grinned a boyish grin.

"Oh, really?"

He nodded, "The only thing that could destroy me is dark magic, it could destroy my soul or the orb I need to fill to move on", he laughed at the look on my face, "But that isn't going to happen, not to me, not to us".

"Right", I nodded looking away, the lava caught my attention again, I had seen something shimmering out of the corner of my eye so I took a step forward to peek, I could see below the surface of the lava itself was swirling and dancing with shining red, orange and yellow lights, then I realised that was not just lava but souls lighting up and swimming in it, they glistened between the swamp of molten rock.

"How are there souls in there?" I asked Thane.

"Souls make up everything in Junia, you have just become blind to it because Cosima is a manmade city, even the trees and grasses are mostly fake. Everything natural has a soul or many to keep it alive. Lavara runs on fire souls which thrive in the molten rock that you see, it doesn't harm them", he replied.

"I feel so stupid not knowing any of these things".

"You shouldn't, plus you are slowly being awakened to it all, to all what Junia holds in its beauty, you will soon understand it all", he smiled brushing his hand over mine.

I looked deep into his hazel coloured eyes and felt warm inside, I was glad I had Thane now. I felt…Normal I guess.

We sat for a while by the lake just talking and getting to know one another again although it felt like we had never been apart, the views of the lava rising and falling were breath taking and the heat soon became bearable as my body got used to the hot temperatures. A little while later more people began to arrive taking their seats, the whole place was a seating arena with rows and rows of chairs moulded to the ground out of the cooled molten rock for performances, we had been lucky to come when we did as we were right at the front. Miners, trades people, women and children all took their seats and waited. Some rather religious looking men soon arrived, they wore special garments which showed their religious status, long dress like cloaks which were embroidered with flames, in deep fire reds, burnt oranges and flashing yellows. They bowed to the crowd before heading to the lake and setting up a few things for the show, some of them walked through the crowd holding trays full of food for sale, Thane purchased some for me and passed them over, I took a large bite before looking questioningly at him, he wasn't eating but surely he must be hungry too.

He grinned, "I'm dead I don't need to eat".

"Oh, right", I blushed feeling stupid for looking at him like that.

Suddenly the audience fell silent, taking in a baited breath as we could feel something flow through the crowd, it was a presence like I had never felt before, it was hot but cool and fresh and made the hairs on the back of my neck stand on end and tingle. A red glow emitted from the tree line just behind the crowd, she appeared in a glowing red flame which as she passed me by was cool to the touch. She glanced down at me smiling with an amused look on her dark, delicate features before she reached the bank of the lake and bowed to us all.

"Praise I send to my humble Junia and to my flame heart".

Some people stood and bowed back, others cheered and sang out her name in a chorus, "Fire Queen, Fire Queen, Fire Queen". Bowing one last time she then took her first step onto the lake and I didn't know it but I instantly held my breath, she sank below the boiling skin meltingly hot liquid and disappeared, I let out a sigh of fear but no one else did, no one else was worried for her safety in the lava. Then as quickly as she had gone she reappeared and she looked amazing, the lava dripped away from her almost naked body before it fizzled and started to spiral around her flesh creating the most beautiful dress I had ever laid my eyes on, more beautiful than the ones I saw every day at the palace. The dress of course was made entirely out of flames, bursting with colour, hot reds, crisp yellows and burnt oranges. The hot flickers of the flames danced along her dark skin, the dress trailed down her figure and flared out behind her as she approached the granite platform, she twirled up and the flames twirled with her catching her up and re positioning themselves as the dress once again. Her hair was long and flowing, itself looking like a long mane of fire, her roots were dark but the mid lengths and ends had all been bleached by the heat into a glowing burnt yellow colour with bright copper highlights.

The atmosphere was electric with a hot current as she paused and held herself on her stage, she looked the whole crowd over as if taking us all in, taking all our delight and happiness into her soul, her eyes glistened with the lava that shone around her. She motioned her hands towards the lava and I watched as it reached her hands and moulded down into what looked to me like a microphone but there could be no wires or speakers in the molten liquid, as I thought this she waved her other hand and out appeared some dome looking shapes which began to vibrate as she put her mouth to the microphone, a gentle rhythmic chant echoed out from her lips down the flame microphone and surrounded us all in her flame lullaby. She turned and twisted her body in time with the song she chanted, moving her free hand and commanding the lava to dance around her and with her lighting up the sky with a brighter, fiercer array of colour. The chant was nothing like the usual pop songs I would hear being drummed out of the radio back in Cosima, this one was more of an opera coated dance chant but it was beautiful and sent chills up my spine, as she reached a certain point in the song the religious helpers she had with her sang a background chorus which echoed in tune with her own.

She sent the lava back down into the lake and then called upon the fire souls creating magical sparks which jumped out and flew all around the arena like stars in the skies, they twinkled and flashed before diving back in and out of the lake, she created a dancing light orchestra that danced in tune with her own fire soul, the flames licked at her arms from the souls and she used them to propel the warmth from the light to shower over us in the audience which got a cheer from some in the crowd.

Raising her hand she sang towards it making a lone flame appear which she threw up into the air and called to it then it shattered like glass and flew off into hundreds of directions shimmering and fizzing like fireworks.

She then changed the tune of the chant going into a new song which was more upbeat and bouncy and the people in the crowd couldn't help but move to the strange new beat, as she did this she waved her hand over her body changing the dress from a flame read to a cold flaming ice blue, the dress weaved itself around her body changing shape and turning into a more shorter but fuller skirted frock which swished as she moved. The lights surrounding us and the trees also turned to a shade of blue and purple from where the lava shone red creating the mixture of colours.

Turning and moving her body she sang her heart out to us, her voice was crystal clear and ear splittingly beautiful, it weaved its way into your heart filling you with something that wasn't there before, I had no idea what these strange fluttering feelings where sweeping through my chest but I had an inkling this girl could make you fall in love with her just by using her voice.

Using her movements she commanded the souls to settle back into the lava causing the arena to darken by a shade or two but without the light of the souls she was able to change her outfit without anyone noticing until she flickered the lights in the sky back to a red and the red bounced off her new dress which was stunning, everyone cooed at the beautiful new garment she had on. This one was white almost like a wedding type dress, the flames burnt a soft off white colour and flickered giving the illusion of feathers. The dress sat under her collarbone and tapered in at the waist before flowing down to her heels and casting a magical train behind her which pooled in the hot red lava. She twirled and sang out her last song which was just as mesmerising as the other two, the crowd went wild, this had to be a song she had sang many a time to them.

Her voice hit my soul and pulled at it making it want to dance, I felt her rhythm in my mind and tried to force it out, I didn't like dancing at the best of times let alone in front of a group of strangers but that's what her songs made me want to do, to dance. She was good and the song lingered inside me well after she had finished. Her last song lyric was, "You need to remember", and I couldn't help but think that it was meant for me, for I needed to remember what Junia was all about, what had been kept from me for all my life.

She stood on the platform and bowed once again to her people and smiled showering them with her light from her soul. Then BOOM! A huge thunderous bang echoed through the arena, I slowly opened my eyes which I hadn't realised I'd closed but I could see the Fire Queen was gone, just the falling embers of her flaming concert remained. The crowd cheered loudly and clapped their hands like their lives depended on it. I took to my hands and clapped them in unison with the others, she had been amazing and had taken my breath away, this was truly magical and I knew I wouldn't never forget such a performance.

I turned to Thane who was watching me intently, his eyes studying me, "Did you enjoy the show?"

"Of course I enjoyed the show it was the best thing I've ever laid my eyes on. How she commanded the fire and the lava was amazing and creating those beautiful dresses was just mind blowing".

"Well I'm pretty sure she is the fire converter as only they have that much control over the elements like that", he said looking around, "My guess is she's headed back to the temple so shall we try to catch her up?"

"It was truly wow, I wish I had a power like that", I said biting my lip realising that I was on this journey to ask all the converters of the elements to help me quest when I had no power myself to show. *Surely they would all laugh in my face at my request for their help?*

"You do have a power, it's just not a physical elemental power, you have a royal power that many would die to have", he smiled.

"That's not real power its fake compared to this", I moved my hands to show the lava arena.

"It's not fake at all, people have cowered at the feet of the royal family for over a century and that power is yours but I know inside you that you would not command it to create fear".

"I don't understand?"

He shrugged, "You will one day, when you need to".

I just looked at him then said, "Well no one would want to live like me, utterly clueless as to what her world is really about", I sighed, ". I know nothing of the kingdom I am to become ruler of, I am still a laughing stock whichever way you look at it and a friendless laughing stock at that".

"You have me", he whispered, "And you know, it's more quality over quantity when it comes to friends".

I went to reply but I was stopped by a flurry of lights that filtered through the trees, they sang to us in a quiet melody only we could seem to hear, either that or no one else cared, "Come to the temple, Come to the temple, Let the flame guide your heart, come and see me before you depart, Come to the temple, Come to the temple, we have something to start, oh lady of Junia's heart".

"I think the Fire Queen knows you are here", Thane smiled.

"Well come on", I took his hand dragging him along with excitement, "Let's go".

~

The Fire Temple itself was rather different looking to the rest of the buildings in the town of Lavara which were now hundreds of feet below us, it was extremely grand in its setting with its flaming backdrop and smoky clouds which floated around the horizon. The temple was built in a large triangle shape, built with no surprise from the granite the volcano produced, large columns decorated the outside with flames carved into all them. Through the bottom half of the building triangular shaped windows were scattered around with stained glass images decorating them of flames, a woman and a man commanding the fire and the people in the town below all praying to them.

Nudging Thane I asked, "The image shows a man and a woman commanding fire, are there two converters?"

He shook his head, "No only one at any one time, the next heir to the converter will be male, it goes in order of female then male so the imagery on the glass reminds people of that".

As we walked up the huge granite steps I put my hand out to the door which was huge and wooden which looked just as charred as everything else in this country, the door handles were small orbs of fire light along with a huge metal knocker which was shaped into a flame. I picked up the knocker and let it drop back down three times, the knocks echoed loudly inside and I thought for a moment the temple was going to be empty and hollow inside but I was so wrong, as I saw when the door was opened by a rather stern looking older man. Rows of pews aligned the centre all facing towards a statue of a bird or rather more a huge Phoenix, the birds wings were spread wide and a glowing orb of fire sat at its beating, flickering heart. Other statues lined some small crevices which had been carved out under the stained glass windows giving each of them an eerie red glow, the other statues were not of the Phoenix but of people, people that looked to be fighting and wielding the fire element, *maybe they were past converters?*

The man let us inside and bowed to greet us, "Come inside Lady Mira the Fire Queen has been expecting you but first please pray to the fire element".

"Um thank you but how do you know who I am?" I asked the man.

"The Fire Queen knows many things...Please go and pray".

Thane took me to the statue which as I neared it I felt it watching me even though its eyes were made of granite and didn't move. Thane knelt down and bowed in a similar way to how the man had greeted us at the door, I followed Thanes actions before we both clasped our hands together and Thane began to speak, "Oh element god of flame, our hearts burn with the desire, to rid Junia of evil, please help us and guide us on our journey and we will forever be in your debt". I repeated what Thane said and we both bowed once more before standing, the man came over and led us away from the statue and to a small side room which housed some chairs and a table with some tea and spiced bread awaiting us.

"Please take a seat the Fire Queen will be with you shortly", he said bowing and exiting the room.

"Wow this is, different", I said looking around the small but cosy room, rows and rows of books lined the small walls with rickety looking shelfs, a desk sat at the other end with a writing pad and inkwell with a large feathered pen. A small stained glass window shone some of the Lavarian light inside making it feel warm and friendly. Pictures were also scattered over the desk and I looked them over, one was of the Fire Queen looking a lot less done up, her hair tied back and she was happy smiling with a few other people, the others I guessed must be of her family and friends. I took a look at Thane who had picked up a book from a pile that had been stacked in a corner, he looked calm and relaxed, the glow from the light outside hit his dark hair giving it a bronzed hazed glow. In the glow of the Lavarian flame he looked charming, handsome and kind.

My thoughts about Thane were interrupted as the door opened and in came the girl from the lake, no older than myself, she had long burnt yellow hair and dark roots which she had braided into many braids and tied up out the way of her face, she wore temple robes and smiled kindly at us her dark features glowing in the warmth, "Lady Mira what a pleasure it is to have you come to my temple, please rest as desired".

"Thank you for having us, we saw your performance it was mesmerising", I said trying to flatter her, we really needed her on side.

"Aww you are too polite, my performance is just a show to cheer the people of Lavara up…" she paused for a moment pouring herself a mug of tea and taking a slice of the spiced bread, "but you do not have to use flattery on me Lady Mira".

"Um what do you mean?"

"I know why it is you are here".

"Oh right", I said feeling my face blush beetroot red.

"I know you need all the element souls to help save your parents and Junia", she took a swig from her tea placing the cup neatly down and finishing her bread, "We here at the Fire Temple know all about Andromeda and her plans for Junia".

"You do?"

"Yes she came here a few weeks ago claiming to be a lost soul that needed guidance but her plan was to infiltrate the temple and take the element soul by force, but we fought her off and banished her from here so she fled taking her goonies with her".

"Goonies?" I asked confused.

"She has many people working for her Mira, she does not work alone".

"How many?" Thane asked.

"Enough to cause us concern, so we looked into her more deeply, Master Cinder the man who let you into the temple can have premonitions when he calls upon the fire element. He prayed for days and was finally granted with a vision, the vision showed us that Andromeda is poisoning the fault lines of the magical pentacle that runs all through Junia. Her plan is to poison each one and take Cosima by force once it has crumbled under her darkness, as soon as she has done that she plans to take the palace and crown herself Queen and use the element souls as her own personal dark guardians, but first she must destroy the final element soul otherwise it could over power her and all would revert back to normal".

"I thought the final element soul was all of them together?" Thane said.

She shrugged, "Legend has it that way but if destroyed they would all perish but her plan is to use them. Maybe she has a way to defeat the final one and keep them alive?"

"Or maybe the final one isn't them all together but another one?" I said turning to Thane but he looked lost in thought.

"There isn't another one my lady", she replied.

I shrugged, "There was meant to be another one though...Right? Thane showed me".

She nodded, "Your right there was meant to be another one but it never flourished, it disappeared".

"Maybe it will appear one day?"

"We cannot count on that Lady Mira, it has never appeared in the whole time Junia has been born and I don't think it ever will".

"Maybe", I whispered more to myself. Suddenly I felt a tingle go through my body, like a whisper of something or someone from the past...I felt like I knew it and I felt like I knew something the others didn't but what? "So what does that mean for us? What do we do now?" I asked.

"It means we have to get all the element souls before she does, she will try the other temples to see if they are weaker and will fall to her tricks but I'm pretty certain she won't succeed that way her other option will be to wait till you have greeted all the converters and then attack us while we have the souls away from their temples".

"We won't let her get them", I said.

"No we won't but there is something you must know before we take the element soul away from the temple".

"Go on?" Thane said.

"Once I have taken the soul out from its chamber the power it possess will be lost from Lavara's fault line, eventually rendering Cosima powerless when all the other countries have also taken their souls. Cosima will become a country of darkness but that should only be temporary until we have succeeded and put them back", she paused and then spoke again, "It will also render Lavara in danger".

"How?" I asked.

But Thane answered for her, "With the fault line down the enemies and monsters it prevents from coming into Lavara will be able to gain access and the town's people will be under threat".

The Fire Queen nodded, "My people will be in danger I must consider how to do this the best way, I cannot take the soul until at least tomorrow, I need to give them enough time to either stand and fight or to evacuate".

"Where will they go?" I asked concerned.

"They will come here to the temple, it will be the safest place, I will put up protection around it and Master Cinder will be able to keep it going with the help of a few others".

I felt so guilty inside, the people here were going to be put in danger for me, because of me and my royal family.

"What's wrong?" she asked me.

"I feel responsible for this".

"Well you can't, you didn't create Andromeda and you are trying to help", she smiled, "Plus it's not just to help save your parents, it is about saving the whole of Junia too".

I just shrugged, somehow deep inside I felt responsible.

"What I don't get is how she has managed to tap into the fault lines to poison Junia?" Thane said to her.

She spoke up, "The faults lines run all through Junia, the pentacle star joins every country together, the lines in Lavara connect to Cosima, Skye, Emerald Valley, Spirit and Beach Haven, no country is alone, they are all connected which is what makes Junia the powerful and magical world it is. Yes it's had wars and powerful ones at that but no matter what it cannot be forced apart, even with the rift between Cosima and the religions of the other countries it is still together in the star shape but... Andromeda has found a second fault line, a dark sided pentacle which runs opposite to our own but she has managed to harness its power and infiltrate ours, if she is left to her own devices she will consume Junia and turn our beloved heavenly world in a Nether world".

Thane nodded, "Makes sense now I guess but how did she find this dark pentacle?"

"No one knows, but legend has it Andromeda's family have been searching for centuries". She replied.

"So what now?" I asked.

"Now I go and explain to my people whilst you to get some rest, the journey ahead is going to be a long one and only Junia knows when rest will be happening again. You need to be strong Lady Mira, my people will not understand like I do what is happening and at first they might point the finger at you but you must keep your head up, I will try to explain the best I can but be prepared for an uproar, you might never be able to come to Lavara again".

"Ok, thank you Fire Queen for being so understanding".

She giggled, "Oh please called me Fira, Fire Queen is just my stage name". And with that she stood up and left.

Thane looked worried.

"You alright?" I asked him.

"I'm a little more worried now I know what Andromeda is really up to but I'm sure with everyone's help we will defeat her".

Staring off into space I tried to imagine the world without Andromeda and going back to normal with my parents back by my side, it won't be long just a few weeks, I hoped.

The door opened again and Master Cinder approached us, "I have prepared you both a room in the housing chambers, I will serve supper at seven please be ready to pray by six thirty".

Agreeing we followed him as he led us through the temple, I spotted many doors which were all closed and locked tight, past the main prayer chamber was a small door which Master Cinder opened and led us through, a small spiral staircase led upwards to the first floor which opened up to be the housing chambers. There were about twenty or so rooms all with beds, there were only two bathrooms one located at each end of the corridor but they were very clean and tiny. He showed me to my room and told Thane his was next door to mine on the left, we thanked him before he left us to our own devices.

I sat down on the small single bed and looked at Thane, "Get some rest Mira you will need it".

"What about you?" I asked as he sat down on a small chair at the end of my room.

"I don't sleep", he replied.

"Oh…So you don't eat and you don't sleep, what will you do? You must get so bored?"

"Not really, you get used to it but I'm going to try and work out a plan", he said, "Now sleep tomorrow is a big day, Fira will call the element soul and we will be set to leave for Beach Haven".

Doing as he said I rested my head on the pillow, it didn't take long for sleep to take me as I hadn't slept the night before, my dreams were filled with Fira's fire dance and the guards at the palace chasing me.

~The Temple Of Fire~

The next morning was full of hustle and bustle, Thane woke me up around seven and after freshening up we headed down to the dining hall where Master Cinder had laid out a massive breakfast feast, he had also packed us some bags filled with food, water and money for our trip that Fira had kindly donated for our cause. We took to completing morning prayer with all the temple helpers which included Fira and Master Cinder, they all wore the decorative temple robes and took their role seriously making sure our prayers were up to the standard they believed the fire element would consider good enough.

As we left the main prayer chamber Fira led us to a large door at the end of the main hall which was locked and could only be opened by a seal on a necklace she wore round her neck, the necklace itself was a beautifully crafted piece of bronze which suited her features. I looked at Fira in wonderment, today she had changed out of her temple robes and wore a rather decorative robe, the colour was a crisp burnt orange with golden embroidered flames and symbols along with a ruby red flame coloured belt around her waist which had been tied into a bow, it didn't falter or flap around as the material looked rather stiff. The ruby red colouring also appeared on her boots which were leather and strong looking, flames flowed over the leather giving it a fake burning look. She had tied her many braided locks into a huge bun with a few stray braids falling around her shoulders which bounced as she walked.

I walked up beside her as she led us further down a long hall, "So this element soul, you just collect it and we can go? How big is it and how will you carry it?"

Fira gave me a playful smile, "So many questions so early in the morning".

"Sorry", I said feeling my cheeks flush again, this was becoming a bit of a habit this blushing business.

"Don't be sorry I'm glad you feel you can ask me but no I don't just collect it, I have to summon it", she replied.

"How?"

"I'll show you in the Chamber of Fire and I'll need to use this", she held up the necklace which could open the seals on the doors we had to pass through, "This is a family heirloom and has been passed down through all the generations of the converters of fire".

"So all the other converters too will have these family heirlooms?"

She nodded, "Yes".

"Are they alive?" I asked intrigued.

"The element souls?"

I nodded.

Maybe", she smiled, "I never really put much thought into it, I look after it and control it, I never thought of it was alive, maybe in a sense of the power it can wield and the souls that are drawn to it, it could well be alive".

"They are not alive as such", Thane spoke up, "They are a mixture of many hundreds of souls pulled together by the element, creating a larger conscience of a soul. To be alive they would be able to think, breathe, eat and make choices but the element is controlled by the converter and told what to do by them and them only. It cannot act alone unless all the elements are summoned together all at once, then they merge and become more of a… how can I put it…ghostly magical being".

"How do you know so much?" I asked him.

"When you have been around as long as me you find out things or read them from history books or accidently stumble across people's past memories", he grinned like a mischievous boy, this pulled his lips into a cute curve and I had to look away, *how could I find a dead guy cute?*

Fira smiled and carried us on with our journey to the chamber until one of the temple helpers stumbled across us but judging by the look on his face it wasn't accidental, he had obviously been looking for us, "Fira!" he sounded cross.

"Yes Dante?" she said sounding a little agitated by his tone.

"Do you think this is a good idea taking the likes of her into the fire chamber?" he said pouting at me.

I felt a little stung but she had warned me the people of the Lavara would not be so understanding.

"She is our future Queen Dante, what better way to give her an understanding of the religions than to have her witness how the summoning works and what the element soul really is".

"And why would the Queen want to know these things?" his voice was threatening and his dark eyes focused on mine. He was a tall young man with gun metal grey hair and strong dark features.

"Because she plans on bringing the knowledge of the religions back to Cosima", Fira answered.

"Huh yeah right", he grumbled, "The element chose you and you should be the only one to enter the Chamber of Fire, no one else, not even me or Cinder".

Fira looked Dante deep in the eyes until he couldn't hold her stare anymore and looked away, "I am the converter and I will say who can and who cannot go to the chamber".

Dante bowed and said nothing more before leaving.

"What's his problem?" Thane laughed jokingly.

"He and his family don't like the Royal family or Cosima and have never left Lavara because of that reason. He believes only in what he has been told by his fore fathers and will do whatever it takes to keep Lavara safe. He's not a nasty person really", Fira told us. "Just over protective".

"So is he right? Should I not enter the Chamber?"

Fira laughed, "Yes in his mind and by the standards of Cosima but in my view, so you can learn our ways, I believe you should".

She continued with the walk to the chamber when finally we reached a door which had pure white steam flowing off of it, she used the necklace again and opened the door slowly, I could feel the heat of the volcano whoosh around me and it made me feel light headed but somehow I managed to fight through it and follow Fira and Thane who both had already started to walk down some huge granite stairs which went down for what felt like miles, flaming torches lit up as we went down, just like the ones in the corridor to the soul chamber in the palace, "Wow how do they light themselves?"

Fira looked back at me, "There is a fire stone within each torch which lights up when someone walks past which are mined from the volcano".

"There were torches like that in a hidden part of the palace", I told her.

"There probably is, once upon a time the palace was alive with the magic of Junia, not the machines it's full of now".

The rest of the walk down the staircase was a silent one as Fira looked to be lost in her own thoughts and Thane was deathly quiet even for a dead guy and me well I just followed on like a little lost puppy. We reached the bottom and came to yet another door but this one was huge and reached up to the top of the ceiling which by my standards could have been a mile high above us but in reality was maybe a few hundred feet or so. Fira swiped the necklace over another seal and the door slowly creaked open, as it did I watched as the torches in this room all lit up at once revealing an extraordinary sight.

The room was indeed the Fire Chamber and everything in it represented the flame in some form or another, rows of large pillars led us through the large room towards the centre which was glowing red, a large orb of crystalized liquid was set into a large chunk of granite which stood standing almost to half the height of the room. Inside the solid liquid was a glowing mixture of souls and a shape, a form of something. "What is it?" I asked.

"A Phoenix", I gasped, "Is it real?"

Thane then spoke, "Yes it's very much real Mira, A real life Phoenix that rises from the flames and ashes".

"Like the statue you all pray to?" I added.

Fira nodded, "If you can stand back I will summon the Phoenix to my necklace but I warn you once the element soul is gone the enemy will come and our journey out of Lavara will not be an easy one. The monsters will try to take the soul away from us but we must fight hard to make sure we stay on the right path. Dante, Master Cinder and the others will try to protect the temple and the town's folk who wish to evacuate to here". She looked saddened by the thought of her town being attacked but it was something we had to do.

"Why will all the monsters come?" I asked, "What are the monsters, I've not seen any before?"

She took a deep breath and then spoke, "The world of Junia is such a magically divine place that when the world was formed the element souls banished most of the evil souls from its lands but to keep those permanently evil souls out the element souls had to be used to create force fields around the countries to keep the people safe. Once the element soul has been removed from its resting place in the temple the force field will vanish, which will mean…"

"All the monsters will be able to come in", I finished for her.

She nodded, "Yes".

"So all the dark souls, they are the monsters that roam outside the force field?"

"Yeah", Thane joined in, "These souls were born of darkness from the evil depths of a void between Junia and another world. No one knows where this void is but its outside of Junia's force fields. They take on many forms too, they could be animal, human or simply a power".

"Animal", I shivered.

Thane looked at me, "You couldn't have seen one Mira they cannot access Cosima it's too heavily guarded".

I turned to him, "The night the palace was attacked, when I was leaving my rooms I did see one, a beast, almost wolf or dog like with red eyes…It…It killed a guard who was saving my life".

Thane gripped my shoulders, "Don't feel guilty it was his duty".

"Like it had been yours?" I asked with a choked voice.

He looked taken aback by my emotions, I knew that I was a wimp, a scared child who could barely stand on her own two feet but to have people sacrifice their lives for me just didn't sit right, whether I was royalty or not their lives should matter too. "Yes, like it was and still is mine".

"Mira, it's not your fault, those people would have declared an oath to the throne…They knew what they were doing".

"Still doesn't make it fair, all life is important…Right?"

"Maybe not all", Thane sniffed.

We both looked at him confused, "What do you mean?"

"Well Andromeda's life is not important, she will kill many innocents for her evil desires. Not all life is important Mira, only those who deserve it".

I didn't know what to say so I turned to Fira who shrugged, "Shall I summon the soul or is there still more to discuss?"

"Summon it, we're ready", Thane nodded glancing at me with a weak smile. I gave him a weak smile back and turned to watch Fira summon her element soul.

She took a deep breath and opened her mouth, a sweet un-lyrical song left her lips, almost immediately the Phoenix inside the crystallised liquid glowed brighter and twitched, its feathers extended and felt around its solid home. The eyes on the bird flew open and they peered out at the three of us, Fira walked closer to the bird and stroked the solid stone, she sang to the being inside and called to it before kneeling down in submission to the beast, the beast looked dead at me and I too knelt in submission along with Thane who for once followed my decision, I didn't want to upset the process in any way and I knew I was in no way above this thing in the hierarchy.

Fira's song grew louder and louder and soon enough the song was no longer being sung by just her but also by the flaming souls who lined the walls of the temple, who swam in the crystallised liquid and who made up the Phoenix element soul itself, the song was powerful and beautiful and made me want to join in but I held my tongue just in case my out of tune singing caused the whole process to rewind. The song reached the loudest it had been, echoing off the temple walls and around the strong pillars. I could feel the ground beneath my feet vibrate, stones that littered the floor shook and rattled then as it reached a final push Fira raised her hand with the pendant of the necklaced clasped firmly in her grasp, she called to it, willing it to accept her plea for help. Finally with a burst of flaming force the crystallised liquid exploded into thousands of shards and pieces, they flew past my ears whizzing so fast they glittered in the flaming light before clattering to the temple floor.

I looked up to see the Phoenix with its wings wide and flapping slowly so it could hover momentarily, the colours of the great bird were magical, bright yellows flickered through the reds of the grand beast, burnt oranges bled through from the underneath. The bird also had strange flaming gems strategically places around its neck which all glowed and grew brighter when the beast landed on its claws.

Fira looked at the bird and willed it into the necklace but it didn't acknowledge her in the slightest, instead it walked over to me and leant down on its claws to get a closer look at me. I felt my heart flutter in my chest, *what if it attacked me? What if it didn't like me and chose not to help? What if...?*

I suddenly felt a whisper on the air around me, a soft melodic voice, "What do you wish my young Queen?"

I peered into the things eyes and wondered whether it had really spoken to me or whether I was imagining things, "Huh?"

"What do you wish my Queen?" It repeated to me.

Staying in my knelt down position I spoke back, "Please I need your help".

It swayed on its claws for a moment before answering back, "So it was you whose prayer I heard that was different to the norm, well my help is granted to you oh Queen of Junia", and it then knelt down to me.

"Oh I'm not the Queen, not yet", I said not wanting it to think I was something I'm not.

The beast either ignored what I said or didn't care, either way it didn't matter as it flew up into the air and lifted its wings to the highest point it could reach and stayed there frozen for a moment before suddenly it began to fall apart bit by bit, it fell into tiny orbs and drifted down from where its shadow still loomed above us, they all came into the necklace Fira held and absorbed itself inside it. The last thing to fall down was a lone Royal Red feather which landed in the palm of my hand, then the whisper echoed again around me, "This is a gift to you Queen of Junia, a feather of a Phoenix is not just a gift for you but a gift for life. Use it wisely and you will be rewarded". Then the room fell silent around us, the only thing giving away that there had been life here was the brightly glowing Fire Pendant that Fira clung on tightly to.

"Wow I wasn't expecting that", Fira laughed.

"Really, why?"

"The Element Soul has never actually spoken to me before so I didn't know it could", she smiled, "You must really mean something to the future of Junia for it to do so".

"Oh…right", I said feeling confused, it was just me how could I mean so much for Junia's future, yes I was the future Queen but I was still just me, scaredy cat, cry baby…me. I lifted the feather up and said, "What do you think it's for?"

She shrugged, "Beats me, we'll find out though".

"It said something about the gift of life right?" Thane said.

"Yeah it did".

"Well maybe you need it to bring someone or something back to the world of the living? Keep it safe", he suggested.

"Hmm maybe", I said still feeling weirded out by the whole Phoenix talking to me thing, clutching the feather I gently placed it in my bag.

Thane laughed gently from beside me.

"What's so funny?" I asked.

"Well I guess I was wrong about the element souls…It turns out they are…Alive…It made the decision to help us, it wasn't told to do it by Fira, it had a choice and then it also gave you what seems to be a powerful gift, the gift of life".

"It's strange", Fira added, "In all the teachings it never stated the element souls were alive but I can see they truly are".

"Maybe the element souls didn't show it before?" I suggested.

"Why only now?" She asked.

I shrugged, "Beats me".

"Maybe something big is coming, something that has woken them up properly", Thane said but didn't say another word as someone else spoke for him.

"Something big is coming, something so powerful only the element souls can stop me...or help me if I control them."

We all spun round to find a woman standing there looking menacing, she had hold of Dante and threw him to the ground, "I'm sorry Fira they were too strong", he sobbed. She then placed a delicate long leg and high heeled shoe onto his back and dug in with the heel so he let out a whimper.

"Let him go", Fira ordered but it just made her cackle.

"You do not order me what to do little girl", the woman said whose voice I recognised immediately, it was Andromeda, she was a tall woman with Crow black hair which was tied up tightly into a ponytail with a leather bound rope, along with three braids which were tightly wound to her scalp either side of her temples. Her makeup was dark and fierce along with her stare, she wore a tight leather bound corset with a black feathered skirt which flapped as she moved.

"It's you", I snapped taking a step forward.

Andromeda laughed and flicked out her finger sending out a flurry of darkness, it wasn't until it was upon me that I realised it was crows, a whole murder of them attacking me, they pecked at my skin and clawed at my arms until Fira sent out a ball of fire which ripped through the birds, Andromeda wailed and called back the ones that were still alive.

"How dare you", she glared at Fira.

"I banished you from my temple", Fira hissed at her angrily, "How dare you return here".

"I do not take orders young child, I'm the one who gives them".

"Then order your crows to back down before I toast them", Fira threatened as she lit up another fire ball and was about to launch it when Andromeda burst apart and vanished into a flurry of rustling dry wings and laughter.

"Lumi I leave it up to you and your army to take down these pathetic excuses of foe", Andromeda commanded and flew out of the chamber and back up the stairs.

Lumi turned out to be a rather cute faced girl who was at least three years my senior, her hair was fuchsia pink and had been cut into a rather odd bowl shape with long strands coming down and framing her delicate but cheeky features. Her dress was a black netted material which just covered most of her private parts with a thin layer of delicate pink velvet, she held onto bag which she threw up into the air and chanted, the bag opened in mid-air and we watched in wonderment as five glowing soul orbs glided out, she twirled her fingers and the orbs began to rotate then she clicked her fingers and then the rotation slowed until one ball seemed to lose its gravitational pull and dropped into her open palm. She smiled a bright pink lipstick smile which then pouted and laughed, "Looks like Rush is up for the fight today girls and guy" and she crushed the orb in her hand which puffed into a strange pink smog.

A woman appeared out of the mist, she had wild off green almost yellow eyes that looked everywhere and nowhere all at once, her body was covered in scales like a suit of armour and her hair was a mixture of blues, greens and oranges, she smiled showing venomous fangs and her arms bled into claws and in one of those clawed hands she held a Sceptre, a Sceptre I recognised, a Sceptre that had belonged to my mother, which should have been locked away in her private chamber.

"You can't have that", I said taking a step forward but Thane held me back.

"Careful Mira", he warned.

"She has my mother's Sceptre", I told him, "But how?"

Rush laughed which wasn't a nice cuddle laugh like Lumi's, this one sounded reptilian and sent a shiver down my spine, she flicked out her tongue from side to side as if tasting the air around her.

"The palace will be ours", she hissed, "The Sceptre was a gift from the guards who feared for their lives under the command of General Gorgio".

"You monster", I shouted and lunged forward trying to grab hold of it but my finger nails just scraped the gold star at the top of the orb.

Rush laughed and swung it round hard and smashed it into my skull, I heard the hiss of the metal glide through the air before I felt the whack. Black dots fizzled in my vision making me want to vomit. Thane rushed forward and grabbed me pulling me back and leaning me up against a pillar whilst Fira went into a full fury mode, attacking left, right and centre sending out fire balls in the path of the lizard like woman. Rush hissed as a few pounded into her scaly flesh but they didn't do too much harm other than slightly burn her scales of armour.

She came for me again and this time Thane opened up fire by releasing a smoke of souls which clouded around her and me, for a moment she couldn't see me and relentlessly tried to smash her way through, she crunched the Sceptre into a pillar which made my blood boil as I knew it would damage it. Feeling dizzy and disorientated so I didn't really know what I was doing I flung myself forward still hidden in the haze of souls, I jumped onto her back and pulled at her arms to free the family heirloom which was rightfully mine. She squealed and shook her body flinging me to one side, I landed heavily on my side and winded myself and then she was on me sending her claws out to tear at me, suddenly a wall of flames appeared in front of me it was cool to the touch myside but for Rush it tore into her. She screamed and thrashed around as the flames ate away at her getting hotter and more painful by the second, she threw her arms out around herself trying to put the flames out and as she did she threw the Sceptre to one side and I watched it clink away behind another pillar.

I jumped up and ran for the Sceptre only to be greeted by Lumi who smiled and punched me in the face, I flew back and tasted blood in my mouth, coughing I spat some out onto the floor of the chamber but before Lumi could reach the Sceptre I was up and running again slamming my small frame into hers but she wasn't much bigger than me and we both went flying. She snarled as I snatched a handful of her ridiculously pink hair as she tried to reach what it was I so desperately desired.

Then without warning a roaring squawk echoed around the temple we both looked up at the same time to see Fira had called upon the Phoenix to help us, Rush was still fighting even though half her body had been melted to a mulch, her armour now giving up the fight and melting down her lizard like body. Thane was now resorting to punching and kicking her but still she wouldn't go down. Fira cooed to the Phoenix and I watch as it made its wings go rigid and tight, the feathers all went rock solid and solidified flames burst from them before it flapped causing them all to fly out and smash right into Rush who screamed louder than before and fell to her knees flapping her clawed hands tearing at her own body to put it out.

Lumi leered into my face, "Sorry Rush guess this is your show now", and she got up pushing me to the ground and headed to the door. She took one last look at me, "This ain't over Princess", and she vanished in a swirl of mist that she created by crushing another orb, leaving her wounded soldier behind.

Rush's eyes looked betrayed and hurt before her body finally gave in and she fell to the floor in a pool of molten flesh and blood. It simmered and bubbled on the floor before Thane waved his hand over her, he was absorbing her soul into his own and recycling the dark soul meaning all evidence of her being was gone, he then came running over to me, "Mira your hurt".

"But I got this", I smiled lifting up the Sceptre, it shone in the fires glow.

As Thane helped me to my feet Fira prayed to the Phoenix and asked him to go back into the necklace, within seconds his orbing soul body vanish back to where it had come from, around Fira's neck. She then ran to Dante who had been hiding in the back of the chamber the whole time.

"Are you hurt?" she asked him.

He nodded and pointed to his leg which had a large gash and was bleeding heavily, "We need to get him to Master Cinder", Fira commanded and I let Thane go to help her.

We all slowly made our way back up to the main temple where a worried Master Cinder and the others were waiting, they took Dante off of Fira and Thane and rushed him to a nearby room. Fira then took my hand and led me into the same room, it was a small medical room with potions, lotions and herbs. She quickly made a paste of clear liquid and smothered it over some wounds I had before checking me over but I was fine compared to Dante who was crying out in pain.

"Will he be ok?" I asked her.

She nodded, "Yes Master Cinder will know what to do".

Then a girl who was also a temple helper rushed in, "It's happening, the enemy is here!"

Fira sighed, "The time to leave is now Princess before too many of the enemy appear". Thane dropped back to grab the bags Master Cinder had prepared for us and Fira led us to the main doors.

"Fira", the girl rushed up again, "Good luck and let Junia be with you".

Fira bowed to the girl before she ran off to help with Dante, just as Fira opened the main doors we could hear the people of Lavara coming to the temple for safety, screams and worried cries filled the atmosphere making my stomach churn, "This way", Fira said taking us round the back, "The people will be angry and scared its best you come this way Mira".

I followed slowly on her tail as I was still in shock and recovering from our first attack, Thane was close behind me but urged me on quicker. We ran down the side of the volcano along some manmade steps which led us through parts of the burnt out forest. The forest sang with a breezy tune of wails and cries of pain and fear, my blood ran cold at the thought of what might be out there but we had to move on, we had to get out of Lavara.

Fira raised her hand stopping me just as I heard a loud roar in the not too far distance, "What was that?"

"An enemy", she replied, "And its close".

"ROAR".

The menacing sound sent Goosebumps up my spine and over the base of my neck making all the hairs stand on end, Fira didn't look so scared but was on edge as she paused scanning the scenery around us, then out of a rumbling burning and bursting tree what I presumed was the enemy appeared.

It was a three headed wolf looking animal, all the heads and eyes were latched onto me, Fira and Thane their jaws dribbled with saliva as they licked their lips, they wanted our flesh and to stop us leaving Lavara. I saw a flash of something behind one of the mutt's eyes and heard a cackle of laughter, "Andromeda", I cried out, the cackled sounded again before the mutts howled and charged right for us.

Fira went right into the fight and threw up a wall of fire to protect us, she then spun on the spot and threw out her hands in quick succession blasting a dozen or so fireballs right at the enemy, the beasts howled and roared as the blasts hit them square on. The wall of fire subsided as

Fira pulled it down to reveal what damage she had done to the monsters, two of the dog's heads were dead, one was lolling around uselessly and the other had been burnt to crisp, its fur melted and pooling underneath it like a gruesome puddle of dog muck. The last head was unharmed but looked angered by the death of its two siblings, it howled louder than before and pounced for us.

I had no choice but to run as did Thane but Fira tried to blast it but the thing was fast and knocked her flying with its tail before it then clamped its jaws down on her arm with its fangs digging into her flesh, she screamed out in pain. Thane ran back and blasted it with a smog of souls but the thing held on tightly, not bothered in the slightest by his attempts to distract it.

I stood there frozen in fear *what could I do? I didn't have a power like she did?* I done the only thing I could think of and ran at the beast screaming and shouting then jumped on its back like I had tried to with Rush smashing my fists into its rock hard skull but it was no use the creature didn't even flinch at any of my blows. It shook me off and sent me flying into the undergrowth next to the steps, Fira screamed again and I knew she was in a lot of pain, I felt like crying and curling into a ball but I couldn't let her die not now, not right at the beginning of our journey. Looking around I spotted a large branch which had fallen from a dead tree, I didn't know how strong it was but I had to try something. Snatching it up I felt the heaviness of the branch, the ash and charcoaled ruins of the forest had strengthened it, causing it to harden. I ran for the creature and yelled again at it, this time it turned to me almost smiling with the satisfaction that it had us where it wanted us but as it turned I launched my body, the branch I held onto tightly dug into one of its eyes piercing in deep, the eyeball popped and an inky mess snailed down its fur. It howled and thrashed its head from side to side letting go of poor Fira but it was her chance, she called out and conjured a large fire ball and blasted it right at the mutts head and we stood there as it exploded in a flash of blood, bones and fur.

We all stood there for a moment gasping for our breath and in shock, I'd never experienced anything like this before and now I was covered in a strange beings blood.

"Thanks", Fira breathed standing up right and flinching as her arm had been bitten deeply by the mutt's teeth, she had two large gouges and they were bleeding heavily.

"Oh no, you're really hurt!" I exclaimed panicking over her.

"It's fine don't worry", she said reaching into her own bag which Mr Cinder had given her, inside she pulled out some bandages and some alcohol to clean the wound with, she set to work getting me to help her and she was soon ready to go again. Thane lifted all the bags onto his shoulders so I could help Fira as we stumbled towards the end of the steps which came to the road not too far from the main gate.

"You sure you're alright?" I asked her.

She nodded, "I'm fine and once we get to Beach Haven I can find a doctor to take a proper look".

Keeping her steady we slowly made it to the border gate which was clear of any enemies, monsters or any of Andromeda's goonies. I just hoped we didn't get spotted by any of the palace guards either, all I needed was to be caught now…*Not.*

We left the not so safety of Lavara behind us and walked straight into the busy bustling world that was Cosima, it was late morning nearly noon but the city was always moving even when everyone was at work or school, the idea of a city never sleeps rings true to the centre of Cosima as there is always something going on whether it be a show at a theatre, a dance at a local night spot or a dashing meal out, not that I had ever been to any but I could watch from my room at the palace and I dreamed of going to them all.

We walked for about ten minutes before Fira asked to sit down, she looked a rather pale shade of her normal self and sweat was beading on her brow yet Cosima was ten times cooler than Lavara. "Fira are you sure you're alright? You don't look too good", I asked feeling nervous to be stationary, Cosima was full of cameras and I didn't need to be caught on one.

"No I don't think I am", she wheezed breathlessly, "I think the mutt may have poisoned me".

"We need to get her to a doctor", I said looking at Thane who agreed.

"How?" Fira said, "Where? Beach Haven is still a long way from here and I don't think I will make it that far."

"The Medical district which is only a few blocks from here, come on take my arm", I said lifting her back up and helping her along. People looked at us with strange creased up faces as we passed them by but I just kept my head down.

"Mira I wouldn't worry too much about being spotted", Thane smiled, "Have you seen the state you're in?"

He was smiling at me as I told him I hadn't, we passed a shop window which was extremely reflective and I then saw how messed up I looked and why people had been giving me strange looks, my hair was dishevelled from all the fighting and was covered in a fine layer of soot from Lavara, my skin too was covered in soot along with blood and other exploded parts from the mutt. I looked a mess. It did relax me a little to know that this might help in terms of a disguise but the looks we got from everyone did make me feel uncomfortable.

I led Fira and Thane through the city centre walking right through the concrete city, only broken up by the strategically placed false trees and flower boxes along with some beautifully carved benches. The whole city around us was unnatural, all cement and manmade inventions holding homes together, there were not many 'Houses' in Cosima most people's home were apartments and not just one or two but hundreds all piled up on top of one another, yet we were classed as the richest country in Junia yet from what I had seen of Lavara I counted them as pretty rich by their simple way of life, yes it was dirty work but their homes were made from natural things and it was spread out, you had breathing space. Although I cannot exactly moan I live in the grand palace which could house thousands of people, we have so many rooms I have lost count of them.

As I watched Fira stare at all the flats and their flowering window boxes, the city people's tiny green spaces I didn't want to let this feeling that was coming over me go, the feeling of having a friend, another girl to run riot round the town with even if she was ill and I covered in grime.

I led her deeper into what we call the 'Medical District' it's basically just a group of plush, clinical looking medical centres with loads of doctors and healers all competing against one another to get the most money, the city scape that surrounded us liked to feed off money and had become so much of a rat race. Some centres catered for the poorest of pockets and some went right up to the royal and famous status.

"So the medical district huh?" Fira said looking unimpressed, "It's all concrete and glass".

"Yes it is", I replied, "Most of Cosima is concrete and glass, you'll get bored of it pretty quickly".

She nodded, "Yeah think I will but it's all still pretty cool at the moment though", she smiled, "So how many districts are there in Cosima".

I had to think and count in my head, "Ten".

"Wow ten districts all in one country?" she looked impressed again, "Lavara only has the town and temple and even then they aren't classed as districts".

"Well Cosima is a huge place", I said holding out my hands and counting down the districts on each finger, "We have the Royal District which is where I live at the palace, mainly for tourists to go to but most tourists are Cosiman's anyway", I smiled at that shyly.

"That could one day change", Thane added from beside me.

I nodded and carried on, "Then you have the Medical District, Beach Haven Port, Lavara, River Skye,

94

Emerald Bridge, Gate of Spirit, those are the main ones people use daily along with The Education Centre where all our mainstream schools and colleges reside along with Cosima's University. Then there's the Green Lands district which is mainly farming land way up towards Emerald Bridge and finally The Residential Home District which is basically as it sounds, a large district just full of homes but some of those are houses not just apartments like the city centre".

"So many", Fira wheezed, "Educational sounds different".

"What schools and colleges?" I asked her.

She nodded, "You go to them?"

I shrugged, "Not really I was mainly home schooled at the palace. How about you?"

"We don't really have much of a school system in Lavara, once you are old enough to muck in and work you work. I was trained at the temple".

"Oh", I said not really knowing what to say, here it was illegal for kids to not go to school, they had to stay till they were fifteen and then they had to move onto college or a work placement. I was about to open my mouth to say something when I spotted something across the street from me and immediately grabbed their arms and pulled them back, we ducked behind some benches and the false bushes. I pointed to some palace guards who were exiting one of the richest medical centres, they were carry bags and bags of medical equipment and potions. *What were they up to?* We waited for them to pass before I spoke, "I think we should head to one of those ones", I pointed to a more run down looking part of the district, the one I had in mind I knew would cater to the poor and I hoped that the guards wouldn't think to go there.

We dashed over the concrete pathways which lined the streets and ducked inside, a small bell chimed as we walked in and a man with large glasses, balding grey hair and a white uniform looked up from a desk and pile of paperwork. He smiled politely and stood to help us as we struggled with Fira as her legs went weak, "What happened?" he asked lowering his glasses and looking carefully at her wounds.

"She was attacked but a mutt", I told him.

He eyed me over suspiciously, "The only place I know that has had sightings of mutts is Lavara, it's all over the news".

I looked down and the doctor studied me closer, "You're the Princess?" It sounded more like a statement than a question.

I nodded looking at Thane.

"Princess Mira you cannot be here bad things are happening to Cosima and the…Palace".

"Please don't shop us in", I pleaded, "My friend needs help and I'm hoping to find a way to bring the King and Queen back to stop…her", as I spoke the small television set the man had in the waiting room flashed to the news with Andromeda and her gang of poisonous witches all standing outside the palace waving like royalty.

"You can trust me Princess but we must hurry she has sent out the palace guards to take all medical supplies so the people of Cosima have to go to the palace and pay larger amounts than normal if they are sick or unwell. I do not condone such practice which is why I vowed to help the poorer people of our country".

"Thank you", I said to him, "Do you think you can help her".

"Yes come this way", he ushered us through a door and led us all into a small side room where he sat her down, he washed and cleaned her wounds again before bandaging her up. He then vanished to a cupboard at the back of the room and found a potion which he shook and handed to Fira, "Drink this, it doesn't taste nice but in a few hours you will be fully healed".

She took it and sipped at it wincing at the gross taste but I knew it would work, I had seen these potions before and I knew they were miracles in bottles. The more expensive clinics had ones that could heal you in a heartbeat, fully with no scars but we would have to make do. Just as she finished and handed the doctor the bottle back the front door chimed, the doctor placed his finger to his lips and whispered, "Wait here", he then exited the room and closed the door behind him.

Thane stood by the door and listened, "It's the guards", he whispered. I joined Thane at the door listening in I could hear the doctor argue that his stuff was not to be taken and we heard him lock the door we stood behind as he argued more loudly, obviously as a warning to us.

"Now what?" Fira asked standing up and flexing her arms, she already looked more her usual self.

"We use the window", Thane said opening the window as wide as it would go.

"But we haven't paid him for the treatment", I exclaimed.

Thane replied with, "I don't think he will mind this time around, it won't take long for them to break in here anyway, he's giving us the chance to escape". And with that he hoisted me up and out the window followed by Fira and lastly by him. He then passed us our bags as we ran down the alleyway behind the doctor's clinic and back out onto the street which was now crawling with palace guards. Looking around I could just make out a sign, *'Train Station'*, I pointed and they nodded in agreement, we had to chance it or risk being found hiding anyway.

We took to a run across the pavements as the guards looked in all the medical practices around them, we ducked behind suitable hiding places when needed before finally making the last mad dash to the train station. The station itself is a very polished building with whitewashed walls which shine in the light like marble, windows sat all around the building which I knew were cleaned on a weekly basis to make sure everything in Cosima stayed pristine. Around a hundred steps led up to the main entrance although there was a lift at the side for women with children or for the disabled citizens but we needed speed on our side and calling the lift would take too long especially if we came across a queue, we took to the stairs taking two at a time Thane taking a quick glance behind us, "I think we're fine for now", he said as we reached the top, two large ornate street lamps loomed above us in their shimmering silver metal, casting long shadows over the ground. Chancing a look I spotted some guards but they couldn't have taken any notice of us or maybe they just thought we were running to catch our train. Keeping up appearances we ran inside and went straight for the ticket kiosk, the woman behind it looked rather disgusted at how we looked but served us anyway, "Where to?" she spoke in her posh Cosiman accent.

"Beach Haven Port district please", I said, "For three".

She handed over the tickets, "As you are, dirty...you will have to sit in second class".

I felt like jumping through the glass ticket counter and telling her who did she think she was talking to but being in second would conceal us more so I took them without tipping her. We went to our designated platform and sat on benches whilst we waited for the train to arrive.

A train soon hovered into the station making just the slight whooshing noise of the electric, the station master called out over the speakers to alert us that our train was boarding now. Taking Fira's hand I led her to the train she was now ogling with amazement, the train itself to me was a rather boring machine, it was streamline and white with windows at the front for the driver but the carriages were all blocked in due to the speed of the train, people before had suffered motion sickness from the view of the whizzing world flying past. The track the train hovered over was merely so people didn't walk out in front of one by accident as the train didn't need to use the track as it hovered, these trains pretty much flew to their destinations but with supersonic speed. The doors appeared like magic flashing to show people it was time to board, when the train is moving the doors virtually disappear so people can't jump out on suicide missions but it is a little frightening on the few occasions one has broken down, which was very rare according to the books I read.

We all headed to second class which was virtually empty other than a few homeless people which had been doing their daily rounds of begging on Cosima's streets, now it was time for them to go back to their shelters before coming back tonight when all the night owls would be out, apparently the night is easier for them to beg as drunk people are more likely to hand money over than during the day but it does come with risks as there have been times were the homeless have been beaten and mugged of the money they had begged for, I guess Cosima was not the heavenly like place it liked to make out it was.

The seats we sat on were hard and not very comfortable, there was a toilet at the end of the carriage which smelt like urine and a disused food cart with inedible food moulding away. We sat alone by ourselves and waited as the smoothness of the train took over, hopefully it wouldn't take too long as there was only one stop which was the Educational District.

~ The Country of Beach Haven ~

The sunlight was so bright and streamed onto my skin instantly warming me to my soul as we climbed off the train and immediately glided unnoticed through the border gate, I shielded my eyes and tried to take in my surroundings but it was just all so new and glorious that my eyes couldn't scan quickly enough. Beach Haven was as the name foretold, it was a beach and a haven, a heaven by the sea and I wanted to stay here, the warmth was smooth and bearable not like Lavara where it was chokingly hot.

The sea itself was fresh blue and crystal clear, I could make out individual fish swimming around below the planks of wood we all stood on. Beach Haven was a strange and happy looking country and town, it had all been built on the water on stilts, wooden planks scattered the water like roads and pathways all leading to people's homes and the town centre which was risen up on higher stilts with rows of shops which were all wooden shacks with twig roofs and flurries of flowers giving the place some bright colours, fuchsia pinks, lemon yellows, leafy greens and pearlescent purples.

We took the path towards the town centre, none of us knew where the Water Temple resided or the Element Converter but surely someone might notice us looking lost around the town and want to help us out? *Maybe?*

The main street of the town centre was crammed with shops, to me this place looked more like a tourist attraction than a town that people could possibly live in day in and day out, one shop sold handmade and beautifully woven fabrics which all hung up on racks in the window but also out on the decking on rails, the sunlight as we passed showed off all the glorious colours and I couldn't help but touch one, it was as soft as anything I might find at the palace. A small woman came out shouting at us for touching the rugs, for a moment I was confused why, then I remembered how dirty and grubby we all were, she must have thought us as tramps. Thane managed to locate a small restroom where we managed to freshen up a little. I scrubbed the soot and grime from my skin and hair and tied it all back up but my dress was still dirty but I couldn't do much about that for now. Fira and Thane both too looked much cleaner as we strolled through the town and onto the next shop which caught my eye, it sold nick knacks. All the small shelves of the shop were so full and over stocked it looked like the shelves might collapse at any time, a woman with bright blonde hair and shocking blue eyes came out the shop, "You buy? Any two for price of one ya!"

"Er…"

"Maybe later", Thane cut in with his charming smile, "Um do you happen to know where the Water Temple is?"

The woman smirked, "You buy I tell".

Thane scowled but I cut in this time, "Sure thing", I looked around at all the trinkets when I spotted a small ring which looked to be made of silver, it didn't look very feminine it was more masculine, at the tip of the ring it had a circular shape and a tiny coin inserted inside I picked it up to examine it.

"That coin is from treasure, we find below sea bed, maybe from before war ya, old Junia money", the woman smiled putting it on my finger.

I laughed, "I don't think this is very me".

The woman tutted, "Then no tell".

But I turned to Thane and grabbed his hand and placed the ring on his index finger, "Hey", he said going to take it off but the woman butted it.

"65 Junians".

"65!" Fira exclaimed horrified by the amount.

I glanced from where I had picked it up and on the shelf the tag said '45' so she added on more Junians because we were outsiders, not wanting to cause a ruckus as I was trying to smooth the relationship between the countries and Cosima I paid the amount with the last of Thanes money, "Now can you help us?"

She nodded, "Yes Water Temple is at the end of the Haven road ya".

"Oh right", I said looking down at all the roads that sprung off from the town centre, "And which one is the Haven road?"

She pointed, "Central ya".

As I stared at the roads before me I could see one was thicker than the others, its planks built slightly wider than the others, so my guess was that one had to be the central Haven road, "Thank you", I said and bowed.

"Hey wait a sec what about our second item for free?" Fira asked.

The woman smirked, "I tell you central road, that is for free ya" and with that the woman left us standing like fools on the decking.

"Well she was rather charming", I laughed.

Thane just eyeballed the shop as if willing the woman his bad thoughts, "No she was not charming, she is a scam artist, no way is this trash worth 65 Junians".

"Trash?" I said quietly with a saddened tone to my voice but I could feel something bubbling up inside me and Fira noticed too.

"Oh no I didn't mean…" He stammered, "It's lovely…Really…It is…Are you two laughing at me?"

I started giggling uncontrollably and so did Fira, Thane's face blushed beet root read and he stormed off down the decking towards the central road. Still giggling Fira and I started after him passing many more shops, some were food shops selling strange looking appetisers, another was a smoke shop, it sold strange items people could smoke or that they could put round their homes like incense.

We caught up to Thane who was still marching on, I got the indication he didn't like Beach Haven very much or being laughed up, "Hey Thane slow down, look I didn't mean to annoy you".

He turned to me, "Don't worry about it, its fine", he smiled at me, "I guess I'll treasure this ring forever", he mocked me and I stuck my tongue out at him and he stuck his out back before all three of us burst into another fit of giggles.

As we walked down the central decked pathway I couldn't help but take in everything around me, Beach Haven was so exotic in its appearance, all the wood that made the homes of people all neatly and expertly compacted and crafted together, the roofs too were expertly made, some thatch like, others were more modern with wooden tiles and high points. But what I noticed more was how everyone had the colourful flowers all scattered around, they wrapped them around the columns and pillars which held up the front roofs of some of the homes, or railings down foot wells and stairs, everything here reflected the beauty and light of nature and water. I spotted some sailors out on their boats fishing, some had rods, others had spears but either way it worked as their boats were stocked up with fish which they either took to the port to export to the rest of Junia or back to the decked shore to be sold at the large fish food shop which we were slowly passing by, the smell of the sea and fish hung heavily in the air around us. They sold everything from raw fish 'Sushi' to cooked fish, smoked fish to roasted fish, there was a few restaurants that specialised in certain recipes one of which I felt my mouth watering at, "Thane, Fira, I so need some fish and Coconut sauce", I said pointing to the takeaway point in the restaurant.

Fira pulled a face.

"It's delicious", I beamed, "The chef at the palace makes it for me and it's wonderful…Your love it I know you will".

"The one here should be even better", Thane added, "Cooked by the people who invented the recipe".

So they both agreed as Fira was also hungry, we soon had some in our hands and were sitting on the end of the decking with our legs in the warm water. Every now and then some fish would swim up to us and Thane threw in some food which they gobbled up and swam off tickling our feet with their tail fins. This was the happiest I had felt in such a long time, sitting in the warm sun, talking and eating with friends, this is what I imagine normal girls my age doing. Thane picked up on my cheery mood and kicked some water at me the drops splatting all up my clothes, Fira didn't look too amused as some went on her food but she just sat back whilst I kicked up a splash soaking him to the bone.

"Hey, Hey", he called out laughing, "That's not fair you cheated". He stood up and Fira nodded at me grinning so I grabbed his hand, he turned to me and smiled, "Oh no you don't", and as we play fought we pulled each other into the calm, warm waters below us. Fira was on the decking laughing so hard she choked on her fish.

"Haha", I said pushing him under and he grabbed me pulling me under with him, he smiled at me under the water with his dark hair floating wildly, his smile made me feel all warm inside. I smiled back and he stroked my cheek before I needed air and swam back up, I felt my cheeks flush from his touch and I looked away from both of them until I felt them calm down once again.

"Hey if you two are finished with your water fight we need to go and find the water converter", Fira said with a mocking stern look.

"Yes mum", Thane joked and I felt myself suddenly sink back into our reality, here was me having fun when I needed to keep a level head to save my mum and dad, not just that but the whole of Junia depended on me to do it. *How could I be having fun now with so much needing to be done?*

Climbing out of the water dripping wet we tried to squeeze some of the excess water out of our now fairly clean clothes but it was no use we were soaked to the bone but Fira commented the sun would soon dry us as we walked and she was right, within an hour I was mostly dry but I did feel tired and my legs were aching now, I hadn't been out on such a long trip since...forever and even then I was with royal escorts who either drove or took me on transportation.

The route through the rest of the central road was a long one and before we knew it the sun was starting to set and a chill had set in sending the nice warm temperature plummeting, people were climbing into their homes and shutting their doors tight, closing their windows and hanging the beautiful Beach Haven fabric over the gaps like curtains.

"Do you think we've been had? By that scamming lady?" Thane asked looking a little worried, "I don't think this road goes anywhere other than to homes".

"Should we turn back?" I asked.

Fira spoke up shivering, "No we should just find somewhere to stay for the night". As she said it a bright blond haired man with fishing clothing walked past us, she collared him down and asked him if there was anywhere travellers could stay the night.

"Only place that will take people now is the Old Haven Bar", he told us and pointed to a large hut on stilts that had lights flickering through the windows and music filling the air.

"Oh really? Nowhere else?" She said not liking the drunken atmosphere that was radiating from it.

He shook his head, "No sorry, the light show will be on tomorrow and people have come from all over Junia to watch it".

"Light show?" I asked but he was already walking off towards his own home.

"Well what should we do?" Fira asked.

Thane answered, "We have no choice but to go there, before long it's going to be freezing".

Myself and Fira sighed but we set off towards the Old Haven Bar, as we neared it I could hear singing and shouting, I knew instantly we were not going to get much sleep here tonight. Thane opened the saloon style doors and ushered us inside away from the cool breeze, the bar was full to the brim with people drinking, singing, eating and partying. The smell of alcohol filled the air even with the many sticks of incense that filled the room with the dulling smoke. Making our way to the bar we found a rather crazy and chubby looking fellow who was singing just as loud as the punters, "Oh here, be thee, be some, be show, me…" I had no clue as to what the song was or even what it meant as it made no sense to me.

"Hello", I called over to him and he smiled at us and came thundering over, he was a large man with a rather large alcohol induced belly, his hair was as bright as the woman's at the shop and the man we had seen on the decking, *maybe it was a country trait?*

"What can ye do for ye?" he asked in a weird accent.

"Um we need a place to stay for the night", I told him.

He shook his head, "No can do ye, we full for week, for the lights ya".

"Lights?"

"Ye great shimmering lights of yonder", he told us.

Feeling deflated we stood back from the bar, "What do we do now?"

"We can't just sleep on the street its freezing", Fira said with a worried look on her face, she looked chilled to the bone already, she wasn't used to this milder atmosphere.

"We could just stay in here for the night and order lots of drinks so they don't kick us out?" I suggested but before they could answer a small voice spoke up.

"Excuse me?"

I turned to find a young blond haired boy no older than twelve, "If you need somewhere to stay I can help. My gramps has a spare room at his, I could ask for you?"

"Would you mind?" I asked him, "If it's no trouble?"

He nodded and ran off to a rather drunk looking man, he was old and frail but I could see drink was his life source, they spoke for a few moments before the boy came running back, "He said yes but you must set up a tab at the bar for him", the boy's face flushed and he looked incredibly embarrassed.

"Do we have enough?" I asked Fira who opened the purse strings for the money she had donated from the temple.

"I think so but tell him 100 Junians is our limit", she said to the boy who ran back to the old man before rushing back to us.

"He said that will do", the boy sniffed, "Anything for a few free drinks", he looked ashamed of how this old man was acting but who were we to grumble, in the long run it may have been cheaper than hiring out a room to sleep in at the bar itself.

The young boy took the house keys from his gramps whilst Fira set up the 100 Junian limit tab. The boy then led us out of the bar and to his home, it took us ten minutes to walk to it by which time Fira was nearly frozen solid. The house was like the others a wooden hut with a thatched roof, as we entered inside I saw how very homely these things looked inside, the boy went round and turned on some oil lanterns which made the home flare up and look instantly warm, even Fira relaxed a little now. The main room was full of the beautifully coloured fabrics like we had seen at the shops, some were hanging from the windows, one on the floor in front of a fire place and another strewn over a small wicker style seat just big enough for two people. I hadn't noticed from the outside but a stone chimney went up into the roof, it curved around the fireplace making it the theme wall in the room, hundreds of trinkets and pictures had been hung from the brickwork. The boy tended to the fire and soon had it up and running, he grabbed some fish from his kitchen area which was a few cupboards and an ice bucket to keep the fish cool in before skewering them and roasting them over the fire. Whilst the fish was cooking away he led us to the spare room, we passed three rooms which were hidden behind fabric which was hung up over the frames, the last room we came to he pushed the fabric aside and we found two single beds with yet more of the fabric.

"Sorry there's only two beds but er, you don't need to sleep right?" he looked at Thane.

Thane nodded, "I'll sit in the front room tonight if you don't mind?"

The boy nodded, "Sure gramps probably won't be home till sunrise anyway".

"You stay here alone?" I asked him.

He shook his head, "Not always I have my older sisters, Brooklyn but she works at the temple and Nisha who is setting things up for the light show tomorrow but normally she works at the fabric hut weaving and is normally home by supper time, they share this room normally".

"Will they mind us staying here?" I asked.

"No they won't mind you are paying for gramps drinks so we can at least save one nights worth of Junians", he smiled wearily.

My heart went out to this young boy, his gramps certainly had a bad drinking problem and they struggled for money *but what could I do?*

"Is there anything we can help with as we are staying tonight?" I asked him.

He shook his head, "Oh no Nisha tidied up before she left and Brooklyn made sure I have food".

"So Brooklyn works at the temple? Will she be back soon as we would really like to see it?" I asked him.

The boy nodded, "Yes she will be back in the morning with more food...Oh no the fish". He ran off in a hurry to go check the fish that was roasting away.

I turned to the others, "Poor kid".

Fira smiled, "He's fine most kids are used to mucking in".

"Yes but he's alone".

"A lot of kids in Lavara do things alone, they have to whilst their parents work in the mines or doing other duties, sometimes at the temple were hold child only prayer days were basically they come and pray to the element soul and then they can play all day until home time", Fira told me, "Things in the other countries are really different to Cosima, you will get used to it".

I felt so bad that these children had to stay alone whilst their parents worked or that they too had to muck in and not carry on with schooling but at the same time they were learning the way of their own country but what if that wasn't what they wanted to do with their life? How would they get into other jobs? Maybe they couldn't? I wonder if this boy even went to school?

"Hope you're all hungry, the fish is ready", the boy said looking in from the fabric doorway, we hadn't told him we had eaten but he had prepared us some of his family's precious food, *how could we not eat it?*

We sat down together with me and Fira on the seat and Thane and the boy sitting on the rug that lined the wooden floor, the fish was cooked to perfection and he had even poured us some of his dads wine, I had declined at first worried for him but he assured us his dad wouldn't notice, "He would just think he drank it already", he laughed.

Soon enough we got chatting and found out the boy was called Kenton, he did go to school twice a week as that was all Brooklyn could afford on her temple wages as Nisha didn't want to chip in as she was saving for her own home with her boyfriend, which as Kenton went on had caused a rift between the family.

"Brooklyn and Nisha always fight especially over who has to give gramps his drink money", he said playing with his fish's roasting stick in the fire pit.

"Can't he get some help, for his problem?" I asked.

He shrugged, "My mum already tried that when she was alive but since she died he's gone back to drinking again"

"Oh, I'm sorry", I said.

He nodded thanks before changing the subject as to why we were here, we told him part of the truth other than me being Royal just in case someone overheard or he decided to shop us in.

"Brooklyn's the converter at the temple", he told us but he shook his head, "But she probably won't help you".

"Why not?" Thane asked.

He shrugged again it looked to me like a nervous thing, "She takes her job of looking after the temple very seriously, if she knows taking the element soul would mean bringing enemies to Beach Haven and not being here to watch over the temple she will refuse. The temple is like her home, family and children all in one".

"Well we might need your help in trying to persuade her", Thane smiled.

Kenton nodded, "I will try but she rarely listens to me, both she and Nisha are very hot headed".

I smiled, this Brooklyn and her sister sounded like right characters but I was nervous, what if we couldn't persuade her to help, *then what?*

Before long Kenton was tired and had fallen asleep in front of the fire, Thane carefully lifted him and took him to his room to sleep before coming back to us and ushering us off to bed.

"But I'm not tired", Fira moaned yawning, wanting to sit and talk some more.

"You both need your rest, now go", Thane ordered which was funny as he normally sounded so chilled out and laid back but his tone gave off a more parenting tone which showed how much older he really was to us. Saying good night we vanished into the sister's room and lay down on their beds.

I lay there for a while but I felt wrong sleeping in someone else's bed, Fira on the other hand was already in a deep slumber even though she had stated not feeling sleepy, feeling like I wanted to talk I decided to go and see Thane.

Thane was sitting on the seat reading a book he must have found lying around somewhere, "Mira you should be resting".

"I can't sleep".

He moved over and gave me room to perch next to him, "Any particular reason?"

"Not really", I shrugged.

"Want me to tell you a short story?" he asked, that same playful boyish grin plastered on his features.

I smiled back, "I'm a bit old for fairy tales don't you think?"

He laughed, "It's not quite a fairy tale but about the lights they keep going on about here, well legend is that the lights come from another world that echoes our own. Every few hundred years it is said that the other world comes so close to Junia that its atmosphere collides with our own causing a chemical reaction in the skies above us making the shimmering lights that appear".

"What is this other world?" I asked him intrigued.

"Some people call it Azure, another form of heaven, another Junia but some people believe it to be the mirrored reflection of Junia, we are the heavenly world and they represent a hell. I think it is something else altogether, another world that is unlike our own but no one knows. No one has travelled out of Junia and come back to tell the tale".

"I didn't know you could leave Junia?"

"There is meant to be a certain location where there is a void and you can supposedly leave Junia but the people who have claimed that they are going to go and do it leave and never come back".

"Do you think they died?" I asked him.

"Maybe", He shrugged, "But people have been to Spirit to see if their loved one has gone there after saying they were going to the void but they cannot be found".

"Maybe they can't travel back to our Spirit maybe they had to settle at another one?"

"Who knows?"

We spoke some more about the lights before I finally fell asleep but instead of going back to the room with Fira I fell asleep on the seat with Thane next to me. He let me rest my head on his shoulder and he stroked my hair to make me stay sleepy as I kept trying to talk to him to stay awake but he was having none of it and ignored me until I was in a deep slumber.

When morning arrived we were all up and ready way before the young boy got up and when he did we had him some food ready which myself and Fira had gone out to a small shop nearby with the last of our money to say thanks. He looked made up by the food we had chosen as he told us he couldn't afford this type of food normally. It wasn't long after he had finished eating that the door opened and a young girl around my age walked in carrying a large tub of fish, vegetables and water, she looked surprised to see us all sitting here but she smiled anyway.

"Hey Kenton whose your friends?" she asked looking at us.

"They needed somewhere to stay last night and gramps agreed as the royal lady paid for his drink", he replied.

"Er how do you know I'm a royal lady?" I felt gob smacked and even Fira and Thane looked nervous.

Kenton smiled and grabbed a book he had hidden under the seat, he turned to a page which showed a picture of me with my parents all dressed in royal attire. "I thought I recognised you and I was right. Don't worry though I know that you are being hunted by the wicked Queen who lives at the palace now so I won't tell anyone".

"We would much appreciate it if you didn't tell anyone", Thane said also looking at the girl who had walked in.

"I won't tell", she said giving us a questioning look, "But why exactly are you here in my home and in Beach Haven? Especially if you are being hunted by some evil Queen, my brother could have gotten hurt".

"She's not an evil Queen", I said, "Just a grand evil witch", I added trying to make it sound better but failed as her faced showed me how unimpressed by me she now was.

"Anyway to defeat the evil Queen they need you to take them to the temple and call the element soul", Kenton blurted out.

She looked angered by this, her long bright blonde hair swaying in its high ponytail which had been almost cornrowed from the sides into the band where all the hair hung loosely. "So who are your friends here?" She motioned to Thane and Fira, "And why do you even think I would give up my element soul to help?"

"Mira needs all the element souls to come together to call the final element soul to defeat Andromeda, if we do not do it she is going to poison Junia and destroy it. She needs to be stopped. Anyway I'm Thane Mira's soul guardian and this is Fira..."

"Fira, as in the Fire converter?" she sounded pissed cutting off Thane, "Why did you leave your temple?"

"I had to, to help Mira and Junia".

"But you have left your element soul vulnerable", Brooklyn said.

Fira shook her head and pointed to her necklace, "The element soul is safe with me, always".

"What!" she shouted, "You took it away from Lavara, didn't all the enemies and fiends come to attack?"

Fira nodded, "Yes they did but my town's people are ready to fight them along with the temple Masters".

"And they just let you walk out of there with it", she looked disgusted, "No way am I doing that, putting my home, my town, my country at risk of enemies appearing and killing them. The temple is my responsibility and I need to keep it safe".

"But if you don't Andromeda will win and she will destroy Junia as we know it", Fira exclaimed.

"Lie's she can't do that", Brooklyn sounded so sure of herself.

"She can and she will", I added, "We need your help and that of all the other converters".

"And why should I trust you, you're a royal, and royals are bad news, they disregard the religions and all that Junia stands for".

"I'm trying to fix that, I want to know about the religion and what it stands for, I want to bring something back to Cosima to stop the rift between us all", I told her.

"That will never happen, once the king and Queen are back they will put a stop to it and we would have helped destroy our own homes to save yours!"

"No that's not true, it's to save all of ours", I cried out.

"No, I will not help, you will need to find another way".

"At least take us to the temple", Thane suggested.

"Why?"

"Well at least his way Mira can see what it is your part of the religion is about, if she doesn't she will never know and can never try and change anything", he said.

"Whatever, but you will not change my mind, but before I do I'm helping Nisha with preparations for the light show tonight so you will have to wait until tomorrow till we can go".

I was about to say that we didn't have time for games or to be waiting around but Thane spoke up first, "That's fine as you wish".

I looked at him questioningly but he said nothing, maybe he just knew that this was the only way to try and break her by letting her have her own way for a while, I just hoped it didn't take too long to get her on side, Junia and my parents needed us and Andromeda had given us a time limit and every second I could hear ticking away.

"Can we possibly stay here another night?" Thane asked Brooklyn.

She looked at Kenton who nodded, "I like them they can stay".

"Fine, you can all look after him but any trouble and it's on your heads".

Thane nodded, "Sure thing".

"I mean at the light show too, we will both be helping otherwise he will have to stay with us and he won't be able to enjoy the atmosphere", she told me.

"That's fine he can show us around", I replied.

"YEAH!" he cheered jumping up and down on the spot.

"I don't know why he likes you guys so much but it has cheered him up", she bit her lip and glanced at us all before storming off into her room and vanishing behind the fabric, I soon saw it was to get changed, she came out not wearing her temple clothes anymore but wearing a light parade uniform. She wore a mid-length dress which had bended tubes of florescent glow stick light around the shoulders forming short puffed up sleeves, the top was black with an off yellow wording on it which clashed a little with her bright blonde hair but she had a stunning figure and managed to make it look good on her, with a belt at the waist and knee high black boots with yellow tubes of light as the laces.

"Wow", Thane said looking her up and down, his eyes studying her and taking her all in.

Brooklyn smiled a very girly smile, she was stunning with long lashes, perfect skin and lovely bright ocean blue eyes. I felt something in the pit of my stomach pull at me and I felt sick, I felt emotions bubbling up to the surface and I wanted to scream out in a rage and cry all at the same time but why, *why was I feeling these emotions? Was it jealousy?* Shrugging them off I turned back to them and tried to look forward to the day and eventually the night to see the mysterious light show. This trip was becoming somewhat of a great knowledgeable journey for me with all these shows and events but still something was nagging at me, *the way he looked at her.*

"You ok Mira?" Thane asked looking deep into my eyes.

I tried to speak but only a squeak came out, "Yes".

"You sure you look upset?"

"I'm fine", I said breaking the eye contact and looking away from his glorious eyes.

Brooklyn jumped in, my blood instantly boiling yet she wasn't doing anything wrong, "Right well you guys should probably head out, gramps will be home soon and will want to crash out".

We all left their home and stood on the decking road and waited for Kenton to say goodbye to his sister before we could leave to explore. Brooklyn hugged her little brother bending over slightly and showing off a rather lot of leg before swanning off, swaying her hips as she left. I had to bite my tongue and look away, especially when I caught Thane's eyes watching her leave.

"Where should we go?" Asked Fira who looked keen to explore now the weather was warmer once again.

"The beach, you should all see the beach before you leave", Kenton cheered and charged off in the direction we had to go.

We all trailed after him walking what felt like miles of wood before he stopped and pointed down some rather weather worn looking steps, "Here we are".

I looked down to what was the beach and felt my eyes glow and my jaw drop to the ground, the beach was gorgeous, full of fluffy white sand, the pure blue water lapped at the shore line it was something from a dream of paradise, it was pure, clean and exotic and I wanted to run over the soft sands bare foot like a child but I had to uphold my composure.

Slowly we took the steps down, the sand was warm I could feel it through my boots. I spotted some fishing boats off the shore line all with their rods and lines hooked into the sea, there were also some guys in the shallower water with spears, their fit athletic bodies arching as they threw the spears to catch their meal. At the other end of the beach was a small wood land with palm trees full coconuts, running over to them Kenton scrambled up as fast as he could and rummaged through until he found some ripe ones throwing them down, Thane caught them and passed them around to us girls. Kenton jumped back down and showed us how to open them whilst preserving the milk inside, the taste that hit me when I took a gulp was fresh and natural, not like the foods and drinks I had back at the palace which mostly had been man made.

Soon we all took shelter under the palm trees and watched the day go by, the waves lapping at the shore were so peaceful and it made me feel so calm inside. *How could I expect them to give up their Element Soul and have all this peacefulness destroyed? But Lavara had given up theirs without a moment's thought*, I sighed feeling stuck but at least the atmosphere was serene.

"You alright?" Fira asked snuggling in closer to me under the tree as Thane got up to play ball with Kenton on the beach.

"Yes why'd you ask?"

"You looked really upset back at the hut, when Thane looked at Brooklyn".

I bit my lip, this was silly stuff, kids talk, "Oh, you noticed that huh? It was nothing".

"You might be a good Queen one day but you're a bad liar now", Fira smiled the sun bouncing off her burnt dark and yellow hair, "You can tell me, I promise not to spill any beans".

I shrugged, "Maybe...Well I...I guess I like him".

"Oh", she smiled, "Well I guessed that".

"Was I really that obvious?"

"A little", she beamed, "But he is nice looking".

"But how can I like him like that?" I said throwing my hands up in the air in despair, "He's a soul guardian, once he's finished helping me he'll go. How? Why would I develop feelings for someone who's not going to be with me forever?"

Fira put her hand on my shoulder, "Love works in mysterious ways Mira".

I shook my head, "It's not love".

"Then what is it?"

"A...A...crush...?"

"Well I don't think it's just a crush. A crush is different to love, love stirs feelings deep down inside you. If you think it's love...Maybe you should tell him".

"And what will telling him do?" I snapped, "Oh that's nice I like you too but I gotta go forever or thanks but you're not my type or..."

She cut me off, "Mira, you're a girl, a teenager, we have these weird raging hormones but maybe telling him will be good for both of you, it could make him feel good for helping you for when he moves on?"

"Fira...I don't know what love feels like...What would be the point in telling him if it wasn't love like I thought…It might hurt him more than make him happy", I pondered, "Plus I only met him a few days ago".

"Really? See way I see it is that you two have known each other a long time but just haven't seen each other for a while. These feelings aren't fake Mira, they have happened for a reason, because you do love him…You love him so much you don't want to hurt him".

I knew inside this wasn't just a crush but then who was I to know, I hadn't really been around boys so how would I know what a crush really feels like, to me a crush and love could be the same thing. Before we could talk anymore Kenton came to tell us it was time to leave and that we needed to get to the stands if we were to have any chance of getting a good seat.

I watched Thane and Kenton as they walked together along the wooden road, they looked like old friends laughing and chatting, Thane had such an easy going way about him, he turned to look at me and winked making my stomach do back flips. Fira nudged my ribs and I nudged her back, she hooked my arm and we walked just behind the boy's together arm in arm until we reached the stands.

The stands were exactly as Kenton said they would be, there were rows and rows of seats all centred around a circular dome, it had walls but they were only as tall as the seats themselves more to keep the youngsters in whilst the show was on and to give the place a slight structure to it.

The sun was still in the sky but was getting lower with every passing minute, the temperature soon dropped and Fira was soon shaking but Kenton pulled out a blanket from a box at the end of the stands which housed many blankets and passed it to her before passing me one to. We took our seats and waited as others began to turn up and took up the seats around us. Suddenly Kenton jumped up and shouted out to his two sisters who were adding the final touches, the surrounding decking had been showered with fabrics, flowers and glowing lanterns which made the whole area look magical. They then came over with boxes tied to rope around their necks filled with food and sweet treats, amongst other things like glow sticks and binoculars.

Soon the dark had completely set in and even Nisha and Brooklyn had taken to some seats at the end of the line, everyone had gone still and quiet, we done the same not quite knowing what to expect.

BOOM!

A flash of thunder and lightning ruptured the air and a few people let out mild screams, the others just let out the breath they had been holding. Within seconds of the noise and the flashing thunder the lights flared up into the nights sky, they were bright and vibrant showering the sky in a depth of colour that I had only thought possible by manmade materials. They weaved across the sky like sky serpents, dancing from one point of the heavens to another, shimmering their way across even brighter than the sparkling stars. The light was at first a bright illuminous green which shifted between blue, purple, pink and red before swirling back to the green and starting its sky dance once again. Shapes and spirals appeared before us showing random pictures from the lights, as I looked deeper into the lights I felt a breeze wash over me, I felt my eyes dim and flicker as if they were being controlled by someone other than myself.

Then I began to shrink and to fall, I slid from my chair to the decking and through the gaps into the cool sparkling gem of blue ocean below, I was still falling though once I was in the water, deeper and deeper but instead of it becoming darker the deeper I got, I felt the light penetrate the water and made it brighter, so bright I was surrounded by an intense white flash. It felt like the water had changed from the dense liquid it really was to a chilling breeze, I blinked my eyes closed and then opened them again and I found myself falling from the skies above in the lights, I was dancing and falling with the stars in the heavens, in the very universe that wrapped itself so tightly around our small world. I let my hand drift away from me, I felt it brush through the star nearest to me which shivered and sparkled brighter just for me, there was some heat but it was a cool heat which showered my whole body in its cool light, I could see myself sparkling and I felt like an angel.

I passed the moon and curtseyed to it in the sky, I wasn't expecting a response but I got one, it was a shower of moon dust which filtered all around me clinging to my clothes, looking down at myself I now saw that my dress had transformed from its dismal hues to a pastel white and shimmer dust, the dress had lengthened on one side where the dust particles had all stuck together. I admired it for a moment before the lights flashed before my eyes and struck my soul, I felt a stab of pain in my chest and let out a scream but nothing came out, only a gargle of bubbles. Again and again the pain came heaving onto my chest, I tried to fight it pushing it away then I heard his voice, "Come on Mira don't leave us now!"

"Thane?" I coughed out spluttering and heaving salt water.

"Mira can you hear me?" his voice sounded worried.

I opened my eyes slowly to see Thane was looking down at me, his hands pressed to my chest, I went to talk again but coughed up loads of sea water.

"Just nod, can you hear me?"

I nodded, the salt water was burning my throat and my lungs, I felt sick and tired, "Whhh….at?" was all I could muster up.

"What happened?"

I nodded again.

Thane's voice suddenly sounded distant as he tried to explain to me what happened and I knew I was falling asleep, "Let's get her to the medical hut".

~

I awoke with a start in a strange room that was dark, only a small patch of filtered light was spilling through a gap in some fabric that had been hung up at a small window, dust particles, warmth and fresh air all breathing in. Looking around slowly not moving too much as I could feel my chest aching and my head spin I found the room to be filled with jars, potions and a weird incense smell, sitting myself up a little I spotted Fira asleep on a chair opposite my bed but also a surprise was Brooklyn also asleep in a chair by Fira's side.

"You're awake!" Thane said from my side.

I turned to him, "Where am I? What happened?"

"You're at the medical hut in Beach Haven, they've done well and made you better again, we nearly lost you, you nearly drowned but we're not sure what happened...You were watching the light show when suddenly you got up and ran for the side, you jumped right into the sea below. The light show gave us some hope of finding you but the ocean was so dark and you kept sinking deeper and deeper, we got you back up to the shore on the beach but you were unconscious...Do you remember anything?"

"Yeah I do... But I don't remember jumping though", and I explained to him all what happened to me, before long the others were awake and listening in.

"What do you think it could be?" Brooklyn asked looking between me, Thane and Fira.

"A spell?" Fira suggested, "When me and my family studied Junia's history we found knowledge of grand witches that can encase a victim into a trance and get them to do things they wouldn't normally do, but most of them died out during the war the only witch I know now is..."

"Andromeda", I said.

She nodded.

"Could she be that powerful?" Brooklyn asked sceptical.

"Why not, she has started to poison Junia from within using another pentacle so it can access the fault lines, why could she not access Mira's mind? She could have known at that certain point we would all be watching the light show and not Mira".

"But why take Mira out now, what threat is she to her really?" Brooklyn asked.

"She has the first Element Soul", Fira said waving her necklace in Brooklyn's face, "So she is already on the path to winning if Mira can get us all together with the Element Souls we can defeat her and stop her plan for destroying Junia".

"But she wanted me to get the souls for her? Why kill me now?" I asked feeling confused.

"She knows you will not hand over the element souls to her, you're not the silly child she thought you were, she knows that we will all try to destroy her using the element souls...You are no longer needed in her eyes I guess". Thane answered, "I also think it was a test".

"A test?"

"To see if we could protect you till the end, if we can't and you're out the way she has a straight run and taking over Junia".

"No offence but why is Mira so important to all this? Surely Andromeda has a straight run anyway, Mira has no element or magic to her soul to stop her".

"It's what's foretold in Mira's destiny, its why I was assigned to her, I don't know why but Mira is important to all of this", Thane stated.

"And who assigned you?" Brooklyn asked.

"The converter of Spirit", he told her.

"Great that nut job, well then Junia is done for".

"The converter of Spirit is no nut job, she is beyond all us other converters", Fira snapped.

"Who says?" Brooklyn snapped back.

"The Temple Masters, they have met and adore her. If she assigned Thane to assist Mira and knows Mira is to do this journey then we will abide by what she has said. Her word is pretty much stone".

"Either way it doesn't matter, all of us are united to protect Mira till the end".

Brooklyn just huffed, "I don't think so".

But I just whispered, "Protect me? Why?"

"I'm your soul guardian, Fira is the fire element converter and now a friend, I have seen you two grow closer", he smiled, "And Brooklyn…Well she's the next converter…Maybe she is testing to see what we would all do and whether Brooklyn will stay or take the element soul and go".

"But why me?"

"It's just what has to happen", he shrugged not giving me a total answer.

"There's just one problem, I won't give it to you", Brooklyn said.

"You don't have to give it to her, I haven't, I still have hold of mine", Fira stated.

"For now", Brooklyn pouted, "But soon she will want it and use it because she doesn't have one of her own. I will never give YOU mine!"

"Yes but Andromeda doesn't know that, she will know the Temple of Fire is unstable and that the enemy has arrived on my soil meaning I have taken the Element Soul away she believes you will to for Beach Haven".

"Will you not reconsider?" Thane asked her, "You've seen what she can do when she is not near, what could she do when she is right next to us?"

Brooklyn shook her head, "No I will not reconsider but I presume when this witch see's that my own temple is not unstable or vulnerable she will know that I haven't played a part in the princess's silly game, then she will leave me and my home alone".

"Or maybe she will just come collect it herself", Fira said.

"This *'silly game'* is not something I made up Brooklyn, she was the one who actually commanded me to do this, she is the one who wants the element souls, I had no idea what they were until a few days ago", I told her.

"So you did plan on bringing them to her to make it easier for her then?" She tutted, "All in the name of Junia? Or just for you to get mummy and daddy back?"

"Not quite", Thane said, "It might have seemed that way to you but surely it cannot now, we have told you why we are doing this to safe Junia and you have seen what Andromeda is capable of. If Mira can secure all the elemental souls without Andromeda poisoning them then they can be used to defeat her, either way they need to be brought together, they are Junia's safety net and saviours".

"I know nothing of this in the teachings at the temple, not once has it been written in the manuscripts that line my library walls, never has it been whispered down the generations to be passed down to me, this knowledge of yours is false and I will not condone it here", she snapped, "I know of no final element soul, there are only five…No more…You all tell me lies".

"It isn't false", Fira said.

"So what, was it written in your temple?" she asked her.

Fira didn't nod or shake her head, "I just know, my ancestors knew and passed it down to me, my temple Master, Master Cinder had a premonition and knows that this is the truth".

Brooklyn just gave Fira an I don't believe you look.

"Either way can you take us to your temple?" I asked, "I would still really like to see it and learn about your teachings".

"Right…because you think once there I will give in? Well I will not".

"Does it matter right now? If that witch can get into Mira's head then she can most probably gain access to a temple", Fira added, playing with words to make Brooklyn think.

"She will not gain access to mine".

"How do you know that?" Fira stated, "She managed to get into my temple…Twice…We had to fight her off both times".

"Two times, my, my", Brooklyn sneered, "You obviously don't look after it well enough", her hands pointed to the necklace around Fira's neck trying to taunt her over that.

"I do look after my temple but Andromeda is strong and powerful, with their help I managed to fight her off to save my element soul".

"And to let the enemy in…To save 'Junia'…To kill your so called beloved people", Brooklyn's tone was nasty and I could see Fira was at boiling point with her temper.

"Believe what you want", Fira snapped.

"Oh believe me I will", Brooklyn replied.

"Can we please just visit your temple?" Thane asked losing his composure slightly, obviously not used to the bickering of girls.

"Fine we will go and check but don't think you can be touching anything".

She stormed out the medical hut with us all following after her, she walked quickly down the main decked road of Beach Haven passing the beach, I knew she was angry as I could see the water rippling as she rushed past it, it concaved in a little before bubbling back to how it should be.

"Hey Brooklyn wait up", I shouted out running to try and catch her up.

She stopped dead on the decking and I almost collided into her but I caught myself at the last moment, "What?" she hissed into my face.

"Where's Kenton is he ok? After the light show I mean".

She studied my face for a moment, looking deep into my eyes to see what I was meaning by asking after him, "He's fine, he's at the temple with my sister".

"That's great", I replied.

"Is it, for some reason princess my brother seems smitten by you and your little fan club, so much so that he sat by your side all night last night until I sent him with Nisha to sleep but he would only leave you if I promised to sit there with you too".

Ouch that must have been hard for her but I didn't say it instead I said, "Oh, well thanks".

"I didn't do it for you".

"No but thanks anyway and to Kenton".

"You can tell him yourself on your way out of town", Huffing she turned and skulked off leaving us to trail behind her.

We walked for what must have been another couple of hours to the very end of the decking road, down this part there was hardly any people, a few huts had been built but had been abandoned.

"What's with all the empty houses?" I said looking at them all.

"We had a hurricane hit a few months back which destroyed most of the huts down this way and killed a few hundred people", She replied.

"I'm sorry to hear that".

"Sure you are, see back in the old days when Cosima was a nice capital with nice royals, money and aid would have been sent in to help repair the broken part of town, medical supplies would have been given to the sick and wounded so they didn't die".

"The King and Queen didn't even know that this happened", I replied.

"Sure".

"No really they didn't, I didn't, no one did. It wasn't on the news and no one spoke of it happening".

"Would it have mattered if they did know? Would your parents have helped?" She looked me dead in the eye but I couldn't say a thing because we both knew what that answer was, "No they wouldn't have".

We came to the end of what looked like a jetty with small row boats tied to large pillars at the end, a few were bobbing close to us but Brooklyn obviously had her favourite and pulled it in closer to where we stood. She climbed in whilst Thane held it steady for me and Fira to join her, climbing in last he joined Brooklyn with the rows and helped paddle to her coordinates which turned out to be a strange looking dark patch in the normally crystal clear ocean. She signalled to stop paddling before she stood and climbed out standing on the water, I couldn't believe my eyes as she stood there on the liquid like it was a pure solid platform. She lifted her hand and revealed a ring which was stylised similar to Fira's pendant on her necklace, the fine detail smaller but just as pretty. A glowing and rippling seal appeared in the ocean below her feet and as she hummed a hymn similar to one of the songs Fira sang back in Lavara she knelt down exposing the ring to the lightened shade of water and waited as it all drained away from where she stood. Stairs appeared below her feet all made from the sea water, the water ran down each step before circling back up to keep it going.

"Right come out you get we haven't got all day", she commanded.

"You want us to go down there?" Fira asked looking a little put off by the water, *would it distinguish her flame if she did get wet?*

Brooklyn just gave her a look and she obliged by climbing out and following her down, followed by me and lastly Thane. As we neared the bottom Brooklyn gave a wicked smile and flicked her ring causing the water to disperse and float back up to the ocean, "Go", Thane urged me and I jumped the last few steps landing harshly on my feet, he jumped too but done a professional looking tumbled roll before gliding back to his feet. As the stairs vanished I felt a small amount of sea spray cover us.

"What'd you do that for?" he said annoyed but Brooklyn just ignored him and carried on walking down a narrow walkway which was damp, cold, a little slimy and I could taste the salty air on my tongue. I couldn't help but know that was meant for me but Thane just happened to be behind me, Brooklyn didn't care she had made me move for her.

We exited the small narrow tunnel and I had to hold my hands up to shield my eyes from the quivering and shaking light that penetrate the ocean from above, the view that greeted me was breath taking and I stood there speechless as Brooklyn announced, "Welcome to the Temple of Water".

~ The Temple Of Water ~

"Welcome to the Temple of Water", Brooklyn said with not so much as a hint of enthusiasm for showing us but I couldn't help but feel excited at seeing this one. I had thought the Temple of Fire was cool with all its flames and smoke but this was something else altogether, a temple under the ocean which we could walk around like it was above the sea with oxygen and light. I could see Fira out of the corner of my eye sniff in distaste at the opposing temple to hers but she stayed polite and walked with us not saying a word.

My eyes widened as we approached the grand structure in front of us, the water tight dome we walked through which surrounded the whole upper part of the temple and reached down to the ground so it wouldn't flood gave us some obscured light from the sun light above which cascaded through the waves over our heads. Little fish and other sea creatures swam around like it was normal for us humans to be walking under the water. The ground was damp and squelched and crunched under foot with tiny damp pebbles and soggy patches of sand. Some small torches had been lit on short pillars that led up to the temple, the light echoed back off the building making the world around us shimmer even more.

The Temple of Water was a huge structure and looked like something out of a fairy tale, large wooden doors were the centre point which opened into a large grand hall. Outside a curved and bubbling wall structure with pillars grew up high into the dome with large trident like spears stationed at the end of each one, they all had bubbles frothing away inside rising and falling along with unnaturally large pearls fitted inside which glided up and down them, along with each point of the trident held what looked like hundreds of sparkling white pearls or diamonds it was hard to see from all the way down here. Large arches swooped over head with stained glass windows looking into the grand hall, the pictures on the glass showed some sort of story about a large sea monster attacking Beach Haven but being tamed by a shining white haired goddess with a large trident in her hands, on the opposite window was the same image but of a male god.

Inside was just as glorious, large pearl like orbs sat like statues along the walls on pillars, with vases on smaller styled pillars, some strange looking sea flowers grew out of of them brightening the place up and giving it a homely, earthly yet watery feel to it. The grand hall had many doors leading off from it all going round in a circular shape. In the centre was a large statue of a creature which looked to be half man half fish, rows of pews sat in front of it along with damp puddles and other coral looking sea growths spread all over the wooden pews. Brooklyn headed to one door and opened it leading us all down it, the hallway was more like an arched tunnel which I could sense led us down deeper into the sea bed, water dripped from above and made the tunnel smell of salt, there were even salt crystals littered all over the walls. We came to another door and she knocked on it and waited.

A small frail old man with wrinkled skin and ghostly grey hair opened up, "Brooklyn", he bowed to her, "Who are your friends?" I couldn't help but stifle a giggle as deep down I thought he did rather look a small bit like a fish with wide eyes and glistening damp skin.

"This is Mira the Princess of Cosima and her friends", Brooklyn said referring to me.

I curtseyed to the man who simple shunned my attempt to show him some respect, "Tell them to leave they have no business here".

Brooklyn nodded, "Yes Master Serpentine, but I request a visit to the Chamber of Water. I need to check the Element Soul is safe".

"The Element Soul is always safe, we never let anyone in", his raspy sea voice ordered.

She bowed again, "Yes but Master Serpentine there is a grand witch who may have been able to enter the Chamber unnoticed and may be poisoning the Soul as we speak".

He hissed, "Poppycock".

I coughed clearing my throat and then spoke up, "Please Master Serpentine I do not wish the Element Soul any harm, I am here to make sure it stays safe", but he ignored my pleas.

Suddenly the ground beneath our feet began to shake violently knocking me over but Thane caught me before I hit the damp floor.

"What's that?" Fira asked looking around, "An earthquake? I thought those only happened in Skye"

"They do only happen there", Brooklyn looked alarmed, "Master the Element Soul!"

"Go!" he ordered her and she took off at a run, going some speed back through the tunnel, the ground started to shake again with more force this time.

"Come on!" Brooklyn cried out to us.

We reached the end of the tunnel and she charged to the most central door in the building, using the ring on her finger she flashed it over a seal and the door flew open just as the ground gave another almighty shake knocking us all down this time.

"Get up, come on", she ordered and we were all up and running down some more of the strange watery steps, she led us deeper into the darkest depths of the ocean, torches flashing on as we made our way down. Finally we reached another large door like the one from the Temple of Fire but this one had swirls of water carved into the heavy wood. She flashed her hand over the seal again and the door opened revealing a horror to her eyes.

Inside was a dark spiralling mist which was crashing into a crystallised liquid statue similar to the one I had seen at the Fire Temple, inside of this one was a rather beautiful but strange looking sea creature, I could sense it was awake but it couldn't fend off the power that was attacking it, it needed Brooklyn to summon it for it to be able to have the power to fight.

"Hey!" Brooklyn shouted gaining the attention of the dark mist which turned out to not be a dark mist at all but was hundreds of crows, all of them were pecking and pounding their wings against the crystallised liquid to get the Element Soul out. It was her, Andromeda.

A wicked and blood chilling laugh erupted through the room, "Well you took your time, I nearly have the poor little Water Element Soul and once it is in my grasp you will never be able to summon it again little Water Converter".

Brooklyn hissed, "I will stop you".

"With what?" She laughed and the murder of crows flapped madly before landing together in front of the Element Soul. The crows all bled together and began to form a shape, the shape of a woman. The last crow on her face melted back and she threw her head up and howled with laughter. Andromeda! She was still just as tall and menacing since I saw her the other day but she looked to be darker, more powerful somehow. The crows had all vanished but had left a rather evilly perfect woman in their place, "So little Mira how are you getting on with the hunt for the element souls? I see you have Fire already but Water...Did little Brooky Wooky not wanna play?" she smiled showing sharp white teeth, she licked her lips as she spoke to me which made me want to shiver.

Thane stood in front of me as if to show he was my protector.

"Ah so you still have yourself that soul guardian, first in your family for over a century", she grinned, "But even he won't be able to save you".

She raised her arm and slung it down so fast I didn't have time to see the flurry of black feathers glide for me gripping their claws into my clothes and dragging me into the air so I was hovering over everyone's heads. Thane turned and raised his own hands and brought down a thunder of screams as hundreds of souls appeared around me fighting off the crows.

"Hahahaha you think you can keep that up forever soul boy?"

BOOM…A large flare of flames erupted up around Andromeda as she cackled making her laugh turn to screams. She shouted and the crows left me and attacked the flames putting them out by the air that whooshed from their wings, leaving me to fall to the ground heavily but unharmed.

"You dare to attack me once again fire girl", She boomed through the chamber.

Fira just smiled sweetly at her, "Why not fight back then sweetheart", she taunted and clicked her finger making a fire ball appear in each hand, "I thought you might have learnt from last time".

"I have, which is why Lumi is sending in our best to defeat you all so I can take the element souls. Then your elements will be mine to control".

I turned to see the pink haired girl standing by the door smiling at me, she had already commanded the bag and a lone ball of light flowed out revealing to her whose turn it was to fight us. "Volt I believe today is your day to shine my love", Lumi smiled crushing the orb in her slim fingers and bowing to a woman who appeared looking angry and electric, her name said it all, Volt, like a Volt or bolt of lightning. She had long electric blue hair which if you looked carefully enough had an actual electrical current running through it. She wore silver armour but held no weapons, her hands and her electrical current where her only weapons.

She moved fast, too fast like a crackle of thunder in the skies and she was upon Thane and shocking him so he shivered violently from the force of her power stopping him from summoning any more souls. Turning to Andromeda I saw she had decided to stay behind for this one with Lumi and they were now both attacking the element soul.

Brooklyn ran up to Volt and raised her hands but Volt shook her finger, "A ha ha, that might not be wise young converter, what can conduct electricity?"

Brooklyn went to flood her anyway but I threw my self forward knocking her down, "What the…" she went to say something angrily but I cut her off.

"Water, Water can conduct electricity you flood the place and she will fry us all", I breathed.

Reasoning flowed over her face and I could see now she felt utterly useless, she had a power but couldn't use it to save her element soul or temple. The ground shook with thunder as Volt sent out some huge waves of power, she sent sparks out to zap us all but luckily I managed to duck behind a pillar along with Fira. Brooklyn was sent back in shock and looked to be fitting from the current zapping away at her vulnerable body. Thane was on the floor, alive as much as a soul guardian could be but a little fried, his hair standing on end and his skin looked a little burnt. I felt so vulnerable, I had nothing to defend myself with, feeling around my body I then came to my mother's Sceptre tied to my belt, well I guess it was better than nothing I could still hit Volt with it.

Before I could truly consider hitting Volt, Fira suddenly jumped out from her hiding place and blasted Volt right in the face who tumbled back and sent out a flurry of sparks Fira's way but she dodged back behind her pillar. Volt was on her feet in a quick rush of movement running to Fira's column, she was commanding large electric energy balls to hit my friend with. I stepped up and charged running as fast as I could towards them, I skidded on my feet just as Volt hit home with the pillar and I knew I wasn't going to make it so I threw the Sceptre. It was like everything slowed down, time had gone into slow motion, the sceptre glided through the air which collided with the electricity before it hit Fira, sparks shot all around the room hitting the walls of the chamber of water and smashing into things causing them to break. But one good thing was one of the bolts hit Andromeda who squealed in pain and yelled at Volt but Volt ignored her as she now came after me.

Thane was now on his feet and shot out a load of angry souls who blocked Volts way, Fira then combined her power with his making a huge swirling vortex fire wall which Volt was locked into. Brooklyn too was back on her toes looking a bit toasted, then she sent out a surge of power like a Tsunami of water which slammed into Lumi and Andromeda who were angry and shocked that their plan now seemed to be failing them. Andromeda howled into the air before exploding into a mob of crows and vanishing from the chamber, Lumi placed her bag on her hip and ran, she dodged all our attempts at preventing her freedom and she was gone with her mistress.

"Go Brooklyn now!" Thane commanded and she nodded running to her element soul and praying for forgiveness at her failing it and asking it for help on our quest.

A song erupted through the chamber around us and we all turned to see Brooklyn dance and sing to the Element Soul, she waved her arms in a fluid motion and the crystallised liquid began to melt away.

I turned to Thane, "The people of Beach Haven…Kenton!"

"I'm on it", and he swirled away in a ghostly haze weakening the wall around Volt but the fire still held her at bay for now but she was fighting it.

Brooklyn sang her heart out to the sea creature that was locked inside and that was slowly revealing itself, her voice was not as strong as Fira's but her body gliding with the fluid moves so gracefully I had to admire her for that. Then as the last of the liquid melted away the Element Soul broke free, I felt my heart thump in my chest at the sight of this one, he looked strong and tough. He had a long scaled tail which flicked from side to side keeping him afloat in the air like he was swimming in his own little bubble, his muscular arms crossed over his muscular but hairless chest, he had strange markings like tattoo's that glided down his arms, they spiralled like the waves of the sea. His face was strong and hard set, his hair was long and blond and wavered behind his body like a cloak, his eyes deep blue like the darkest depths of the ocean.

Brooklyn bowed to the sea creature and showed forth her hand which contained the ring but he ignored her at first and pointed to me.

I gulped hard and slowly walked towards him, I knelt down with Brooklyn and bowed my head and waited for what he might do. He opened his hand and came down to my level, "Take this, gift for my Queen".

He bowed his head and placed the gift in my palm before turning to Brooklyn and accepting her token of the ring and absorbing himself inside.

"What did he give you?" Fira asked intrigued.

I opened my palm to see a small glittering scale, my thoughts were that it came from his own tail, "What is he Brooklyn? A mermaid?"

She shook her head, "No he is a male Siren, they normally sing out at sea. People used to think they were bad that they used to sing to call sailors to their deaths but actually they sing to calm the dead of the sea. They know the sailors would die anyway and sing so they go peacefully".

I looked at her ring and watched as it now glowed a deep blue, "Brooklyn you took the Element Soul, you know what that means?"

She nodded, "Yes, the enemy will come".

"But why did you do it?"

"Because your friends tried to help me save him, he called to me and said I needed to help, even if it means sacrificing some of my people and my home to do so", she looked down and depressed at that thought.

"Thane will help them and get them to a safe place", I said, "Could they come here?"

She shook her head, "No there are too many people for the temple to cope with and under the ocean? People will go mad with claustrophobia. No there is a secondary temple like structure hidden in the forest on the beach, they will most likely go there".

A haze of souls hushed into the chamber and Thane came back to us but he wasn't alone, "I have alerted the town to the enemy and initiated evacuation to where ever they deem a safe place... but someone wouldn't leave", Kenton came out from behind Thane, he looked sheepish.

"I thought you were here with Nisha?" Brooklyn said.

"I was but she left me to find her boyfriend, Thane found me helping gramps".

"Where is gramps?" but she didn't need telling.

"The pub".

"Oh that man, that girl, this family! Why can't they just do as they are told and THEM", She hissed angrily, "Leaving you alone yet again".

"I'm not a kid", he said but there was more than just the actual meaning behind it by the sound of his tone.

"But you are", Brooklyn told him kneeling down to his level, "They shouldn't leave you alone especially at a time like this".

"That's not what I mean", his looked at his toes in a rather childlike way before stepping one foot in front of the other, raising his fist trying to show strength and shouting, "I wanna come with you guys, I wanna fight for Junia".

Brooklyn just scowled but it took me a back just a little, "But you have no powers, you cannot fight the enemy, the fiends or the monsters", I told him.

"Neither do you but you still get to fight".

"That's different I'm…I'm…the princess…I have to fight".

"Why?"

"Because it's what I'm meant to do", I shrugged.

"Maybe it's what I'm meant to do too, I can fight if you guys let me".

"No you cannot and you are not coming", Brooklyn told her brother with her arms folded.

"Does this mean that you, will?" I asked her.

She nodded, "What was the point in me taking the element soul if I wasn't to come".

"But if you go and leave me I will be all alone, Gramps will drink himself into a coma and Nisha only has eyes for her boyfriend. Me, her little brother she does not care for, I will be left alone and then what? The enemy could come for me then anyway".

"He has a point", Thane said trying to sway her mind, for some reason Thane wanted the kid with us.

She bit her lower lip, "I can't let anything happen to you though".

"It won't, not if I'm with you guys", he smiled, "And if you give me a weapon I can fight the monsters to".

She didn't look convinced but Thane was and rushed out of the room and came back in with a trident passing it to Kenton.

"Where did you get that?" she scolded him.

"From a statue".

She gave him an angry look, "Defacing a statue of the element soul is…"

"What he's not gonna use it is he, the statue I mean? The element soul is too powerful to use a menial little piece of metal like that", Thane smiled twisting her arm, at last she cracked and smiled, smiled at him in a way that made me feel jealous again, made me want to push her away, made me feel…*angry*.

"Ok fine you can come but you do exactly as we say, when we say".

Kenton nodded and jumped for joy smashing the trident down on the ground, just as he did the ground beneath our feet began to shake once again, violently. "Did I do that?"

"I don't think so", Thane whispered back to him.

"What now?" Brooklyn asked.

"The enemy", Fira answered.

They both looked at each other ready for the fight and ran off back into the tunnel, Thane and Kenton were right behind them whilst I strolled along behind them ducking down and grabbing my sceptre. As I slowly caught up to them I saw a strange glow dancing along the walls as I moved, looking down I saw the Sceptre was glowing from my belt. I grasped it up and studied it more closely, the golden wand of the Sceptre was stunningly beautiful in its craftsmanship, not a scratch or blemish in sight even though it had been used to hit people and had been struck by Volt's lightning, the orb at the top held a replica of the pentacle of Junia inside, the different sections of the star were in different coloured gems to represent the element that resided there. On the top of the orb was a sharp pointed golden star which shone brightly, almost flowing a current of energy through it which if I blinked I would have missed. The bottom was more decorative with two long chains hanging from the bottom with the star of Junia to represent the king and a half moon along with a smaller golden star to represent me and my mother. Clasping it tightly in my hands I thought of my mother and felt my chest go tight, I so wished she was here with me to help me, she would know exactly what to do. As I thought of her an apparition of her appeared in front of me, swirling in the soul orbs that Thane could summon.

"Mum?" I said feeling numb and stupid, how could it be her she was with Andromeda? Unless Andromeda had found a way to get her to be in two places at once or she was … Dead*…No don't think like that she's fine, she's safe with my dad and they are both fine…Together.*

The apparition didn't talk to me but instead placed one of her hands on my right cheek as she did I tilted my head into it, it was her hand, so warm and comforting but also wispy, it was a strange butterfly wing type feeling, not quite whole, *I knew it was really her but how?*

"How? Why are you here? Are you safe?" I asked her.

Her eyes dimmed and looked down, I guessed that meant no.

"And dad", her eyes lit up, which meant he was ok still.

I felt my heart shred into pieces inside, *did this mean my mum really was in Spirit now?*

"Are you…Are you gone?" I asked her.

She nodded slowly.

"Nooo!" I cried out and fell sharply to my knees, the stab of pain etched through them as tiny pebbles cut into them. "No you can't be gone, I need you, Junia needs you...This isn't real!"

"It...Is...Real...But...I'm...Still...With...You", she whispered slowly, like it took all her energy to do so.

"I don't want you with me in soul, I want you here with me in person, forever".

"Just the way...It has to...be", she breathed with a little more strength.

"No, Wait!" I said grabbing my bag, "The Phoenix feather, it said it is the gift of life...It can bring you back!"

She stopped me, "No...Mira...You will need it...For someone else".

"What? Who?" I sobbed, "I don't want anyone else I want you".

"It has to be...This way", she said gently, "It has to be this way to make you fight on".

"But what do I do?" I sobbed, I couldn't help it the tears just came and rolled down my cheeks.

"Defeat...her..." she whispered into my hair.

"But how, I have no powers? I have no element to use?"

She pressed her hand harder onto my cheek and then her other hand onto the Sceptre, "This is not just a pretty stick", she smiled, "Call upon the stars of ancestors passed, they will guide the shining light, take you down the narrow path, to kill the unsightly blight".

"I don't understand what you mean?"

She turned the Sceptre to its side and swirled some of her soul orbs around it which revealed what she had just said, '*Call upon the stars of ancestors passed, they will*

*guide the shining light, take you down the narrow path, to
kill the unsightly blight'* .

"But how that wasn't there before?"

She smiled, "Magic…Religion…Junia".

"But you never believed in all that? Wait mum no
don't leave me", I called out but her apparition began to
disperse into the air and I was left with just myself and my
thoughts.

"Mira you alright? The enemy is here but you didn't
follow and…Mira?" Fira asked before her eyes widened at
the glowing Sceptre.

"I think Andromeda just took my mum".

"I thought she already had her?" she asked confused
before it dawned on her. "Oh, oh no Mira I'm so sorry".

"I need to find her and stop her no matter what!" I
sounded determined even for me, lifting the Sceptre I
smiled, "I will have her by my side to help me".

I took off at a run with Fira behind me struggling to
keep up, I charged into the main hall where a battle had
broken out between the enemy and the others, Brooklyn
was flushing them out with floods but they were soon
swimming back inside, Thane and Kenton were fighting
some at the main doors along with Fira who charged past
me and threw up a wall of flames and smashed it into the
door area but unwillingly destroying the doors.

"The temple", Master Serpentine shouted out as he
appeared with some of the temple staff with swords and
staffs trying to fend the fiends off.

We took to a small formation with Fira and
Brooklyn at the front, Thane and Kenton at the sides and
me at the back, they struck them all down one by one

slowly forcing ourselves out of the temple and into the underwater cavern that was alive with howls and clashes of power. Kenton was charging around swinging his trident at the closest ones, he took them down along with Thane who never left his side, it was like he was trying to be a big brother figure to him and to protect his young soul. A wall of flames erupted up again as Fira cast an almighty fire incantation which took out hundreds of enemies but as the flames died down more of the enemy appeared to take their place. We had to get out of here now.

A laugh chilled my already cool skin and I looked up to see Lumi sending out waves of fiends to fight us, she was summoning them from somewhere deep inside Junia, as I looked I saw we had no hope in fighting our way out we would tire before too long and they would over run us. The Sceptre shook in my hands and glowed brighter, I felt my mother's presence with me, I knew what I had to do, my voice as strong as I could muster I called out the incantation, "I Call upon the stars of ancestors passed, they will guide the shining light, take you down the narrow path, to kill the unsightly blight".

A bright beam of energy rocketed around me then burst all through all the enemy wiping them out and turning them to dust, it carried on going flowing up the walls and all around the dome above us wiping out all the evil in the temples surroundings other than Lumi who snarled at me then vanished in a puff of pink smoke just as my light cascaded where she had sat hovering in the air. The light flickered and went out, the Sceptre had done its work here, I slowly lowered it and looked around there wasn't an evil soul left in sight, just mounds of dust and drops, lots and lots of drops of water coming from…A huge crack in the domes ceiling and the ocean above us was threatening to flood in.

"What have you done?" Brooklyn said to me looking horrified.

"I…I…"

"Does it matter we need to get everyone out now", Thane ordered shoving Kenton and Fira towards the tunnel to the watery steps to the surface which Brooklyn called upon.

Brooklyn turned to Master Serpentine and the temple staff, "We have to leave, the temple is going to flood".

"I cannot leave my ship, a caption never abandons his ship", he said looking determined, "My life is here whether I be alive or dead, my soul belongs here".

"No please come on we have to go", she begged him.

He motioned for the other members of temple staff to leave and they ran for the stairs, "Good luck Brooklyn and my Queen of Junia, may you all conquer in defeating the monsters who try to destroy our world". He bowed to me which I found strange as just a little while ago he had ignored me as someone not worthy of his time.

"No!" she shouted running for him but Thane appeared grabbing her waist and dragging her away, she cried and shouted for him to stop but he took her away.

"There is no saving the captain", Thane told her.

She turned and glared at me as she vanished into the tunnel.

I turned back to Master Serpentine, "I'm so sorry, your temple I didn't mean to…"

"You have the light of the elders in your grasp, if they deem it so to sink this temple then it must be done, now leave before you drown", he bowed again to me and walked back into the temple alone.

Spinning on my heel I heard the first hiss of a large crush of water coming, I had to move and now. I ran over the dusty pebbles and sand pits jumping over large obstacles that fell or erupted before me, my heart raced so hard in my chest I couldn't hear the loud thunder cracks as the whole force field dome came crashing down around me, I only noticed because everything before me became a blur as the water took hold and began to carry me away from where I wanted to go. I pumped my legs in the water trying to swim back to the way I needed to go but the current of the crashing waves was too strong and I couldn't push hard enough. I felt the muscles in my arms and legs burn out, the acid tearing into them trying to stop me before I hurt them but if I didn't I would drown. I held up the Sceptre to see if it could help me now but there was no glow and the writing on the side had faded away, there was no power in it to aid me now. I gave a few more struggled kicks before my body gave in and tried to take a breath, I could see my whole life flash before my eyes, it was like a water coloured dream, all splashes of colour that dripped and faded away when I tried to take a closer look in.

'I could see myself as a baby in my mother's arms looking up at her sweet, young face. She had been young to marry the King but she had been his liking in the courtship and she had accepted, I came along a year after their marriage. My mother's arms were always warm and comforting even if at times she was distant with me. She sang a song to me as she laid me down in my crib to sleep, 'A royal baby sleep takes you, drift away were the magic grows, the secret city beneath is true, is where the magic in you really shows, a royal baby true and pure, the seeds of time will watch you glow, time for magic, religion and a cure, a royal baby sleep then magic awakes you'.

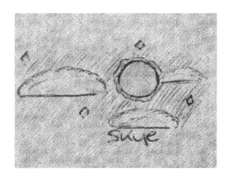

~ The Country of Skye ~

A hand reached out through the gloom and encircled itself in mine, I couldn't see well through the waves and frothy bubbles around me but I knew it was her, I knew it was my mother who had come to take me with her, yes I had failed but surely that was what was meant to happen? I had started the chain reaction for the element souls to be gathered surely the others could still go on and fight without me, they didn't really need me, *did they?*

The hand pulled me close and I felt dizzy as bubbles and stars danced around in my vision obscuring my mother's delicate features, I felt safe in her arms, I knew I belonged there with her, floating in the ocean lost and gone. I closed my eyes and drifted into a sleep which felt so peaceful it was bliss.

~

"Come on we're losing her", Thane snapped shoving Fira out the way as Brooklyn sent out another wave of power at the enemy that had stopped them in their tracks on the main decking road.

Fira stood up from beside the body of Mira, she had watched Thane trying so hard to keep her alive until Kenton could return with a potion from the medical hut. Brooklyn hadn't wanted him to go alone but he had fled into the army ahead of them and soon vanished.

She watched as Thane pumped her chest and breathed into her lungs like a repeat of the light show just last night, was water such an omen for Mira, twice in her stay in Beach Haven she had nearly drowned but today it looked like she had and that water had finally won.

Suddenly a cry of achievement filled the air and Kenton stormed through the inner layer of enemies slaying them where they stood, he ran back into the circle with a bottle of healing liquid and quickly passed it to Thane who begged Fira and Brooklyn to keep the monsters at bay until this was done, they couldn't lose her now.

Thane unfastened the bottle lifting Mira's neck and poured the liquid down her throat gently stroking her neck as if to guide the liquid down to where it should go. As he did that Fira sent up a wall of fire which encircled them all keeping the fiends at bay... For now.

Brooklyn hugged her younger brother and told him how stupid he was before then changing her tune and telling him how brave he also was but to not do that again to her. But he wasn't listening, he was watching with hope in his heart that he hadn't taken too long and that Mira would be fine. Thane stood back and bowed his head, it didn't look like she was going to make it.

"No", Kenton cried out running to her lifeless body, "Come on Lady Mira you can do this, you can wake up".

"Come on Mira don't give up now", Thane whispered, "We need you…I need you".

Shocking them all she arched her back involuntary, water spilled out her mouth being forced out by the healing potion pushing it all out from her lungs, she took in a sharp and painful breath before opening her eyes, "I'm not dead yet?"

~

I opened my eyes and the light from the sun hurt them but I blinked and opened my mouth taking another gulp of air.

"No Mira you are very much alive, thank Junia", Thane said kneeling at my side.

"But how? I saw my mother she came for me".

Thane was a little taken a back, "What do you mean your mother?"

"She came for me in the water but I saw her before, just before the water temple battle", and so I told him all about my mum and the Sceptre. Fira backed me up saying she found me looking weirded out just before I flooded the joint.

He looked concerned, "So does this mean Andromeda has taken your mother's life?"

I nodded feeling a pain in my chest but not from the water but from my heart silently breaking, "She has which was why she was able to come to me and again in the water, she saved me".

Thane smiled, "She sure did".

"No she didn't you saved her, you dived back in to get her before swirling back out", Brooklyn snapped, "Back out from the hole of the temple you destroyed, my temple".

Thane looked a little annoyed, "Yes I did, I saved you Mira it was my hand in the water but I do think your mother was with you too, if you say you felt her then she was there".

"What about my temple though you couldn't save that, or Master Serpentine", Brooklyn hissed at me.

"Hey Brooklyn lay off her she saved all our skins by what she done back there, all those enemies gone that we didn't have to fight. What do you think would have happened if she hadn't? We'd all be dead by now and the enemy would have torn down the temple anyway", Fira snapped.

"Your only saying that because it wasn't your temple that got destroyed", She hissed back at her.

"Your temple is not destroyed Brooklyn, it's just sunk at the bottom of the ocean. Once this is all over we can visit it and maybe build a new one in its honour or try to raise it somehow", Kenton added trying to calm his sister but it only angered her more.

"You cannot replace a temple with a new one, they were created by the element souls themselves", she shouted shoving Kenton to his knees, "You will never understand because you are a kid, just a stupid kid. Running off like that to save the life of this…Idiot", she pointed at me, "You held no responsibility for your own life or for mine, how could I go on if you got killed?"

"She's my friend Brook and that what friends do for each other", he swallowed hard trying not to cry, he was braver than me by a long shot as I would never have stood up to her and I would have cried already by now.

"Friend, you only met her the other night, how can she be a friend, she is merely an acquaintance".

"I'd rather have her as an acquaintance than not here at all", he cried out.

"That's just silly", she sniffed and then walked off towards the horde of monsters, Fira's wall was nearly down and out of power so Brooklyn called upon her ring, she summoned the great element soul of water, the proud Siren come mermaid man who swam in the air and bowed to us all before tackling the problem of the fiends. He opened his large muscular arms and brought them down showering the world before us with rain drops but not just any rain drops these ones hit the fiends and melted them down to puddles of nothing.

"If you could do that why didn't you do it before?" Fira asked her, "You could have saved your own temple?"

Brooklyn looked shocked that Fira said that, "But I had only just summoned him to the ring, he would not have been powerful enough yet".

"Yes he would have been powerful enough, I had only just summoned the fire element soul to my necklace when I called her to help at my temple when the enemy attacked", Fira told her.

This angered Brooklyn even more so, she called the element soul back into the ring before she fled down the decking road to the border gate of Beach Haven, not once looking back to see if we were following. Thane rushed after her leaving me and the others behind, I felt a sense of heartache at the fact he had run after her and didn't stay with me, he was my soul guardian not hers! I felt ashamed at myself for thinking that way and mentally beat myself for it I shouldn't be thinking of him but her the one I had lost. I felt so angry inside he was swanning around after her but I needed him, my heart was shattering inside, I had just found out I had lost my mother and he was with *her*. It had been him dragging her away from her temple that had caused me to nearly drown, he should have been dragging me. I felt anger well up in my veins at Brooklyn, I felt anger because I thought he liked her, liked her like how I liked him, when I should have been focusing my anger elsewhere, at *her* at Andromeda. It was all so messed up. I shook my head again I couldn't be thinking like that, it was childish, selfish and what did it matter…He was dead and so was she… Queen Espinosia.

Sighing to myself I ran with Fira and Kenton soon reaching the border gate where Thane and Brooklyn stood in deep conversation. As we approached Brooklyn glared at me and stormed through but Thane held the gate open for us, there were no more enemies behind us but that didn't mean they wouldn't reappear if we left it too long.

Once back in Cosima we set off towards the train station which was just a small walk, the walk itself was a silent one as no one really knew what to say. Brooklyn could have eliminated the threat before I had, she could have used her element soul instead of me using whatever that power was my mother had given me in the Sceptre, the temple could still be here and I wouldn't be feeling like rubbish. Unless that was her plan all along, get me to trip and stumble over something like that so Thane would feel sorry for her and look at me badly, that way she could make him fall for her and have him all to herself. I shook myself mentally again scolding my inner voice, *no that couldn't be right why would she do that, he was a soul guardian and would leave us soon, why would she go to all that trouble to get him to fall for her?* But the idea was now embedded in my mind and it wasn't going away, I could feel myself staring daggers at her back like a silly little school girl but the funny thing was I guess I was still a silly little school girl, fifteen made me nowhere near being an adult whether I was royalty or not.

Soon enough we arrived at the station and we waited for the train to arrive to take us to the district of River Skye, Thane sat talking to Brooklyn trying to calm her down but it was no use she too had daggers for me in her eyes.

"Don't take any notice of her", Fira smiled, "She just can't handle the fact that you took matters into your own hands to save us when she could have done it all along. She's really angry at herself, not you".

"Doesn't look that way", I said looking down at the Sceptre, *was it my mother who had given it power? Or was it the lightning that Volt had struck it with*? Either way I had no idea although I did wonder if it would come back again if I or we truly needed it. The train whooshed into the station, Kenton was super excited to climb aboard even if it was second class, couldn't risk being found by the palace guard and well second class wasn't too bad really, once you got used to it. The journey to Skye was a long one, although the train was quick on its hovers it was still a long journey to cross from Beach Haven back past Lavara, through Cosima's green rural lands and onto Skye, if we had walked it would have taken maybe all week and maybe more. Spirit of course might have been the logical one to go to next as it was closer to Beach Haven but Thane assured us that Skye was the better option as taking the element soul from Spirit will make it unsteady and unlike Lavara and all the other countries when Spirit becomes unsteady so do the souls inside it and the longer they are left without their element soul they can become dark and dangerous, so that was becoming the last place of interest for us until the final journey back into Cosima to find her, Andromeda.

We arrived at Skye in the early hours of the next morning, most of us had napped on the train other than Thane and Brooklyn who had been talking most of the night. Getting off I could sense the change in the atmosphere here, it was a lot cooler than what Lavara and Beach Haven had been like.

Thane came over to me, "Hey you alright?"

I shrugged, "Didn't think you were talking to me anymore?"

He smiled, "Of course I am but we need to keep Brooklyn on side or she might depart and we will have no water element soul".

I shrugged again, "I suppose", I tried not to give him too much attention, maybe I could back off a little and it wouldn't be so hard later on or if he did chose her.

"Anyway we need to get some warmer clothes whilst we travel through Skye, it's their winter and its cold".

"Ok", I replied flatly.

"Mira are you sure you're alright?" He sounded genuinely concerned.

"Course she's not alright Thane, she's just lost a parent", Fira snapped at him a little harsher than I would have had the guts to, "Come on Mira", and she took my arm in hers and led me away from him.

"I'm sorry", he whispered, barely audible, almost a whisper of the air but I heard it and wanted to cry but I kept going letting Fira lead the way.

Once in the village we headed to a small shop that sold clothes and other items, we counted how much money we had between us and managed to bargain with the man who owned it into some discounted items. We had to mix and match to try and get the most out of the clothing for all of us. I already had boots so the thick winter boots went to Brooklyn who didn't have any, Fira felt the cold more than most of us so the thick fur jacket went to her and a smaller jacket went to Brooklyn too. Kenton found a small fur coat for him that had been damaged and was sold so cheap it was a steal. I on the other hand knew I was going to freeze, the only thing left was a small fur hat, gloves and scarf. I was only in the dress I had purchased from Lavara and it was meant for hot weather, I just hoped I wouldn't freeze to death on the way to the temple.

We were all set to go when the man approached me, "You cannot go to Skye dressed like that you will perish instantly".

"I have no more money", I told him.

"Do you have anything you can trade?"

I shrugged, "Not really", I opened my bag and looked inside, all I had was the feather from the Phoenix and the scale from the Siren.

"Is that a Siren scale?" he asked me looking in my bag over my shoulder.

"Er yes why?"

"Those are good in medicines to heal, I could make a whole batch with that", he said gesturing to it, "If you trade them to me I will give you a coat".

I looked at Fira who nodded, "Sounds a good deal to me".

"Deal!" I agreed and he rushed to the back room and came out with a lovely if not a little dusty fur coat, the fur was white and black, I had no idea what beast this would have come from, "Here you go my lady".

I smiled trying it on and passing him the Siren scale, "Thank you so much".

"No thank you, please pop by on your way out from Skye, I would like to see you before you leave", he said.

"Ok sure".

We all left the shop a little warmer than before and as we neared the gate I could feel the chill beneath the fur, I think I would have frozen to death just by standing near the gate. Thane approached it and opened it slowly before some hands grabbed hold from the other side. As the gate opened wider a tall strong looking woman stood there, she had the darkest hair and dark jewelled eyes I had seen other than Andromeda but on her it didn't look evil. She was a little weather worn with some wrinkles on her pale skin, she wore a fur coat similar to mine and thick fur boots, her hands wrapped in fur gloves and a thick hat. Her breath steamed in the air as she opened her mouth to speak to us, "I am Stormra I will guide you to the town, we will attend the temple at high sun".

"Whoa", Thane said, "How do you know what we're here for?"

A smile spread over her face, "We have some friends of yours staying with us, they told us you would soon arrive".

"Freya?" I asked.

Stormra nodded.

"Are they well?"

The woman's eyes dipped a little but she did nod too, "They are alive but well maybe not so much".

"I need to see them", I said.

"Then follow me".

Stormra headed up a small path which was cast in shadow by huge looming trees, hills and mountains, snow had been falling recently and sat like a perfect crunching white cushion as our footsteps shifted over them. Small animals and critters alike all sat in trees and other hidey holes all trying to keep warm together from the winters bite. I could hear a river flowing behind a row of trees, as I glanced over I caught sight of the icy cold depths that looked stunning in the white scenery. The snow around us glowed and twinkled in the light as the sun slowly rose up but not reaching the high point in the sky just yet, I hoped it would bring extra warmth with it but it lied to me, it didn't, it stayed the same coldness the higher up we climbed.

I breathed out hard watching as my breath misted and swirled in the air around me, this place was so magical in itself. I had never seen snow or a real winter before, Cosima tends to stay the same temperature all year round other than for the occasional rainy spell. I looked behind me and smiled at all the footprints that trailed behind us, a few smaller ones flitted over ours where animals had made a run for it after we passed by.

A large rocky hillside loomed in front of us along with a snowy field, the trees framed the picturesque landscape perfectly with frozen drops hanging from branches twinkling in the sun light. As we neared I thought the white field was moving but it was in fact full of beautiful white horses.

"Those horses are beautiful", I cooed trying to get closer to the fence to look.

"Won't they get cold?" Fira said shivering, her teeth chattering together.

Stormra looked at her and shook her head smiling, "They are Skye mountain horses, born and bred in the harsh cold snowy hills, to them this is normal".

"N…Normal?" Fira gasped.

"You can light a small fire if you like, the converter of air will not be offended", Stormra suggested.

Fira grinned and threw off her gloves and lit up a small fireball in her palms and sighed at the warmth that now covered her, "Thank you".

"Can we ride one?" Kenton motioned at one of the horses.

"Not without proper training, our horses are not like pony rides at the fair ground. They are strong willed and need to be told what to do", she said as one stuck its pure white face through the fence to say hello, she lifted a fur gloved hand up to it and patted it, "Hey Titan".

Titan lifted his head up and let out a loud nay.

"Here", Stormra smiled passing me something.

I opened my hand to see some sugar cubes.

"Titan will like you for a life time if you feed him them".

I lifted my hand to his mouth and almost jumped out my skin as he chomped down on them. Watching him intently I then lifted my gloved hand and stroked him, his tail whipped around as I patted him before stepping back.

"Come we must go", Stormra instructed and we all turned to follow her.

As I went to keep up with Fira a hand grabbed my arm and pulled me back, I went to protest but Thane lifted a finger to his lips, "Hush Mira I need to show you something".

I looked after the other who hadn't noticed we had stopped, "I just want to see Freya", I told him.

"I'm sorry…I'm so sorry for …"

"I know you are I heard you before", I said trying to pull away again.

"And still you want to ignore me?" he asked, "Mira I truly am sorry but I have a duty to help you on your journey and that means…"

"Keeping Brooklyn onside yeah I guessed that".

"You sound bitter".

"I am bitter…I lost…her…" I used both my hands and pushed at his chest stronger than I expected forcing him to step back.

He then took both my wrists but in a gentle way, "Let me show you something".

"Let go of me", I hissed.

He pulled me closer lifting his arms almost causing me to dangle by my own arms and standing on my toes, we were so close now I could feel his breath on my cheek so warm against the cold. His eyes peered into mine, his hazel eyes shining in the cold light, "Just for a second, trust me…I'm with you Mira, I'm your guardian now let me guide you".

I nodded.

He let me down gently and turned to a small path between the snow clad fields and the purest cold river. I followed him my feet crunching on the soft snow. At the river bed he stopped and knelt down parting patches of snow near the roots of a tree, then he smiled turned to the river and took a handful of the water and washed it over the patch he had made. From the root of the tree a small green seedling lay in wait, the water froze it solid on the spot.

"Thane what are you…?"

He waved his hand to quieten me, "Just watch".

I done as he said and watched and within a minute the seedling grew and burst open, inside was a small twinkling gem, Thane lifted it up and examined it before handing it to me.

"What is it?" I asked looking at the gem, it was tiny but flower shaped with a stem and petals, it mirrored a glass effect ornament like what the glass makers in Cosima would make in their factories.

"A crystal Topaz plant", he said cupping his hand around mine, "They grow all around Skye and nowhere else, with the frozen water it forces the plant to crystalize. The people of Skye call it a metempsychosis plant or crystal Topaz by its look but it basically means the transmigration of the soul, or journey after death of a human soul or animals to some other human or animal body…A form of rebirth, the plant was set to become a green worldly plant but instead it turned into a beautiful crystal".

"Why are you showing me this", I sighed.

"Because although her soul will go to spirit and eventually move on she will relive her life in the heavens and on Junia. Heaven and Junia are as one, she could walk the lands as a new baby soon enough".

"I thought we just went to heaven".

"Heaven, rebirth…" he moved his hands around trying to show me what he meant, "Mira don't you see all our souls are recycled we have all lived here before and will do so again. Heaven is just another term for rebirth really, we will all come back…As someone else".

"Even the bad?"

"Once they have been recycled and cleansed and deemed worthy to come back", he replied.

"So even if I defeat Andromeda she will come back?"

"Maybe…not right away but as someone else, not as the evil she is now".

"And my mum?"

"When she has been to Spirit and moved on".

"But she wouldn't leave me".

"Her essence of life will always live on with you Mira, her love will never leave you".

This to me just made it all worse, *she would move on and become someone else and so would he... They would both end up with other people not me.*

"Hey guys you coming?" Kenton asked peering into the pathway where we stood.

I looked up at Thane and felt like crying and pushing him away again but I knew he was just trying to show me and guide me about the world I lived in. The world I hardly knew.

About forty five minutes later we arrived at a small mountain side village, it sat neatly on top of the mountain surrounded by a large wooden fence which had spikes at the top, all the houses here were wooden cabins with fires all burning inside as the smoke filled out into the air and into the atmosphere. People were all milling around, some were chopping wood and piling it up to put near the houses, others were washing clothes in large tubs of water and hanging them on lines to dry even though I imagine in this temperature nothing dried much. Kids were playing happily building snowmen and other snow animals.

Stormra led us through the village to a large cabin, once inside I instantly felt the heat from the huge burning log fire in the fireplace, we all took off our winter clothing whilst Stormra asked us to sit down as she made up a pot of winter spice tea. She handed us each a mug before she vanished upstairs to do something.

"I wonder where Freya is?" I said turning to Thane who was checking out some of the ornaments in the cabin.

"We'll find out soon enough", he replied lifting a picture up of a young girl, she had dark hair like Stormra's but her eyes were ice grey, she looked to be a very moody type of girl.

The front door opened and Thane placed the picture back down only to come face to face with the girl from the picture, she was definitely as moody as her picture made out and in the cold harsh snow it radiated from her even more. Her eyes studied us all intently as she hung up her coat by the fire place to dry and placed two long hunting knives down on the mantel piece. Her ice grey eyes flicked between us all landing lastly on me, she looked me up and down her eyes giving nothing about what she thought of me, she either hid her emotions well or didn't have any.

"I take it you must be the princess?" she said to me in a flat monotone voice that actually held no interest in the answer I was about to give her.

"Yes I am and who are you?" I tried to say it as polite as possible but she didn't even blink when I said it, she actually just turned took off her thick set boots and put them by the fire to dry.

"I thought princesses wore frilly dresses and drank tea all day…Well I guess the tea bits right", she said half joking half not.

"Er…Well a frilly dress isn't really that good to travel in", I said thinking back to the night me and Thane ran from the palace.

She shrugged, "Ok".

"So who are you?" Fira asked repeating my question.

The girl looked her over, "So you're the Lavarian?"

Fira nodded but clenched her teeth, this girl was rude expecting her questions to be answered when she wouldn't answers ours, "Yes but who are you?"

"Isaura don't be rude, our guests have asked you a question", Stormra snapped coming down the stairs.

"I was about to answer", she huffed.

Stormra huffed back at her before turning her attention to us, "This is my youngest daughter Isaura, she is a defiant, hot headed girl with a chip on her shoulder, but she is my daughter and I love her".

Isaura rolled her eyes, "I don't have a chip on my shoulder".

"Sweetie you do and you know it", her mother replied taking up the hunting knives and cleaning them up, "And you know I hate animal blood on the mantel piece".

"So Isaura what do you do? You a hunter?" I asked trying to make conversation seen as we were in her home.

She smiled, "I'm the Air Converter".

"Really?" Fira said from beside me she sounded shocked and a little rude.

"Fira", I whispered.

She shrugged at me with a grin, "So you hunt to?"

Isaura nodded, "Yes, the temple here is too high in the mountains to stay at all the time as the air is so thin, the teachings here tell us to pray once a week at the temple and the temple will look after us. The rest of the time I hunt for food, forage for berries and other fruits and protect my home from predators".

"You only go to your temple once a week?" Brooklyn sounded disgusted.

"You'll understand when we visit it later".

"Why later? Why not now?" Brooklyn said impatiently.

"Not only is the air thin but it's below the minuses in temperature, you go up before the high sun and you will become one of the frozen statues that stands guard", Isaura told us not caring for Brooklyn's rude tone, I could see this girl had a thick iron skin with rudeness plus she was just as rude.

"Frozen statues? Is that true?" I said.

She nodded, "Yes many people have tried to go before high sun to prove they can survive but they all perish and freeze and by doing so become guardians of the temple".

"It's such a terrible price to pay for wanting to prove a point but the statues are incredibly pretty, the jewelled ice stops the bodies decomposing, they just stand there forever young", Stormra added.

"What if we warmed them up? Would they wake back up?" I said.

Stormra shook her head, "No we tried that once before, they just melt with the ice".

"Oh that sounds…Terrible", I gasped.

Isaura smiled at my words, "Terrible yes but if you go thinking you can prove to the gods you are stronger than them then you deserve to perish and become a guardian".

I bit my lip, this Isaura sounded just as terrifying as the monsters about how she saw the world and its people.

"That's a bit harsh", Thane said, "No one deserves to perish just for a bit of foolishness".

"Think what you want, I don't particularly care…My opinion is no one is greater than the gods so don't think you can do the unthinkable", she told him.

"There's that chip again", Stormra smiled trying to lighten the mood.

Thane just coughed and changed the subject, "Where is Freya?"

"She is upstairs resting, you may see her soon".

Soon wasn't soon enough we sat downstairs for hours until we heard a bell ring from upstairs, Stormra went to check before coming down, "She is awake now, only one at a time".

It was only really me that knew her so I went up first, Stormra led me up the wooden staircase which turned back on itself, it came to a long landing that led to four rooms, one was the bathroom, the next one was a tiny bedroom with just a bed and bedside table, the next one was a master with three beds and a large wardrobe, the last door was shut but Stormra knocked before opening it. Inside the curtains had been pulled shut casting the room in complete gloom, a large bed was placed in the centre which had two people laying in it.

"Freya?" I said trying to see past the gloom.

"M…ira?"

"Yes it's me", I said feeling happy to hear her voice, "What happened to you both?"

She sighed, "We were able to fool the palace guards that you had come this way, they chased us for days through Cosima until we reached here, when we arrived here they already had a patrol waiting for us. A fight broke out and they struck him, he was so badly injured and I tried hard to fight them off but they were too strong so in the end we ran into Skye, blind and in a panic we forgot the winter was here. The cold overtook us and struck us ill, I'm afraid he might not make it and maybe, I will not too".

"No you'll be fine, we can get potions to heal you", I told her panic rising in my chest, *I couldn't lose anyone else.*

"No Mira", she breathed, "You have a more important job than saving us and you are under a time limit. You need to get on with your journey to save Junia. Andromeda will start to play foul soon, you need to hurry".

"She already is".

"What do you mean?"

So I told her all about seeing my mother and how I knew she was gone.

"Mira I'm so sorry".

I bit back tears and dug my nails into my palms trying to prevent the tears from coming. One of my hands went numb and I felt a small warm trickle of blood drip down my fingers. "Can I see you Freya, I hate talking in the dark?" I asked, I needed to see a familiar face to comfort me.

"No".

"No?"

"The cold has done something to me Mira, I have incredibly bad frostbite. If Stormra hadn't of found me when she did I would have been dead sooner. I don't want you to see me like this, I want you to remember me as me".

"Freya I'm so sorry".

"Don't be your still alive and that's all that counts to me".

I put my hand out to where I thought she sat in the gloom, it connected with her shoulder and I squeezed it gently, she took it in her hand and squeezed it back. "I need to rest Mira, go on to the temple, hurry and defeat that witch".

I nodded before realising she couldn't see me, "Yes, for you, for my mother, for Junia!"

"Make sure you make that witch pay for all of this".

"I will…Are you sure you don't want me to collect a potion of some kind to help you?"

"I am too far gone now Mira, plus I can't imagine a life without him by my side…If he goes then I wish it that I go with him too".

I felt hot tears burn at my eyes, *Why did everyone around me have to die? Why couldn't I save them all? Why, why, why?*

I gently gave her a hug and left, I couldn't say goodbye and neither could she. I was too chocked up to go back downstairs straight away so I hid in the bathroom until my emotions where all back in check. My face was tear stained and red as I looked in the bathroom mirror but why should I be afraid of the others seeing that I have feelings, the future Queen of Junia has a heart.

I left the bathroom and made my way down the stairs, I noticed how everyone was in a sombre mood and didn't make fun of my swollen red cheeks, instead they all sat quietly drinking their tea and preparing for our journey to the temple at high sun.

~ The Temple Of Air ~

We set off soon after the sun was high but the temperature was not, I still shivered under my coat and wondered whether I might still become a statue. The walk through the mountain side was peaceful and airy, birds chirped into the breeze, snow occasionally fell from a branch and the water still flowed behind the trees. Nothing could break this peacefulness around us, it was like the world around us was taking a huge quiet breath before the storm.

Thane was up ahead with Brooklyn and Kenton who were chatting away to one another, I walked with Fira whilst Stormra and Isaura both lead the way.

"You ok?" Fira asked.

I turned to her, "Yeah why you ask?"

"You seem a bit quiet and you keep staring at him".

I looked down away from Thane.

"You need to tell him", she told me.

I nodded, "Yeah I guess so but...I'm scared...Everyone around me is dying, I don't get why they have to? I don't want to tell him and then lose him too".

"I guess it's just the way the Queens journey has to go", she replied. "He's going to go no matter what but you could make that time easier on you both, you might regret not telling him otherwise", she looked sad for me and it made me feel a whole lot worse.

"I'm not Queen yet", I reminded her.

"Maybe so...But...The element souls seem to think you are".

"I can't be", I snapped, "Because that would mean... that would mean... My father is gone too".

"I really hope for you he isn't", she placed her hand on my shoulder, "But I think you should prepare for it just in case".

I knew she was right, so much was going on and Andromeda had already proven she didn't keep to her word, "I know, I just don't want to think about it, it's one of the only things I'm holding onto...Plus I have no people to be in my court, I have no friends back home and no one suitable to be my king...I would need to marry you know, within a year of taking the throne and to have a child soon after to keep the royal blood line going...How can I?" I turned to her.

"You do have friends", she smiled, "You have me, Kenton and I'm sure Isaura isn't too bad under all the grumpiness and Brooklyn...Well...She might like you one day..."

I just pouted, "Brooklyn no thanks...But you are like my only friend Fira and Thane".

"It's quality not quantity that makes a friend a friend", Then her eyes travelled to Thane, "And a king might not be too far from you, you know".

"He will leave me when he has completed his journey with me, how can I ask him to be my King? You know that".

"Unless we change it?"

I looked at her confused, "Even if I could what makes you think he would want to be with me?" I looked over at him with Brooklyn who was laughing and giggling and resting her blonde locked hair on his strong shoulder, "He likes her".

"You two have a connection, you've known each other since your childhood you're going to feel something".

"Yeah but is it just me that feels it because I grew up lonely and didn't know anyone else? Is it just because he is the only guy I have met who looks my age? And then…Well I feel so angry that he's walking and talking with her, I want him to be here with me".

"He will when he knows she's not going to run off or do something stupid".

"You really think that is the reason he's with her?"

She nodded, "Of course, she's a loose cannon and needs to be kept an eye on. When he knows she is completely on side he will leave her".

"Maybe and what did you mean by if we change it?"

"Mira we live in a world full of magic, I'm sure something will materialise", she had a knowing look in her eye, like something obvious she wanted to tell me but couldn't.

"Like what?"

"You will work it out", she smiled.

"We're here", I heard Isaura call out taking my attention away.

I looked to where she said here was and felt my jaw drop to the snowy ground, here was exactly a thousand steps up the side of a mountain, it went up so high that the steps vanished into the clouds above. My legs ached just looking at this beast of a staircase, the stone steps gleamed with the snow that had pooled and melted in the middle where the steps had the most use over the thousands of years they had been here. The mountain itself was rocky with a few green patches sticking out through the white. Alongside the mountain was a huge, beautiful and radiant waterfall which fell right from the clouds and into the river below.

Isaura took lead and marched on up, she went on like this didn't burn her leg muscles but then after living here your whole life and doing this once a week the steps would be nothing but a walk in the park. I struggled as we reached the half way point which was signalled by two large statues situated either side of a large step, the statues were of half horse and half winged beasts the eyes glittered with grey gems which dripped with melting snow like tears. We took a five minute break refuelling with water, even though the temperature in Skye was freezing we all sweated like pigs from the walking and at such a steep gradient too it was a mission. As we ventured upwards I felt more tired, my chest was screaming for air but my breathing was shallow which made me feel light headed.

Stormra smiled at me as I puffed up, "The air is thin up here, take your time no need to rush".

"But there is every need to rush".

She shook her head, "No dear child, rushing will get you killed take it slow".

I took notice of her and slowed my pace, the others were all ahead of me but I tried not to let the anxiety that they all thought I was a weak little princess take over. *Take it slow and I will make it to the top with them,* I told myself.

We were soon at the top which I was grateful for, the others were actually all panting and gasping for air just like me which made me feel a little better. I turned to look back the way we had come and my breath was taken away by the view that was bestowed in front of me, the clouds littered the landscape like fluffy cotton candy floss, every now and then they dispersed and showed me glimpses of the country below, I could see for miles over the land, the birds flying in the sky, the mountain top village and its specs of dust for people moving around, the rushing river that flowed relentlessly down towards the border gate. The waterfall started up here as a large lake that circled around the temple. Rocks, reeds and other pond life scattered around and the wind blew harder up here and my hair whipped out in front of me.

The temple itself wasn't much to look at from the outside other than the rows of glittering human statues that guarded it. It had been carved into the mountain it stood on right into the pinnacle point where the roof was the tip with the snow shaken on like the light coating of sugar on a cake, a large gaping hole with two large wooden doors stood locked and chained on the surface of the rock, there were no windows like the other temples this one was purely natural. Isaura open the door with an earring that hung down hidden in her thick dark hair which she had kept tucked away under her warm fur hat. The earring was long with colourful threads leading down from the metal clip and at the base was a small metal seal, which she swiped over the seal on the chains and they fell to the ground with a loud clunk. She threw the doors open and marched in, the others all followed whilst I trailed behind, I turned looking out over the world below. It felt like eyes were burning into the back of my head but I couldn't see anything but those fluffy clouds, then again anything could be hiding behind them and with each temple normally came a friend of Andromeda's, *I wondered who it would be this time round? Or maybe it's just all those statues looking at me? Wondering how pathetic little me had made it this far when they hadn't, when they had become frozen guardians.*

"Mira you coming in?" I turned to see Thane, he was watching me carefully.

"Huh?"

"You just gonna stand out in the cold?" he smiled, the smile instantly melted the ice that was shivering round my heart, *how could I not let myself fall for him? Would it just be better to hurt later when he left and have him fully with me now? Maybe because of what I had to do he would lie for me anyway and pretend he liked me, that way I could carry on with no other fears or unwanted hatred with me?* I bit the inside of my lip, I needed to grow up, I didn't need this now I needed all my focus to save hopefully my father and Junia and me crying over some guy dead or alive was not the Queenly thing to do.

The inside of the temple was no way near as grand as the other two we had seen, this one was just a large room with a tall statue similar to the ones that had been sitting on the steps outside, a few cushions had been placed on the floor for people to kneel down and pray on, a book sat beside each one. Walking past I picked one up and looked inside it but I couldn't read it, everything was written in another language, all in pretty looking swirls and patterns.

"That's our LibriaJun", Isaura said taking the book from me and placing it back down by the cushion I had taken it from.

"A what?"

She huffed, "It's our religions book with all the teachings and things we need to know and understand".

"You can...read that?" I asked looking confused the writing had all been gibberish to me.

She bored her cool eyes into mine looking at them I could have sworn the greyness of them had darkened a little, "Of course I can read it and it's in the tongues of our ancestors, the language of Skye".

To her that explained it all but to me I still felt clueless, *the language of our ancestors? They weren't mine just hers, right?*

She didn't talk to me anymore she just headed off to the only door in the room that wasn't the main door. Stormra on the other hand went to the front door and locked it tight, they obviously didn't want any unannounced visitors. Isaura led us down the narrow and dark tunnel which was burrowed deep into the mountain around us, torches flamed to life leading the way and I got the sense we were going higher into the mountain. Small recesses had been carved out to make way for bookcases, more statues which I presumed to be the past converters of air, their names had been carved onto them but in the strange lingo of the people of Skye. Other things like candles, plants and larger torches than the ones that hung on the walls also decorated our path.

We came to the end of the tunnel but where normally I would have expected a door to lead into the chamber of the element soul there were only large and small pipes all blowing out gushes of air in the doorway. To me it didn't look like much of a safety feature.

"Er is that thing safe?" I said looking to Isaura for an answer.

"What do you mean?" she asked back.

"Does it protect the temple? Do we just walk right through it?" *Maybe it will blow away all our cobwebs* I thought.

Isaura huffed and walked over to a vase which was standing proudly in a recess along with a candle which had burnt down ages ago and was just a puddle of wax. Lifting it she turned to the wind and threw it, within seconds the vase has disintegrated into thousands of sharp tiny pieces, "No the door is not safe does that answer your question?" she huffed at me like I should have known the whole time.

"Yes thank you", I said weakly hearing Brooklyn snigger behind me.

Once again Isaura took her earing and swiped it over the seal to the entrance which was engraved into the wall beside her and the air instantly stopped howling and the wind eased off enough for us to walk through.

The Chamber of Air was dark and dingy with next to no light but Fira took care of that and flicked her fingers and summoned a fire ball to sit in her palm to light the way, the chamber was much smaller than the other two temples, five large pillars sat in a circular position around the crystallised liquid that held the elemental soul for Air. As I looked up I noticed loads more of the large and small pipes, some with chunks sliced out others with holes carved into them, not knowing what they were for I stood still, I didn't want to set off a booby trap and end up sliced to pieces by flying knives of air.

Isaura took control before any of us could ask what she was going to do, she took a few steps towards the pillars she touched the first one which lit up with a coloured flash of air emitting from it, the colour was a grey tinge which I thought might represent the element for the temple air, the next pillar emitted blue for water and the next one red for fire, she spun on her heal and danced to the last two pillars which were green for earth and a slightly light purple colour for spirit. Once all had been touched and alight they zapped beams of light into the middle which all combined together into a rainbow shimmering beam that bled to white and shot out shards of light hitting the pipes around the room within seconds warm gushes of air pulsated around the room and hit the pipes creating a strange, eerie but at the same time beautiful melody which echoed around the room.

Isaura walked to the crystallised liquid and placed a hand on it, she knelt down and prayed with all her heart with her hand still connected to the statue like object, her voice spoke quickly and in a tongue I had never heard before I knew it had to be the language of her ancestors, it was odd sounding to my ears but the thing inside the object understood it and moved lighting up the frozen liquid, the light bounced off something on the wall and the gush of air changed, the direction the wind hit the pipes changed making the melody sound more threatening and high pitched, the song reached such a pitch I thought my ears might burst but it wasn't them that did, the crystallised liquid erupted and exploded everywhere as the noise cracked the solid form.

The Element Soul raised its wings and floated in the air unmoving.

"Wow a Pegasus", Kenton exclaimed from my right.

And he was correct it was a Pegasus and a beautiful one, this one had a silver coat which glittered in the eerie glow of the chamber, its wings were large filling that side of the room, its legs and hooves moved ever so gently like the thing was treading water but actually treading air.

"Please help us oh mighty Element Soul Air", Isaura said to the Pegasus but like the other two Element Souls this one turned its attention to me and came as close as it could get without being on me. I knelt down showing it respect and it showed me the same by bowing down on its two front legs.

I repeated Isaura's question, "Please help us?"

"My Queen the help of Air is granted, please accept this token", the Pegasus said tilting its head to one side and letting a lone tear trail down its silver lined cheek. The tear dropped from the Pegasus and landed on the floor with a tinkering noise, leaning down to retrieve it I found that the tear had solidified into a tear shaped crystal, inside looked to be clear but at an angle I could see specs of silver inside.

"Thank you", I said and placed the token inside my bag with the feather I had received.

Isaura was about to call the element soul into her earring but was stopped by a sudden shrill sound of laughter. I knew that sound now very well as did Thane, Fira and Brooklyn but Isaura and Stormra looked confused. "Lumi", I whispered angrily.

"Oh yes hello little princess, it is I Lumi", she chuckled playfully and popped out from behind the wind door, "Want to play a game?"

"What if I say no?" I said playfully back knowing full well what she would answer with.

She moved making her shocking pink hair bob around her, the long strands she had at the front swished with her, "Then you forfeit". Her voice held just a hint of a threat but I knew it was bad either way she played it.

"What game is it?" Isaura asked, "I don't want my temple harmed".

"What like the poor water temple", she laughed sloping her head to one side and glaring at Brooklyn, "Best not let the little princess play this time then".

There was a silence as we all waited to see what the game was going to be, Lumi walked towards us with no fear in her stance, she took the bag from her hip and circled her hand inside, "The game is…a guessing game. I will sing you three rhymes and you have to finish them, if you guess the endings correctly you get to keep your element souls, if you fail I get to keep them", she smiled.

"I don't like the sound of this", Fira said beside me, "I don't think we should play".

"What's the forfeit?" Thane asked.

"We kill you now anyway and take the souls from your dead bodies", she smiled ever so sweetly.

"How hard can it be?" Brooklyn smiled with determination in her eyes.

"Brooklyn she isn't going to choose rhymes we know", Thane told her but she just scowled at him.

"I take it the water element is first up then?" Lumi smiled taking her hand out the bag and holding up an orb of water, "Hmm let's see…My mind is the ocean, the ocean is the sea, the ocean is in my mind, the ocean is in me…" She stopped and looked at Brooklyn, "So do you know the answer?"

Brooklyn looked shocked, her eyes wide she had no idea and Lumi knew it, but I had heard that rhyme before in the palace, Freya used to sing it whilst cleaning sometimes, told me it was an ancient rhyme from something long since lost where all the countries knew each other's songs but what was the last part? "The Ocean isn't as kind, as Junia used to be, one day Junia and the oceans will be set free", I whispered.

Lumi's head whipped up, "What did you say?"

I repeated myself, "The Ocean isn't as kind, as Junia used to be, one day Junia and the oceans will be set free".

"How do you know it? That rhyme came from the lost city", she remarked. "No one knows of the lost city except us".

"The lost city?" I asked but she snapped back to Brooklyn, "I don't think that's fair, you keeping your element soul when you didn't answer".

"But you never stated any rules?" Fira smiled, "So any one of us can answer a question".

Lumi's face contorted with anger, "Well I'm making a rule, once you have spoken you cannot speak again, the princess is now out of the game", she glared at me as she said it.

"So I get to keep my element soul then", Brooklyn smiled.

"For now child but not for long", Lumi threatened.

She weaved her hand in her bag and revealed the next orb which was red for fire, "How about you Fire Queen, ready for a riddle?"

Fira nodded and looked to her friends, I just hoped it was one they all knew and not me this time.

Lumi opened her mouth and sang out a small tune, "The flames of fire open our hearts desire, the flames of home is what I admire, the truth is what I seek but not from cheek to cheek, the lies burn in the capsule of time…" she smiled showing her white teeth, "So Fire Queen what's the answer to this one then?"

"But the goddess of flames is one so divine", Fira said coolly.

Lumi looked mad, the madness was spreading through her eyes and into her body and an eerie darkness was coming from her shadow and slowly consuming the chamber behind her, "But how?"

"Guess you're not the only one who has riddles from the lost city", Fira told her.

Cursing she then pulled another orb the one for air from her bag, "So the power of Air your turn is now".

Isaura posed her shoulders and awaited her rhyme.

"The air of my elders is the souls of the past, something I cannot contrast, to show you the beginning would be to show you the end, to which my breathing air cannot defend, my last breath and only fight…" she didn't bother asking she just looked at Isaura.

"Will cast away the darkened blight", Thane responded behind Isaura.

To me it sounded similar to the inscription on the Sceptre, *didn't that prove how the religions were connected to Cosima too?*

Her face turned beetroot red with anger, "You got lucky this time kiddo's but your luck is about to run out", she hissed and pulled one last orb from her bag, crushing it she then threw it in the air of the door way and we all watched as this darkened orb split in two and dropped to the floor, two more mixtures of laughter echoed around the room and we all took defensive stances as two shadows glided past the wind door and entered the room. Two people stood there and both looked like each other, *twin's maybe?* One looked to be male but rather feminine, his hair was cut bowled around his head, it was smooth sleek and shiny and similar to Lumi he had two longer strands that hung down around his face, his eye brows were trimmed and looked perfectly manicured for a guy, his pale smooth skin was flawless. He wore dark clothing which consisted of a dark leather sleeveless jacket with a black hooded top underneath exposing pale arms and long fingered hands, on his fingers were long metal rings which covered his nails and gave him the effect of false ones. From his grasp hung a chain with metal spikes tailing down.

The other twin, the sister was more masculine, she had scruffy tasselled hair which had strikes of jet black and grey to it. Her eyes were wide, for a moment it looked like something was moving inside her eyes but as she blinked it went away. She too wore dark clothing but hers was more leather and spikes, her jacket had rows of spikes coming off the shoulders and elbows, I just hoped I didn't get close enough for her to swipe me with them.

"I'd like you to meet brother and sister duo, Salem and Senti", Lumi applauded them as they bowed to their audience.

Salem took a glance at me and sprung with a speed unknown to me before, I thought the other minions of Lumi had been able to move like the speed of light but he was faster and he took hold of me wrapping one slender but strong arm around my chest and holding up a ringed finger which I could feel was so sharp it could slice my throat open in seconds, "Hand over the element souls to Lumi or she gets it", he said snarling at my friends.

Thane went to move but Senti opened her mouth, I expected her to shout at him with the way she moved it but instead a swarm of buzzing flies flew out and swarmed around him, I could make out his soul power thrashing away at the insects but it fared badly against her weird insect magic.

Fira was by my side in a heartbeat her eyes wide and knowing, "Please take it", she said passing her necklace to Salem who sneered but as he went to take it from her grasp she touched his hand, with a feather touch of her finger sending a flame searing up his arm. Shocked and in pain he shot back letting me go but his finger sent the smallest of cuts into my skin, it stung and was bleeding lightly.

"You fool", Lumi snapped at him which angered him to a point I could see the vein at the top of his temple throbbing with the venom of anger.

He whizzed forward flying through the air like a whisper but I was ready this time and ducked and lifted my Sceptre up, causing it to collide with his skull with a solid crack but before I could celebrate Senti sent some of her swarm my way. The noise of the flies was sickening, the rustle of their wings as they flapped past my face, the weird connecting buzz noise that echoed through my mind, they swatted themselves at my face and I tried with all my might to hit them away flailing my hands at them, a few hit my mouth and I felt like gagging as the moving sensation from them made my skin crawl.

A flash of fire hit them and a small patch of air got through to me, "Don't give up the element souls!" I screamed before the swarm came back and closed me off from what was happening outside of my fly bubble. I had no idea what the others were doing but I hoped it was something powerful.

The wings of the flies beat down at me and I felt myself moving to be closer to the floor to close off my eyes, mouth, nose and ears to them all, the thought of one getting inside me and laying eggs which could hatch made me heave. I felt my stomach clench at the thought and my mouth water with the idea of being sick.

I felt something tugging at my hair and I raised my hand blinding trying to swat it away but I felt nothing but cool air, turning slightly I looked to see Isaura commanding the Pegasus to attack Senti and her army of flies, as the beast attacked Senti she lost her connection with the swarm and they began to leave me and fly aimlessly around the room the noise still echoing in my mind. Thane too was coming out from his fly trap and he ran to me taking my hand, "Can you call any power?" he asked.

I shrugged, "I don't know, why?"

He pointed to where Lumi was and I let out a cry of despair she stood there with Fira's necklace and Brooklyn's ring and now Salem was fighting Isaura for her earring but the Pegasus turned and kicked the twin in the chest sending him flying across the room but he was up before Isaura could call on her own power and he was fighting for her earring yet again.

I lifted the Sceptre up and watched as a slow glow grew up the wand side, the incantation returning and lighting up the top, "But what if I destroy the temple?"

"Just do it", Thane said batting off Senti as the Pegasus was now too consumed with Salem and Isaura to stop the fly Queen.

I stood there frozen to the spot for a moment, *should I really risk using it again and falling out with another converter?* Feeling like I had no choice I lifted the Sceptre above my head and chanted the incantation, "I call upon the stars of ancestors passed, they will guide me with the shining light, take me down the narrow path, to kill the unsightly blight".

The Sceptre grew warm in my hands and I felt the power flood through it, the power was flowing right out of me making me feel light headed and dizzy but I stood my ground keeping the Sceptre raised before it emitted out the huge beam of light which rocketed around the room devouring all the insects in its way. The light travelled so fast but Salem was able to dodge out of the way but as he turned to his sister Senti who was fighting off Fira and Brooklyn who had tackled her to the floor to stop any more flies he could see she couldn't physically dodge it.

"SENTI", Salem screamed which echoed around the whole room.

Her eyes flared open wide with horror as the light flashed down towards her but the girls kept her pinned down, the light collided with her body and on impact she imploded into hundreds of shards of miniature black fly wings. They glittered back down to the floor like a shimmering ash.

"NOOOO", he screamed with a pure vengeance in his voice and he rushed for me, I didn't have time to move out the way and he hit me with such force that I was sent flying, winding myself in the process, the Sceptre skittered out of my hand and landed at the foot of Lumi who smiled and went to pick it but as her hand neared it a light flashed from it showering her in the afterglow and it flew away from her hand. Lumi screamed as the light burned her hand, she lifted it to her face in horror as the skin of her hand, wrist and up to her elbow melted and smeared in together instantly drying and scaring her for life.

"Ahhh", she cried dropping the necklace and ring as she examined the true extent of the damage, Thane lunged for the items she had dropped and shoved her over in the process, she sobbed in pain and stared at me, "Oh little princess how I am going to enjoy tearing you apart one day soon", and with that she threw down an orb from her bag which exploded and she was gone in a cloud of mist.

That only left Salem who had his hands around my neck with his ringed claws digging in, "You are going to pay for that, you little bit…Ah, guh", he spat as something went through his back and out through his stomach, blood blossomed down his abdomen and pooled from his lips.

I looked to see Kenton with his trident, he had struck it right in the back of the last twin standing looking shocked at what he had just done. Salem turned and swatted the boy to the floor before pulling out the trident with a thick wet sucking sound. He loomed over Kenton who turned deathly pale as he now had no way to defend himself, Brooklyn ran but I knew she wouldn't make it even as she rose her hands to cast a water spell. I stood and charged just as Salem sped up towards the boy, I pumped my legs faster and jumped just landing in front of Kenton arching my back ready for the impact as Salem brought the trident down home, it hit me in the shoulder and I felt pain sear through where my shoulder blade sat, I let out a scream just as Brooklyn turned up, she threw up her hands and cast a powerful water spell like nothing I had ever seen her cast before, the water flowed from her hands and circled around the twin who tried to run with his speed but Thane hit him with a soul punch which knocked him back. The water twisted into a water spout creating a vortex tunnel, the water rose and span faster and faster until it covered the whole of Salem's body head to foot. She then stopped the twisting and Isaura breathed cold air over it and froze the water in place and watched as Salem thrashed around trying to get out but at every turn Brooklyn was there flooding more water in his face inside the frozen container. Eventually his body began to give up and the water consumed him, his eyes glanced to where Senti's ashes lay and he bowed his head to her before taking a breath of the crystal clear liquid, his lungs flooded instantly and we all watched horrified as Brooklyn drowned him, his eyes bulged with the lack of oxygen and he clawed at his own throat slicing it open flooding the clear water with a red swirl until suddenly, he just stopped moving.

Brooklyn then lowered her hands slowly, Isaura letting the ice crack and all the water washed away around us, his limp and lifeless body dropped to the floor with a wet thud. She turned to Kenton and pulled him close to her. "You need to stop scaring me like that", she sobbed into his shoulder.

"I'm sorry", he sobbed back and holding her close.

Thane went over to the body of Salem and absorbed his evil soul to recycle.

I lay there gasping in pain, "Mira!" I heard Fira shriek just as I watched black dots swarm my vision just like the flies had done before it all went very, very dark.

~

I opened my eyes slowly, the haze of light entered them and made me blink profusely, I looked around at my surroundings and found that I was back in Stormra's cabin. I was laying on a bed, I knew Stormra had given me a potion of sorts as my back and neck were healed, no trace of any marks on my skin.

I stood up from the bed and straightened myself up in a small mirror which hung on the wall before opening the door and heading down the stairs, they all turned to me as I entered the warm front room, they were all sat around the fireplace drinking spice tea and eating what looked like a meat stew, my stomach rumbled and I instantly licked my lips.

"Come child and eat", Stormra said motioning to her seat.

I nodded thanks and sat down, "Is everyone ok", said looking over everyone especially Kenton.

"We are and thank god you are too", Thane replied, "You scared us back there", he placed his hand on my shoulder and looked deep into my eyes, "Don't do that again".

I looked at Kenton who smiled but looked embarrassed.

"Thank you", I said to him and he looked surprised.

"What do you mean?" he responded.

"For saving my life".

"What? No it was you who saved me", he gasped.

I shrugged, "We saved each other, if you hadn't of speared him with your trident then he would have killed me anyway, I had to repay that debt".

He nodded, "You didn't have to repay nothing, you are our Queen and…Well I wanted to save you…You are the only one who can save Junia".

"With all your help not just me", I smiled.

He shrugged his eyes looked like he knew something.

"What do you know?" I asked.

"Nothing", he replied.

Brooklyn looked at him, "Kenton?"

"I don't know anything, I just wanted to save her".

I felt my face burn at how he reacted and how he had saved my life because he thought it was the right thing to do. "So we're even now ok, no more saving each other right, we just stay out of harm's way", I smiled.

"Alright", he blushed, Brooklyn took his hand in hers.

"Alright", she repeated, she looked me dead in the eye with a curiosity in hers but Stormra turned up with my food and I looked away from them.

The food warmed my stomach fully and the spice tea warmed my bones, "So how long was I out?"

"A few hours, but it's nearly dusk now so we cannot leave for Emerald Valley until morning", Fira told me.

I nodded but I felt sick, this journey was taking longer than I had anticipated, Andromeda had given me a two week limit surely I must be on around the week mark now, time was running out and it was making me nervous. I still needed to save my dad, I needed to know that at least he was coming home, that was if Andromeda let him live after the chaos at all the temples between us and her friends.

After supper Stormra took me to one side, "Mira I need to talk to you about Freya".

I knew what was coming, something bad. *Was that what Kenton was hiding?*

"She isn't going to make it past tonight, when we were gone she took a turn for the worst, the potions aren't helping her at all".

"Ok, can I see her?"

She nodded, "But be prepared Mira she is in a really bad way".

"What about him, her boyfriend?"

She shook her head, "He's gone".

I knew why Freya was giving up because he wasn't here anymore and she wanted to be with him, I had seen her reaction at the palace when she thought he was going to be executed. I was going to miss my maid, she was my friend, things just weren't going to be the same when I get to go back home. *My mother gone and now Freya too, what else was going to be taken away from me? From all of us?*

I walked up the stairs alone leaving the warmth and hustle of the voices below, the walk to Freya's room took an age and I could hear my footsteps echo around me, I didn't want to open that door, I didn't want to say goodbye.

Inside the room it was warm and quiet, I could hear Freya's breathing, it was quick, short and shallow, the curtains had been opened wide and Freya was stood next to the window looking out to the world outside. She was taking it all in before…before she left. She turned to me slowly, she had wrapped a silk scarf around her face only revealing her eyes but I could see dark patches around her sockets where the cold and frost bite had eaten away at her skin.

"Freya?" I said to her feeling tears well up in my throat.

"Don't worry about me Mira I'm going to be with him now, I'm going to Spirit".

"But I don't want you to go, I need you back at the palace with me, to be my friend, my maid", I cried.

"You have new friends now Mira they will help you", she said softly raising a gloved hand to my face.

"I'm sure I can find a potion that will cure you".

"Stormra tried but I was too far gone, there is only so much potions can do", she replied, "I need you to be strong for me Mira, I need you to go on and fight. I know that you can do this, all of you".

I tried to talk but I couldn't, my throat had welled up so much all that came out was a strangled cry. Freya suddenly gasped in pain and collapsed to the floor, I ran to her and held her in my arms.

"Mira there is something you need to know, the hidden city…" she breathed so tenderly as her last one escaped her lips, "Your mother…" But she didn't finish what she needed to say as she closed her eyes and left me. I cried and held her tight not letting go, I could feel her soul sweep the room and a prickle of electric current as she flickered gently in front of me, she bowed to me and smiled opening her mouth to tell me what it was I needed to know but nothing came out, she couldn't talk. She looked troubled but there wasn't anything I could do.

"I will find out what it is you mean", I told her and she looked relieved that I knew that I needed to know something but how was I going to find out something I knew nothing about, *what was this hidden or lost city? It wasn't the first time I'd heard of it.*

She bowed to me again and her body flickered and vanished into the cool evening air. I didn't leave her side straight away as I felt too numb to move, she had been like a sister to me, my best friend, my only friend and now she was gone, gone to be with my mother and her one true love.

The lost city

~ The Lost City ~

The next morning we were up bright and early and had left for the gate before the high sun, Stormra had decided she wanted to travel with us to keep Kenton company for when things get messy when we finally reach Cosima for the last time and to fight Andromeda, she knew it had to be our battle and not theirs. She had packed us a small bag each with some food, water and some money, not a lot but enough to hopefully get us by till the end. I had promised to pay them all back with their kind donations to our journey but Stormra had clicked her tongue in dismay and told me that it was her gift to me as Queen. But I wasn't Queen yet, my father was still alive to take the throne, somewhere out there in Junia he had to be alive, he just had to be.

We reached the border gate and left Skye behind, the trickling water was slowly turning dark as the element soul was no longer there to keep it pure and from being tarnished by the enemies, we had been lucky enough that we only encountered a few enemies on the way all of us swiftly taking them down. Isaura and her mother bowed to Skye as they left and prayed at a small statue at the gate which I hadn't noticed when we first arrived. Stormra encouraged us all to pray to the element soul to help us on our journey, we all obliged other than Brooklyn and Kenton. Brooklyn stated it would go against her element soul and her part of the religion, even though Fira reminded her it was all one religion just different elements but Brooklyn was having none of it. Fira prayed and stood up, she then said a small prayer to her own element soul and followed us as we all trailed out and down the path that led to the small village just outside.

"You really should have prayed to our element soul", Stormra said with a worried look on her face, "It's bad luck not to".

"We pray to our own, he will keep us safe", Brooklyn answered with dismissing Stormra's concerns.

Kenton just shrugged doing as his sister wished him to do.

"Um before we go, the shop keeper asked me to pop in before we left".

Stormra nodded, "Then we must see him".

The shop was quiet as we approached and I could see the man working away restocking the rails and pricing clothing up, he smiled as the door chimed open and greeted us with praise of Junia.

"You said to see you, before we left", I said to him.

He nodded, "Yes my lady I think this might come in handy", he nipped behind the counter to the back room and came out holding two bottles of potion, "These I made with the Siren Scale, it's the best potion money can buy but you get these two for free".

I took them and felt my heart shatter, if only I had these last night Freya might still be alive, "Thank you", I smiled.

"I managed to make quite a few and I'm going to visit Skye over the next few days to see if anyone needs help now the element soul is gone", he said.

"You know the soul is gone?" I asked.

He pointed out the window, we all turned to see that beyond the force field that separated Cosima and Skye the normally blue sky was shimmering with darkness, "The Sky in Skye is never that dark and never full of that amount of evil magic, I knew the element soul was gone last night, I take it you lot have something to do with it?" he asked politely and although he was weary he wasn't accusing us as such.

Stormra spoke up for me, "We do. My daughter here is the element converter for Skye. Cosima is in danger and we need all the element souls together to defeat the danger".

"You mean Andromeda?"

She nodded.

"Then I wish you all the luck in Junia, especially you my dear princess".

"You know who I am?"

"It just clicked, I saw the television appearance you made last week".

"Well thank you".

"Any time princess, any time".

With that we left his shop and headed to the train station, it was still a long journey to Emerald Valley and it was only lunch time now, if I was going to speed things up a little to stick within the deadline we needed to move and get the next train.

I didn't really feel like talking and whilst the others picked up on it Brooklyn on the other hand for once actually tried talking to me, "Hey Mira can we talk?"

"Huh?" I said looking at her, "You want to talk to me?"

She smiled shyly and clasped both her hands together, "I just wanted to say, thank you", she said the last part really quickly and I only just heard it.

I smiled, "For what?"

"For saving Kenton, he means the whole of Junia to me and to lose him, well I couldn't bare thinking about it", she sighed, "But thank you Mira I appreciate it".

I nodded and watched as she run up ahead to catch up with her brother who was talking to Fira and Stormra, Isaura was walking behind looking around Cosima, although this part of Cosima is rather well tamed compared to the city centre full of tall buildings and concrete this part actually looked quite green with real trees, grass lands and fresh air. The train station was just up ahead I could see the hulking great white building looking odd against all the greenery. Thane was at my side as Brooklyn ran off and although he said nothing I knew he was trying to be there for me, the pain of losing Freya was still so raw for me.

As we neared the train station though we noticed something was amiss, palace guards were all over the place with lookouts, patrols and gunners all waiting and my guess was for us, "Thane".

"I see them", he said, "We need to find another way to Emerald Valley".

"Another way?" I said, "But we don't have time".

"It's either another way or we get caught by them, Andromeda will have them kill us on sight and with bullets and weapons we stand no chance, yes we have powers but bullets are quick I don't fancy taking our chances".

"I might know a way", Isaura spoke up.

Stormra looked at her daughter confused, "But you've never left Skye how would you know a way?"

"I read in an old book I found on Cosima's history that there is an older disused train line not far from here, we would have to walk it but it would lead us straight to the Abyss near Emerald Valley".

"The Abyss?" I looked at Thane.

"Just in front of Emerald Valley is a large Abyss, a dark canyon. It was created by the Emerald Valley citizens when the great war was raging on, they wanted to be a separate country from Junia altogether, they wanted out and away from Cosima so they started to use machines to dig down into the earth, they cast powers to make the hole wider in the hope they would just snap off the face of Junia but…the fault lines appeared and started to fray causing Emerald Valley to have a magic power outage, they knew if they severed the tie completely then their magic and element soul would be lost forever. So they repaired the fault line but kept the Abyss as a reminder to Cosima of what they would do if war ever spilled on their turf again", Thane told me but looking at Isaura.

"Would it be safe I heard a strange cult live down there?" Fira said from beside me.

"You know of this place?" I asked.

"Not much, only rumours that a murderous cult live below Cosima in an abandoned train line".

"There are people down there but they are not a murderous cult", Thane smiled, "It was a rumour spread by their own people to stop travellers going down there".

"Why?" I asked, "Why don't they want people down there if they are not a strange cult?"

"Because they are hiding a secret", He stated, "A secret that they didn't want the royal family to find out about".

"Is it really safe?" Brooklyn asked, "I have my brother to think about".

"Yes it is safe, for us but I imagine they will be hostile at first. They will not know it is us coming".

"Wait I don't understand", I said, "Know it is us? What is this place Thane?"

"You will see. I didn't think we would end up travelling there, not now, not with our time limit but I guess it wouldn't hurt".

To me he made no sense and by the faces the others were pulling I think they all felt the same as me.

Thane turned to Isaura, "Lead the way".

She nodded and ushered us away from the view of trouble.

At a fork in a crossroads she turned left down a narrow dirt track, trees lined the road hiding what was beyond behind it. A few miles down the track she stopped to get her barring's trying to remember what the book had told her. Without speaking she turned looking at a tree and feeling its bark, a small notch had been carved into it, "This way". We all followed and watched her as she felt trees either nodding to herself or cursing if it wasn't the right one, after an hour or so of looking and walking further away from the eyes of the palace guards we finally came across a hidden entrance, the entrance itself was like a mine shaft, a dank dark looking cave type thing with vines, tall grasses and other plant life hiding it but there had been signs of previous use, some of the grasses were damaged and had been flattened before being fluffed back up along with a small footprint dirt track that led into the cave.

"This is it", she said turning to Fira, "Think you can light the way?"

Fira nodded and strolled straight in holding up her hand and casting a fireball to light the way, inside was so dark and dingy it sent shivers down my spine, it was damp and dripping with moisture from the soil that lay over the top. A small pathway went downwards, I had to brush cobwebs off my bare arms as we ventured further down, I heard Brooklyn tell Kenton to stay close to her, Isaura walked with Fira and Thane walked by me with Stormra at the rear.

"Are you sure this is this safe?" I whispered my voice still echoing even though I spoke so softly.

"I hope so", he said taking my arm in his to keep me close. The warmth of his arm on mine sent flutters running through my stomach, I resisted the urge to place my head on his shoulder.

The path soon led to an underground station which was gloomy, dark and eerie. Pure white and once pristine

Cosiman tiles which had been on the walls of the station were all smashed and broken on the floor, the old marble flooring was covered in dust and some plant life had even managed to find a way to grow back up through the manmade structure. Just past the platform was the old railway track which had an old broken down train all crumpled and rusted to the tracks, the old trains used to run on the tracks with old metal wheels, they even had windows for passengers to see out of as the train moved but they could only go so fast which for most Cosiman's wasn't fast enough. What I didn't know though was that the old trains had run underground only, I thought they had run on the metal tracks that the hovers use for guidance above land.

We all stepped of the platform and started down following the track, Isaura seemed to think that the next station would lead up to the Abyss and we could find our way up from there but with all this darkness and parts of the tunnels old escape routes all boarded up and blocked off I was beginning to feel like the other way might have been a better bet.

After what felt like miles and miles of my feet aching we spotted a small sign for the old train drivers telling them of the station approach, "Not far now", Thane said encouraging everyone to keep moving but as he spoke we heard another noise, it sounded like running feet and it was coming closer from the way we were going. Looking panicked Thane ordered us to hide but we were in a tunnel with boarded up passages, there was nowhere to hide. The others all took defensive stances and I tried to join with them and look menacing but even Kenton looked fiercer than me.

The running noise got closer until we could see the shadows moving as people rushed for us, a clatter of swords, spears, hunting knives and other weapons all scraped the tracks as the people stopped in front of us.

"Who goes there?" A harsh male voice asked from the front, he wore a strange dirtied looking fabric wrapped around him like a robe, his skin was inhumanly pale, his hair whiter than Brooklyn's, I could see him looking at each and every one of us and I breathed slowly hoping that him and his people wouldn't attack. The others who stood behind him showed they were ready for action swinging their weapons in their hands and they too all bore the same characteristics as this leader.

"We mean you and your people no harm", Thane stood forward, "We only need means to get to Emerald Valley".

"Why take this way why not the upper city train?" the man frowned.

"We have special circumstances that make it difficult for us to travel in the city".

"How did you find this place?" the man asked gruffly.

Isaura spoke up, "I knew about it from an old history book".

"No books have this spoken in them, you lie".

Isaura bit her lip and looked at her mother, "Ok fine I didn't read it in a book, I found it a few years ago".

"How?" both Stormra and the man asked.

"I was bored and wanted a different life to the one I lead, I didn't want to be an element converter I wanted to travel and explore Junia but it was forbidden in the teachings for me to do so. So I ran away one night but I got lost and wound up here, I slept in the cave entrance overnight and explored down here a little. I had heard stories of a strange cult down here and wanted to find you to ask if I could join you but I was too scared to go any further and returned home. Mum you just thought I had stayed out too late whilst hunting".

Her mother looked horrified but the man suddenly warmed to us, "Element converter?"

"Yes I'm the converter for air and these are my friends", she said.

Fira waved showing the fireball in her hands, Brooklyn smiled and flicked out some water from her hands, Thane bowed, "I am a soul guardian".

"To whom?" The man asked.

"To me", I said.

"And who are you?"

"I'm the princess of Cosima, my name is Mira".

"Your mother is the Queen Espinosia?"

I nodded, "Yes".

He bowed to me then extended his hand out, I took it and shook it. His palm was chilled and his hand shake showed strength but not enough to make me feel uncomfortable.

"You must come with us, we have much to discuss", he said letting go of my hand, turning to his people he spoke in Skye's tongue.

I looked to Isaura who translated, "He says you've come home and to command a feast".

Home? A feast?

Thane pursed his lips a happy and knowing look in his twinkling eye, "Then we must attend, there must be good reasoning behind it".

"Good reasoning? Are they going to eat us?" I said but the man simply turned and smiled.

"Eat the Princess of Cosima? Not quite what I was thinking more a feast in your honour".

The others around me giggled but I could already feel the atmosphere was changing, these people were allies, they could be trusted, well I hoped so. As I watched Thane giggling at my reaction I knew then that he knew something about these people, he looked comfortable. Like meeting old friends after a long time.

We followed them to another hidden passage, this one was hidden by magic and the man tapped his sword upon a certain stone on the wall and a door appeared, he opened it and we all walked in. My eyes had to adjust as there was still a gloom but it was lighter, lit up by hundreds and thousands of candles along with torches with firestones and other magical light sources such as twinkling orbs and fireflies.

"Where are we?" I asked looking around in wonderment, this place was amazing like a whole city beneath a city. There were hundreds of buildings all grouped together built out of old bricks and other building materials. A small lake flowed through the centre where people sat collecting buckets full of water, they all turned to look at us as we approached. Magical orbs of light floated around the lake as if guiding the people who lived here so they didn't fall in.

"That water, that's from Skye?" Isaura questioned the man.

He nodded, "The River of Skye ends in a Lake at the bottom of the border gate, we have tunnelled a small enough hole to retrieve natural clean water from there but not too much to flood our homes or that you would notice".

"How do you know it's from Skye?" I asked her.

"The orbs, they appear in Skye when magic is being used which means magic is used a lot down here to make the orbs that bright".

I watched as the orbs danced freely around the water like they had a life of their own, which if these were souls then they would but something about these orbs didn't look soul like, just balls of pure magic.

"Please princess this way".

We followed the man whose name I still didn't know but as he was leading us through the trails of the underground city I couldn't bring myself to speak, my eyes darted everywhere all at once taking in the views. This place was enormous almost like Cosima but broken, the disused buildings lay in ruins the further in we went, a few darkened creatures scurried away as we passed, their claws skittering up the brick work but the man didn't seem worried by them so we didn't bother to show our weapons. The path soon came to a dead end rows of broken buildings blocked the way so we couldn't travel any further, the man stopped said nothing and just pointed and I saw what it was he wanted me to see. In the distance a huge building almost identical to my palace, my home, it was sitting quietly in the gloom, strangely above this underground palace a group of tunnels had been built up and connected to the soiled ceiling above, it looked like a rabbit warren full of funny shaped tunnels mostly built of disused bricks from crumbled buildings, they were wonky and a little crocked and held up by magic but they led somewhere and I had a sinking feeling I knew where.

"The lost city", I whispered to myself, then I turned to the man and to Thane, "What is this place? And where do those tunnels lead?"

"My name is Koal and these are my people, we live in this hidden city, the old city…the true lost city of Cosima".

"The true Cosima?"

He nodded, "The old government leaders of Cosima hated the fact that Cosima didn't have its own element soul or magic, even though the true royal family could in fact wield magic and powerful magic at that but it could only be tapped into at times of need it wasn't all the time like the other places and people of Junia could do. They wanted Cosima to become a magic free country to show that it didn't need it to be almighty and powerful. They killed the true royal family and declared the throne theirs tainting the bloodline and abolishing the families magic, they wanted the other countries to fear them and bow down by using weapons made by machines and turning Cosima into the great machine and concrete city it is now, they also wanted the other countries to declare their magic as illegal but instead it started the great war, a war they didn't win because the other countries rebelled and kept their magic. The leaders had to stand down but became ruthless, killing anyone who tried to taint the royal bloodline with magic again or who would push the religion back into Cosima".

He paused looking me over, "But you hold the magic don't you?"

"I don't know what you mean?"

He lifted his hand to my Sceptre, "That is your weapon, it propels your power into it and charges it up. You don't have power all the time but you have enough to fight when you need to, am I right?"

I nodded, "Well sort of I guess, I thought the power was from my mother, she…" I trailed off.

"But how if the magic was spilled from the royal bloodline?" Fira asked beside me.

"Because she is from the true bloodline", Koal stated.

"How?" I whispered.

"Your mother Espinosia".

"My mother", my heart ached at the mention of her and he saw the pain cross my face.

"I take it the great Espinosia is no longer of Junia?"

I shook my head in dismay, "Yes Andromeda took her".

"Do you know who Andromeda really is?"

I shook my head, "Just a grand dark witch?"

"No", he looked at all of us, "She is your mother's aunt and your mother is of true royal decent. We saved her own mother, who was Andromeda's sister long ago at the start of the Great War, keeping her hidden and safe when the leaders took over and killed her family. They thought she died in a tunnel hidden under True Cosima when soldiers stormed in but she was kept hidden, as well as Andromeda".

"No", the others all hushed behind me.

"Andromeda is of royal blood?"

He nodded, "Which is why she has been able to poison Junia by connecting with the opposite pentacle, your mothers magical lineage has spread out to good and evil, Andromeda's magic had been tainted by the maid who saved her, the maid we believe saw so much death in her own life and turned to the evil side whilst fleeing the palace and wanted revenge and set it into Andromeda's brain. She left all her evil plans to Andromeda only in memory and she studied them ever since. She grew up here but fled when we disapproved of her plans to use evil to gain the royal throne again. We had our own plans, to bring up a young woman of true blood and train her to become a princess and send her off to marry the king".

"My mother lived down here?"

"Yes for some years of her life then we took her above ground to get her acclimatised to the atmosphere, we took her to a courting school in Cosima which was open then due to the King needing to marry. She trained there until she was seventeen, she grew into a beautiful young woman and took the young princes fancy, they married and consummated the marriage and she bore you, a true princess now in the royal bloodline".

"So I'm of true royal blood?"

He nodded, "You are a true Queen of Cosima".

"Is that why the element souls address me as Queen and not princess?"

"Yes they know everything that happens around them, they have known that you were born and one day would come to them for help. You must defeat Andromeda so the throne is not of dark magic, the throne needs to be of light and good magic".

"My father will never allow this, not magic on the throne, not his throne".

"No he won't but there comes a time in every Queen's life where she has to make hard decisions".

"You mean overthrow the King? I cannot do that to my own father!"

"Once he sees how powerful you truly are he might abdicate on his own accord".

"I cannot rule Cosima I am just a child".

"I do believe your sixteenth birthday is soon upon us? No?"

I thought…*yes it was in a few days' time*, "How do you know this?"

"Because our religious teachings speak of a young Queen of thus age that will change Junia forever".

"It must be wrong I cannot", I replied, "I do not know how".

"We will guide you, all of us", he motioned to his people and to my own.

I looked to Thane who beamed, "You truly are special, I was meant to help the real Queen".

This was all too much for me to take in, "You have it all wrong, I'm a cry baby wimp who cannot fight her own battles, I rely on my friends to protect me".

"These friends are your ladies in waiting, they are your royal elite, they are here to protect the true Queen of

Cosima, it was written in the stars when Junia was born. When the elements came to Junia they foretold of this day. We are not wrong lady Mira, it is your destiny".

Looking around the hidden underground city of True Cosima I buckled to my knees and Thane caught me, "We are here to help you Mira, all of us, let us help you to the throne and we will forever be by your side".

I looked at them all, Fira, Brooklyn, Stormra, Isaura, Kenton and Thane, they all smiled at me in response and bowed down to me. "But we still have two element souls to collect from Emerald Valley and Spirit".

"And we will guide you to Emerald Valley after the feast", Koal said.

"Wait hang on!" I questioned, "The war happened many, many years ago…That would make Andromeda and my mother… old…"

"Andromeda yes, your mother not so much. She was born by Andromeda's sister many years later, who was a babe herself when she arrived her during the war but in her mind she is older".

"How?"

"Souls are born to live and die and then to be recycled, I imagine your mother is an older generation of recycled souls but it gives her courage and knowledge than a younger soul has yet to learn". He looked at me as he said it, *I was a younger soul and I had much to learn.*

"How old is Andromeda?" I questioned him.

"Around a hundred years old, give or take a few years".

"But she still looks so young, how is that possible?" Brooklyn gasped.

"The royal bloodline. They age slower than most people due to the magic in their blood, not magic like most of us possess but it is a magic only the royals hold and if there is a strong King or Queen then the magic will try to get them to stay on the throne for as long as possible. It is the will of Junia".

As I thought about it Fira butted in and asked, "How is it that the True Cosima is down here?"

Koal responded, "The leaders wanted the people of Cosima to forget all about the magic the country used to hold, so they buried it with *'magic'* funnily enough, they hid the city beneath the soil and cement that Cosima now beholds. Its true beauty and true magic lost down here".

"And those tunnels?" I asked.

"They connect the true palace to the new one, once you are Queen you can come down to the hidden city anytime".

"How did they get there?"

"We built them, as escape tunnels for Espinosia for if she ever needed to flee with you to us".

"Why didn't she?" I said out loud more to myself than them.

Thane took my hand, "She would already have been taken".

I sighed, I didn't want to think about being Queen, I wanted my mum and dad back and now I knew who my mum really was I felt confused, *did she even love my dad like he did her*? He wasn't a cruel man not really, yes he had executed rebels of Junia's religion but that was due to what had been moulded into his brain.

"How is it the people of Cosima didn't revolt?" Isaura asked looking concerned, "Surely they would have known that the 'Leaders' killed for their place on the throne?"

Koal looked haunted by her question, "They despised magic but they used it to help themselves, they were able to cloak themselves to look like the King and Queen of the time so the people thought none the different. The people of Cosima truly believed their 'Royal Family' declared magic and the religion illegal in Cosima. Over the years some magic has seeped in, it always would in the form of healers and potions but that was it, nothing else. The people of that time had no idea their royal family had been brutally murdered".

I felt so sick to my stomach, "But why? Why be so ashamed that they had no element soul?" Then something occurred to me, "But they did didn't they? They did have an element soul just not one that was awake".

"You have seen it?" Koal asked surprised.

I nodded and looked at Thane, "When he pulled me into the mirror he showed me the birth of Junia and I saw the element soul fall to Cosima but it didn't wake like the others…It died but that means Cosima did have one? Doesn't it?"

"It's not dead Mira", Koal corrected me, "But it is lying dormant waiting for the day when someone truly believes and is powerful enough to wake it".

"Is that Mira?" Fira asked from behind me, excitement full in her voice.

Koal shrugged, "We do not know that, all we do know is that Mira should become Queen and rule over

Cosima with magic but whether that is shared from the other countries or through her own element soul I do not know".

"Where is it?" Kenton asked, "Cosima's element soul? We could see if we could wake it up now and be rid of Andromeda for good".

Again Koal shrugged, "Again we do not know where it is located but it is said when the time comes for it to awaken the person will find it without maps or guess work. It will call the Cosiman element converter".

A cold breeze suddenly fluttered around my shoulders and I glanced back at the secret and true palace of Cosima. I knew it couldn't be me, that I wasn't the hidden element converter but for me to be Queen, something I had been trained for my whole life was something I knew, my mother being of true Royal blood and having me to get the magic back into the Royal family I could believe….Just.

A little while later we all were perched on long benches that sat around a long table made up of hundreds of scraps of wood. Goblets of wine, water, spiced tea and plates full of food from roasted pigeon and fish to some strange looking vegetable concoctions were set out on old broken plates and bowls. We ate and spoke in joyed spirits joining in with the hidden city dwellers, they all looked so similar to Koal, all deathly pale and white, colour stripped from them from lack of sunlight and living underground. What confused me was how my mother and Andromeda didn't look like them.

"What troubles you my Queen?" Koal asked.

So I told him.

"The royal blood line is strong, even living underground the vibrancy from their royal souls still shone through. We are not of royal blood, we are descendants from the maids and servants that worked their years ago, so living underground has taken its effect on us".

Having answered my question he went back to cheering around the dinner table and I found myself watching Thane who was gossiping with Kenton and a few of the white haired people. Fira sat beside me shovelling food into her throat, I hadn't realised how much that girl could really chow down. Isaura, Brooklyn and Stormra all sat together, the two element converters talking and Stormra mainly just keeping watch. As I watched Thane I knew he had known about all this, he had tried to avoid me since Koal brought us to the meal, a quick smile and glance and he'd purposely turn away and talk to someone else. *Why didn't he just tell me if he knew most of it? Why leave it to these people, especially since he didn't think we would come this way on his original journey plan?*

Around midnight Koal came to me and ask me to take a walk alone, Thane stood to argue the point that he would accompany me but Koal assured him that I needed to see something for myself and for myself only, without my trusted soul guardian by my side. Thane sat down when I nodded to tell him it was fine, I didn't feel threatened by Koal, in fact he felt familiar like I knew him, he held some of my mother's ways about him, her mannerisms and other qualities but hers had been honed down and trained by the courtship.

He led me away from the table and down a small narrow pathway which was concealed by broken buildings and rubble, we walked for a while the view of Thane and the others vanishing from my sight. I had to tread carefully over some crumbling ruins, my eyes not adjusted to the broken ground like Koal's.

It had been around twenty minutes or so of walking before he spoke. He pointed to a small dark recess in the cavernous wall, "That is the tunnel where Andromeda escaped through with the help of the maid, we believe they were trying to reach Emerald Valley which is just through there. The exit comes out into the Abyss somewhere but we have not entered it for many years due to the lost souls that dwell there they play us memories to show us how terrible it was for them. I have seen many but I feel seeing some for yourself my Ladyship will help you on your journey".

"How so?"

"You will see why Andromeda is the way she is, it might help you to know any weaknesses she may have for the battle that is looming".

"I have a question?" I said and he nodded for me to ask away, "Does Andromeda know I'm of true royal blood?"

"No, if she had she would have killed you already. She wants the throne for herself and will let nothing stand in her way, she wants the final element soul to be able to do so. She will destroy Junia with it and turn it into dark lands. You are the light Mira and she is the dark, always remember that".

"Ok but surely she must know of some of this...She grew up down here and...Did she even know my mother?"

"No...She was exiled from here when her sister was pregnant with your mother. Her sister had been saved by a different palace maid, her wet nurse and was brought up as her own, she didn't tell any of us that the young child was Andromeda's sister as she didn't want to risk the palace guard finding and killing her so she thought it best if only she knew. No one found out until the maid was on her death bed and revealed the truth, by then Andromeda was long gone. Andromeda's sister then fell pregnant with your mother but unfortunately she passed away when your mother was still young".

"So Andromeda has no idea that my mother was her niece?"

"No".

"And she had no idea that her own sister had been alive and living beside her the whole time?"

"No, they had both been really young when the attack happened at the palace. Andromeda's sister was only a tiny baby and believed to have died".

"But how? Didn't they look alike?"

He shifted on his feet, "In a way, some facial features but mostly not but that was due to the trickery of the maid. She disguised her to look like a normal child and not a royal one".

"Disguised her?"

"Most maids and servants used to be called in from the other countries where magic and element power was part of daily life, they could all cast their own magic".

"So does that mean that in a way, the throne really should belong to Andromeda and not me? She is the first heir to the throne?"

He nodded glumly, "It does but she must not take the throne. She would destroy Junia, you know that".

"But how can I be the one to take the throne and save Junia if I am only a watered down version?"

"Because although the blood line might be watered down as you say, it also carries the magic and the magic would not be watered down. The throne would accept you, more so than the people before you, more so than your father".

I looked into the mouth of the tunnel, "Who will I see? The memories?"

"You could see anyone's but I'm hoping because of your connections that Andromeda's family's memories will appear to you".

"Ok I'm ready", I said stepping towards the tunnel.

"Remember this place is just a tunnel full of memories, they cannot hurt you even if they seem to the point they might", he said placing a hand on my shoulder, "Good luck my Queen".

I didn't bother saying anymore to Koal mostly because I was shaking and nervous but I also just wanted this strange memory game to be over with *but if it would show me any weaknesses then I couldn't pass it down could I?* The tunnel was chilly with a strange eerie breeze infiltrating the entrance like what I had felt earlier, it was pitch black and I almost turned back in the thought this was a lie and it was just an elaborate plan to kill me for Andromeda, that everything he said had been lies until I saw her. It was a woman, a palace maid by the looks of things, I could see the elaborate palace uniform which hadn't changed much over the years for maids, she had light mousy brown hair but dark knowing eyes, for a moment she looked lost, shy and innocent, that was until she locked onto my royal red locks and her eyes flashed with an anger, fury and evil. She held out a hand making me pause, *Should I really take it, she looked evil? What if an evil memory could hurt me?* I turned to look back the way I had come but there was no sign of Koal, I had no choice but to try and so I took it and she led me into the tunnel, the breeze slowly becoming distant and warmer. She led me deep down under more ground, the tunnel split off into sections and she knew exactly which one to turn down, her body shimmering with a soul lit glow she turned to a small room. It was an emergency exit door which had been camouflaged to blend in with the walls around it, she ushered me inside and I followed, then she placed both palms on the sides of my face and opened her mind to me.

"Come with me, I will show you all".

~

My vision was black and white like an old fashioned film and I knew by looking at my hands that these hands were not mine, I was back in the palace but the old one. The lay out was similar other than a few changes, randomly placed doors and disused windows.

I walked to the throne room and my hand flew to my mouth in terror, I had only come to see the King to ask to go out to the town for supplies, to the local herbalist for the ingredients for the poison I was making, the poison no one could know about because I had been using it on the oldest princess but now I could never ask to leave again as his blood was spilling over the marble tiled flooring. His neck had been sliced open wide, the dagger still embedded in his throat, the killer still standing there laughing, Edwardo the Kings right hand man had stabbed the king in the back in more than one way. He grasped the dead king's crown and placed it over his head. I heard a cry coming from the throne and spotted the Queen laying limp but alive on the steps, her eyes burned into mine and I knew what she was thinking, the Princesses! My princesses, the two things I cared about for all the wrong reasons, to use them for my own agenda to over throw the King and Queen but it was taking time and now I had run out of it.

Without thinking I ran to the chambers of the young princesses but only one was present, the older one but where was the other, the baby? The Queens chambers maybe? Without explaining anything to the princess I took her hand and ran for the Queens private chambers luckily just missing some of Edwardo's guard's men who were on their way to the princess's chamber to kill her too. I found the baby princess with her wet nurse. I snatched her up from the surprised woman and told her to run, that evil was in the palace but little did the wet nurse know that the evil wasn't just the one she would see very soon in the form of Edwardo and his men but the woman who had rushed before her. Then without taking time to grab anything else I ran with the two girls to the nearest exit tunnel. I found one not too far from my own rooms hidden behind a painting of the Queen and her daughters. Just as I opened it and rushed in I could hear the clattering of swords as the guard's men came this way, I went to close the door behind me when a strong hand grabbed my arm that held the baby. With Andromeda crying and the strong hands pulling hard I lost grip of the baby Princess.

"I will not let you poison them both", the wet nurse screamed at me. How did she know?

With it not really mattering now as the princesses parents were both dead and would never know I screamed back with frustration and slammed the door shut leaving the wet nurse and baby to die by Edwardo's hand not my own.

We turned and filtered through all the tunnels that led in and out of the palace, only a few people other than the actual royal family knew about these tunnels. The guard's men were soon lost trying to break in behind us but I knew it wouldn't take them long to catch up.

We reached the exit which led out to a small stream, from the outside it just looked to be a waste pipe but to the palace it was a concealed entrance or exit. The sun was high in the sky and Andromeda screamed from the sudden glare but I hushed her and ran off into the city. I knew of another secret tunnel a hundred or so miles from here that we could hide down and would eventually lead to another country either Emerald Valley or Skye, I didn't care which one as long as I could keep us safe but the question was how to reach it?

Rushing through the city I spotted some Skye mountain horses tied up outside a healers, travellers not knowing how dangerous the city would soon become for them. Hushing Andromeda I untied one of the horses and boosted her up onto the saddle then climbed on myself taking the reins and charging off into the sunset.

The guard's men were soon on our tail charging on horseback pushing people out the way through the city streets. I grabbed at my uniforms pocket and pulled out my wand, the stick was made from Emerald Fur branches, I was originally from Emerald Valley but not the one here, not the good one that made me want to vomit at how good it was, how reserved the people were with no letting go and just being them, with a hint of dark magic. Holding onto the reins with one hand I half turned and aimed my wand at the horsemen letting my dark earthly magic burst out and kill them on impact, it meant I had lost them for now, I just had to concentrate on her.

We crossed the green lush lands and I knew we were close by to the tunnel I desired to find but by chance so were the palace guard who were roaring towards us, pistols aimed not caring if they hit me or the princess. Women and children screamed as the violent men roared towards us but we were there, we were at the tunnel. I used the royal seal to unlock the door and shoved the princess inside before slamming it shut in the guard's faces and sealing it with my magic but I knew it would hold for long.

Wasting no time we carried on running, tripping and stumbling through the dark tunnel, I heard them as they tore the door from its hinges and smashing their way through and they were gaining I just knew they were gaining, I could feel it in the ground.

I came across the camouflaged door and opened it making the princess sit on the floor in the corner, I kissed her cheek and told her not to worry that someone would find her. I then whispered into her ears as I pointed my wand at her young and good heart, "One day the magic will go and the darkness will come, become the darkness that they fear, tear them shred to shred and not shed a tear, become the Queen of Junia and fight them to the death, bring back the magic that is your destiny's quest".

I had no idea if the poison I had been feeding her would work its magic yet but as I spoke the final work of the spell a darkened light evaporated around the princess and centred over her chest disappearing in a blink of an eye. She sobbed in a panic before the darkness filtered in through her eyes, I knew it then, she was mine.

I didn't have to say anything else to her, she knew what she had to do even if she was so young, so I turned and shut the door, I wavered my wand over it and chanted, "Seal this door, become deaf and blind, for the child inside, only the good will find". A royal seal flashed before me and then faded and I could no longer hear the child's cry then I pulled one my earrings from my ear and laid it flat on the ground, I used the sharp piercing point to pull blood from my finger and dripped it on the earing and imagined the unimaginable, a body appeared one of a child girl with dark royal jet black hair, an illusion of sorts to fool the guard.

The first guard appeared wielding his great sword, "You killed the child?" he asked.

She nodded but said not a word.

"Why?"

"So Edwardo could not have that satisfaction".

The guard shrugged, "As you wish, kill her", he commanded to the others and before me the world went dark and vanished, a familiar rustling noise filled my ears around me, like feather brushing up against each other.

~

I came back to myself in the tunnel that was so dark and silent, I felt my breath coming in quick sharp waves, I looked to find the woman, Andromeda's maid but she was gone, she had shown me what she wanted to, so I could see why Andromeda was the way she was but what was I meant to do with this new information, she was only evil because of what the maid had done to her but I felt confused *why had the maid showed me this? Wasn't it her will for Andromeda to succeed? Why come to me at all?*

I went to turn and stroll out of the tunnel to find the others, I was chilled and in need of some chatter I had to tell them what I had seen but I was stopped by a flickering from the corner of my eye, the camouflaged door opened wide and a shimmering flicker like an old T.V set appeared before me. Like a moth to the flame I let my fingers glide towards it and was instantly taken into another memory but this one was different.

~

I was young and scared hiding away, I knew that my little sister was dead, the traitor guards at the palace had stolen her from my maid's arms. A sob left my mouth and then I froze, what if they heard me crying? I scolded myself for that, I dug my nails into my arm, scratching them harshly down leaving small long trails of crimson coloured blood. I was so young but I knew bad things had happened.

Suddenly a voice whispered in my mind, the voice of my maid echoed inside my head, "Curse them all the heathens of the new bloodline, curse them all for taking the throne away from Junia, from me the rightful dark witch Queen of Junia. Curse them for killing the royal bloodline and tainting the magic. I curse all those born into the bloodline from hence force to be born with the colour of the blood they spilled, so everyone will know who the false bloodlines are. I offer you my darkest magic, the magic and flight of the Crow to help show you to give no mercy or sorrow".

My heart raced, they cursed my family, my bloodline with the blood of those spilt.

Suddenly my own memory flashed before me, my mother was sitting on her chair in her chambers, her long dark jet black hair glimmering in the palace lights, "Mummy why do I have red hair and you have black hair?" I couldn't have been more than five.

She took my hand in hers, "Because my love you have the Royal Red in your blood".

The Royal Red! It wasn't Royal Red at all but the cursed bloodline with the spilt blood of all my past ancestors. I immediately felt dirty, guilty and ashamed, I had always prided myself on the vibrancy of my red hair but now? It just felt so wrong.

~

I stood back in the tunnel shaking, Andromeda had the true bloodline in her soul, she had the true royal coloured hair but me, I had the cursed and fake royal colour. I found it strange how I had seen my own memory, one I had once long forgotten, dismissed because to me it hadn't really meant anything important. I was just a child asking why I had my father's hair colour and not my mothers. When I had been growing up I had wanted to be just like my mother, she was stunningly beautiful, her hair echoed the night sky above, it shone with the glimmering stars, her hair reminded me of the universe that controlled our skies.

But it was strange how had I seen Andromeda's memory? She wasn't dead yet?

Sighing to myself I sluggishly took myself to the main entrance, I had only witnessed two memories and one had been mostly my own but I was tired. Walking at a slow stroll I soon made it to the entrance where Koal was waiting.

"What did you see?" he asked me, "Did you see her?"

"I saw what her maid wanted me to see I suppose and a memory of her but how, Andromeda isn't dead".

"Let's you get you back to your friends, there is much you need to discuss", he told me.

"No wait, you're not telling me something".

He turned to me, "Dear Queen I'm sure you have figured out why Andromeda is the way she is?"

"Yes because of the maid".

He nodded, "The maid killed off the good in Andromeda that day so there for the good in her resides there as a memory".

"And the maid?"

"What do you mean?" he asked his brow furrowing with confusion.

"Why would the maid show me this? She wants Andromeda to succeed in gaining the throne for evil, was it the maids good side that showed me? Because the maid had killed her good side off too?"

He looked lost in thought, "I suppose so".

We walked back to the feast where everyone was still sat waiting for us to return, Thane looked relieved to see me and instantly stood to greet me, "Are you harmed?" he asked glaring at Koal.

"No I'm fine just tired that's all".

"What happened? What did you see?"

The others all grew quiet and waited to hear what I would tell them, "Andromeda, I saw Andromeda and she was pretty much a babe, a young child of the palace, a princess, a 'good' princess. The monsters who took over the palace killed the Queen and King and took the throne and they wanted the princesses and the others dead to so they couldn't take back the throne, so the maid took Andromeda and ran and hid in that tunnel", I said pointing to the direction it was in, "But the maid of Andromeda was not all she seemed, she was evil and had her own agenda for the throne and the royal family, she had been poisoning Andromeda as a child with a potion, then she chanted something to the princess before hiding her in the tunnels and a dark force went into her causing her heart and soul to go to the darkness. It wasn't Andromeda's fault she turned out this way, it was the maids fault…Not helped by my fake royal family bloodline".

"But why was the maid doing it?" Thane said.

"Because she wanted the throne, she wanted to be the evil Queen of Junia but could only do it through

Andromeda, the throne would never accept her, the people would never accept her but through Andromeda she could rule".

"So it wasn't just your so called families fault then", Thane tried to reassure me.

I shrugged, "What is the difference I was born half to the family who thought they killed off the bloodline and half to the real royal bloodline, my family still killed hers in some way".

"Yes but your family are not the reason Andromeda is evil, that is just a fuel to the fire planted there by the maid. Even if they didn't kill off the royal family the maid would have eventually done it".

"But why? How? Where did this maid come from?" Stormra spoke up from beside Isaura.

"Emerald Valley but not our one".

"Huh?" Fira exclaimed, "There is only one Emerald Valley Mira".

"The Void?" Thane answered looking at me, "It's meant to lead to another realm or world…Maybe it's…"

"To the dark side of Junia?" I looked at Koal.

He shrugged, "Junia was born of magic so anything is possible I guess".

"So could that mean that the maid isn't really dead?" I asked, "Maybe she is back in the other Emerald Valley waiting for Andromeda to do her dirty work".

"Didn't you see the maid die?" Fira asked.

I shook my head, "No, it just went dark and I heard feathers, like Crows feathers, like Andromeda…I heard the guards say to kill her but didn't see them do it".

"You most definitely have to prevent Andromeda from taking the throne, especially if it means the evil maid could return", Koal told us, "If she can control Andromeda from another world, another realm then she will be too powerful to defeat if she gets the throne".

"What does that mean for Andromeda? She isn't really evil, she wasn't born that way she was forced to be that way", I said softly my heart going out to the evil witch that had killed my mother, then it shattered and I felt pain break it apart again. *Maybe it wasn't her that killed her but the maid?*

"Nothing changes, she still needs to be defeated", Koal said glumly, "She is too far gone to be saved and brought back. Nothing and no one can help her now".

"But the maid…"

"Will be taken care of I'm sure if she ever shows her face in Junia again but for now Andromeda is your problem".

"But if she comes back?"

"Then I'm sure you and your converters will take care of her. Mira I'm sorry but no one has ever crossed the void and returned, it would be foolish to go looking for her. If she is to be defeated then she must come to you".

Fira looked puzzled changing the subject ever so slightly, "Well we know you're related to her, so do you think it could mean that you two have a kind of connection to each other? If so can you use it against her?"

"I don't know what you mean?" I said, "A connection? Other than for obvious reasoning"

"I'm not sure like your powers, could hers be similar to yours?"

"I don't command crows", I laughed but it wasn't a true one.

"No but deep down, inside the power might be connected", she suggested.

"I don't really have a power though".

"Yes you do, you command the sceptre", Koal stated.

I shrugged, "I don't think I do, when I used it for the first time it was because my mother charged it not me".

"And the second time?"

"Well yes I spoke the incantation on the side and made it work…"

"Well there you have it, you do have power inside you, to make it work you must".

"But it only happens when I'm desperate".

"Because the magic is seeping back into you slowly, it will take time to master it but in all honesty the true royal power was one that charged up and used occasionally, not one to be used all the time".

"We don't have time", I responded.

"Time…Time is a funny thing Mira and I'm sure time will catch up with you…The magic will catch up with you. The closer you get to being Queen the more your powers will grow".

"I guess we will just have to wait and see", Thane reassured me placing a protective hand on my shoulder, "I think you should rest then we shall leave for Emerald Valley in the morning, the real one of course".

I agreed as I was knackered and Koal took me to a makeshift home inside an old building where some beds had been made up, once my head hit the pillow I was gone and the dreams were wild and weird. I distinctly remember one, I had a power, a dark spinning black hole, where time froze or sped up depending on how I commanded it. The black hole boomed around the enemies destroying them in a swirling darkened blast. If only it were true.

~

The wind was whipping wildly at my hair making it hard to see through the solid red mass of strands, something was calling to me, not out loud so the others could hear it but deep in my mind like a shy vibration. It called so dreamily to me that even though I was tired I felt myself move my aching feet and take off in the direction the vibrations were coming from.

My movements were a blur as everything around me faded, I knew I was in the hidden city but everything milked together into browns, reds, greys, blacks and oranges as buildings, ruins, bricks, rubble and soil all passed me by.

I headed into the old palace pushing the old rusted doors open, I didn't bother to see if it was safe or not I just walked right in, cobwebs clawed at my face and spiders hurried away from my presence. The dust was thick and heavy in the air but it too vibrated along with whatever was calling me, deeper into the palace I went not caring about the dark gloom or the strange silvery glow that gave my eyes some light to focus on. Deeper in I went until I came to an old picture of a past King and his family, I knew it wasn't the ones I had seen in the memories these one were even older maybe the first royals to ever be in rule over Junia. The picture was painted in oils and hung heavy in a dented and dusty old golden frame, I placed my hand over the King's Sceptre and the picture swung forward revealing a hidden passage way that wouldn't lead up to the new palace but downwards, further into Cosima's core.

I followed the passage down, flames sparking up as ancient fire stones hung in torches but this wasn't the only element present, all of them were somehow. Tiny trees had been planted in small recesses, they glowed with earthly power but didn't grow out of control they just stayed small, above them hanging along the walls were glittering chains with what I thought were diamonds but they were droplets of water that didn't move, I only knew this as I brushed my finger over one and it came away wet, the droplet I had taken away was instantly replaced by another, they glowed like rain drop necklaces dancing over the walls. As I looked up I noticed souls creeping and whispering past, they circled around as I walked but never came low enough to reach me. The floor as I walked lower down in the passageway became a foggy mist, it chilled my feet but not enough to freeze me. That was it all the elements were here, Earth, Water, Spirit, Fire and Air, all of them working together to protect whatever it was that was hidden down here.

I came to the end of the tunnel and approached a large wooden door, it wasn't fancy or appealing in any way it was just a door, a door that vibrated with the feeling that I needed to go inside and see what was there, I needed to help and let lose what was inside. I reached my fingers up and stroked the handle, I clasped my hands tightly round it and pulled...

"Mira, Mira wake up".

~

I jolted up awake from the strange memory, my mind floating with swirling orbs. I could see Thanes worried face looking over mine.

"Mira, Mira wake up", he said shaking my shoulders.

"I'm awake", I moaned feeling sleepy and groggy, "What happened?"

"I'm not sure?" he answered, "But I came to wake you as we are set to leave soon and there were orbs swirling all around you".

"Orbs?" I asked.

"Yes".

"Memory orbs", I stated.

He nodded, "What did they show you?"

I opened my mouth to answer then closed it, the memory was gone from my lips, it was gone from my mind. The memory hadn't actually happened yet, so I couldn't remember it. "I can't remember".

Thane looked worried, "I'll get Koal". He rushed off and a few moments later Koal was by his side.

He pressed his hand to my head and checked my eyes, "There seems to be no indication of foul play on Andromeda's part".

"You sure?" Thane stammered, "She was able to nearly kill Mira before, she entered her mind and tried to drown her".

"There is no trace of evil here, I would sense it", Koal answered, "Maybe the orbs wanted to show Mira something, something that she cannot process yet".

"What?" Thane sounded stressed.

"Something she doesn't need to use yet".

"Like a premonition?" I asked him.

"Precisely".

"Something from the future?" Thane asked.

Koal nodded, "Yes but it is no use to fully know yet. The orbs tell people things they need to know and when the time comes it will come back to Mira, I'm sure".

I just looked at them both, my mind still floating, I tried to call whatever it was but it was gone.

"Come on, breakfast and then we leave", Koal commanded.

Breakfast was a fast event, we had only been seated for ten or so minutes when a worried Thane came to the table, he had been by the main gate checking the plan over with the guards there.

"We have to leave now, the palace guard have got into the entrance of the train tracks".

No one said a word as we all stood up from our seats, food being strewn around us as hands rushed to grab items that belonged to each other. Within moments we were all grouping together by the main door.

Koal emerged in armour and with plenty of weapons, "Lady Mira we will escort you to Emerald Valley now, are you ready to leave?"

I nodded, "Yes".

"Then let's go but keep quiet the longer we can keep the hidden city hidden the better".

"Wait I thought Andromeda knew about it already?" Brooklyn spoke up.

Koal turned, "She knew about it once as a child but she left when the darkness became too much for her and we exiled her as a teenager, wiping her memory with our magic, she knows of its existence but not exactly of its where bouts. We have heavily concealed it with magic but if she finds out there could be more trouble ahead. If she destroys the hidden city there could be no hope for it is the True Cosima and it needs to be kept alive".

We followed him out of the hidden city and into the train tunnel, they boarded up the wall and cast magic over it to hide and conceal the entrance. We could hear the shouts and the clanking of swords as the palace guards approached but Koal just led us away from their position and down another smaller tunnel which by my guess would run right over the top of the tunnel Andromeda used as young child to escape the guard. I turned to see Koal's small army behind us to keep them away from me, from all of us. Koal turned again and led us down another tunnel which then came to a metal mesh grate which was hung over a small stream, Koal lifted it and the metal screamed, "Hurry they would have heard that". We all climbed through and sloshed in the water outside, it had once been the old drainage system for the old train station.

I looked up and couldn't see anything for miles, we were deep down a bottomless pit but as I looked closely I could see light at the top. "Where are we?" Thane ordered.

"The Abyss, right at the very bottom", Koal answered.

"The Abyss leads here?"

Koal nodded, "It's been called that for a while to keep it secret so no one would discover what lays below. The Abyss to most people means a harsh and horrible death if fallen into but for us, the people of the hidden City it is a means of escape in an emergency".

"But how do we get up there?" Kenton asked looking around.

"Over here", Koal called out and we all looked to see a small royal seal engraved on a small platform.

"What is it?" I asked.

"Climb aboard and find out", Koal instructed, "We need to hurry I can hear them coming".

I could hear the clatter of the guards as they tried to find out where the noise had come from. We all stood over the seal and Koal bashed his sword onto it and calling out a word in Skye's tongue, the royal seal gave a jolt then a shudder and slowly began to move up in the Abyss, it was an old magical lift. My eyes widened as I watched the layers of soil, rock and solid earth fly past before we reached the top.

The top was a welcome sight and we were greeted by fresh air, we were directly at the border between Emerald Valley and Cosima, climbing off I looked to see Koal stayed on.

"Aren't you coming with us?" I asked him, I had got the impression that he was.

"No me and my people will try to hold off the guards for as long as possible and to keep the hidden City protected but hopefully that will give you enough time in the Valley".

I didn't know what to do or say so I just said, "Thank you".

He then bowed, "Good luck my future Queen, may Junia's magic be with you. I shall pray hard for your success…We will meet again", and then he smacked the sword onto the seal and spoke the lingo, I watched as he disappeared back down into the darkness below, I just hoped Koal and his people wouldn't get hurt.

Thane nudged my shoulder, "You ready to go?"

"Can we really leave them to fight our battle?"

Thane smiled but it wasn't a grin, it was a 'don't worry' smile, "We can because they want to, they know you need to go on and if that is their way of helping then we must let them".

I felt something inside me stir, a knowing of things that might come, people were going to get hurt in the crossfire of this battle, *but how many I didn't know?*

~ The Country of Emerald Valley ~

The view before me was all a vibrant green. That was the best and only way to describe the entrance into the Emerald Valley, a sparkling mass of emerald greens, lime greens, apple greens and every other shade of green physically possible.

We had to cross over a large wooden bridge which connected Cosima and the Valley, the bridge itself was a beautiful masterpiece built of solid dark wood and carved into a perfect sweep over the abyss, small carvings of trees, magical beings, power and the valley itself were dotted all over the tough wood and along the railings. At each end stood two small pillars which housed small orb like lights which at night must look beautifully eerie, they glowed an earthly green. Two bridge keepers stood guard at the Emerald Valley end and had their weapons raised as we made our way across.

The first one a small almost elflike man with brown hair and slit like eyes spoke, "Halt, who wishes to enter the sacred valley?"

Thane pushed forward and bowed to the guards, "We have travelled a long journey, we wish to speak to the element converter and visit the temple of earth".

"Why?" was all the second man who was much taller and broader in the shoulders asked.

"Because if we don't the whole of Junia may be lost to the dark forces of Andromeda", I spoke up and came forward holding my Sceptre close.

The guards bowed down to me, "Your grace please forgive us we did not know it was you. Dangerous enemies have been trying to cross over, we can't be too careful".

"Don't worry", I stammered at being called grace outside of the palace, "I…understand".

"Please follow us", the broader one said and started off into the Valley.

I looked at the others confused this was not the welcome I had been expecting, not after how some of the others had reacted to me turning up.

"Do you know of our reasons?" I said rushing up to the guards but at first they ignored me, the shorter one put his hand in his pocket and pulled out a wooden wand similar to the one Freya had and the evil maid from the memories used. He then aimed it into the air causing light and dust to blast out, the particles whizzed up and collided causing a massive crashing sound and light show in the sky like fireworks.

"Yes we know your reasons and our converter has already agreed to be of service but she cannot retrieve the element soul until tomorrow", the shorter one said, as he did I saw flashes of green whip past us, turning to look back at the gate I saw that two new guards had taken the place of the ones we were following.

"How did you know?"

"You mean about you needing our help?"

I nodded.

"Have you been back to Cosima recently?"

"Not really only to travel through the stations to other boarder gates, why?"

"You will see when we reach the castle", he said but he sounded glum, something was wrong.

They led us through a long and narrow path which filtered through all the trees, the light here was darker than normal but that was due to us being under the shelter of all the branches and leaves but it wasn't a problem as the people of Emerald Valley had traced lights over the branches lighting the way, giving it a truly magical feel to the place. Ornaments, orbs and wind chimes all hung from different branches, gently tinkling and swaying in the breeze. We soon twisted down another path winding through the throng of green ferns and the dark brown of tree bark and roots.

A noise whistled in the trees above and I snapped my head up to see people running and jumping around. Now the branches had spread out a little I could see what was really up there, houses! A whole town built within the tree tops, small little wooden tree houses all with small boxed windows, short thatch roofs and rope bridges leading from one tree to another. Thane gently put his hand at the base of my spine to gain my attention to prevent me tripping over huge tree roots which sprung up over our pathway.

The guards soon led us through a huge gateway which had large wooden panelled fencing leading the whole way around a huge castle, the gate itself was also wooden and huge it took three guards either side to open them fully so we could all walk through. Inside the view was daringly different, large stone walls filled the perimeter of the castle, small stained glass windows peered out over the lands, a moat flowed around the base along with a strong wooden draw bridge which had the beautiful carvings all over it of plants, trees and earthly things. The top of the castle had two towers, *was this the Temple of Earth?* If so it didn't looked very earthly to me but maybe they had built over it to conceal it.

We walked over the drawbridge and were taken to a large door which opened as we arrived pulled by more guards, the inside of the castle was enough to compare it to the grandeur of the palace back home, a huge dark metal chandelier hung from the main foyer ceiling, candles lighting each section and showering the room with light. A large wooden staircase led up to the other floors where the same beautifully carved bannister railings looked out over the foyer. A tall gentleman with armour decorating his body stood by the stairwell, his muddy brown hair almost swaying softly in the candle light, he bowed as he saw me and took my hand bringing it to his lips, "Queen Mira it is an honour to have you visit our home".

"I'm not Queen yet", I smiled nervously.

"I'm afraid Lady Mira that you are", his cool golden eyes lowered to the floor and I felt panic and bile rise in my throat.

"What do you mean?"

"I think you'd best follow me", he motioned to a small side room.

I followed him, the others all crowding in after me. The room held a small television set and many seats, it looked to me like a small make shift cinema. The armoured man took me to a seat and made me sit down, "I cannot prepare you Queen for what I must show you but understand that I must. You need to know what is happening to your Kingdom of Cosima".

He turned the television set on and flicked it to a news channel, I recognised the reporter she was regarded as a high status celebrity back home, normally well-manicured and well-groomed but today she looked exhausted, her hair a ruffled mess, her makeup a quick slap on edition to her features. Her voice too was tired, flat and monotone as she addressed the nation, "So the kingdom of Cosima has fallen from grace, Andromeda has declared herself Queen of Junia and is now fully housed in the palace with her entourage. There has been no recent sightings of the princess and rumour has it that she has been killed along with the perpetrators who helped her escape".

As she said it my fists clenched, *Freya and her boyfriend had not been criminals!* Thane touched my hand, just a flicker of movement but it instantly made me feel calmer, although the anger was still dancing below the surface.

As we continued to watch the reporter didn't really say much else for a while just showed us pictures and other news reports of chaos. Buildings were ablaze, people had been made homeless and killed in what Andromeda had called the cleansing, everyone with royal red hair had been murdered, man, woman and child, anyone who resembled the cursed bloodline had been sent to Spirit and she had declared that the other countries would be next, that anyone with royal red hair or just red hair in general was to be handed in for a reward at the local guard post. My stomach twisted in knots, *how could she kill all those innocent people?* Of course I knew how, the maid who had twisted her mind, causing it to become evil and vile.

"A date has been set for the King to be cremated and his soul sent on to Spirit, his death came as a shock to most Cosiman's but Andromeda has assured us all that it was a necessary sacrifice to cleanse Junia", the news reporter even had a tear in her eye as she spoke, "And there have been reports that the Queen too has died but the whereabouts of her body are unknown".

I felt the world around me shake and dance in a blur of a wave, I felt sick and like my brain was going to explode.

"Mira calm down", Thane said trying to sooth me but he couldn't help, not now.

Hot painful tears burned down my cheeks, I'd had no proper time to mourn for my mother and to be honest I guess I hadn't believed it to be true. I had hoped it wasn't real and when I returned she would be there waiting for me but now, seeing that…Made it all real, both my parents now taken from me, my country and my people burning and suffering because of a twisted mind. It wasn't fair, it wasn't the innocents fault, yes my father's bloodline had condemned hers but he himself hadn't been responsible. I felt the anger surge through my body like an electrical current, my body began to shake uncontrollably from all the pain and anger and I fell from the chair to my knees.

"Mira?" Thane said but I couldn't reply, "Everyone stand back", he commanded.

I could feel it, a burning pain at my side. I grasped at it and found my mother's sceptre to be burning hot, it shook in my hands and a spark spat out from the star point. Confusion engulfed me before a knowing flooded me, it was me, my power, it was so hot. I stood from my knees and lifted it up to look properly at it, the sceptre was going crazy jerking in my hands.

"News has just come in...Andromeda has now instructed that the Temples in each country to be destroyed. She will be sending out her armies at first light to Lavara and then to Skye, Beach Haven has already been destroyed. This is in a bid to prevent to element souls ever returning to their homes and ever gaining their full power to be able to stop her. Here is Andromeda now...Queen Andromeda what do you have to say on the matter of the temples?"

Andromeda looked at the screen and smiled, "As I presume the princess to be dead I have commanded all the temple's to be destroyed so no one can ever challenge my position on the throne. It was an easy decision in a way as I hope to bond with the element souls when my companions bring them to me if not I will destroy them too. I know a way and I have the power to do so, then Junia will be completely under my full rule".

My body shook again, more violently this time, I blinked and there was a loud flash and bang as I felt power rip through me. Screams echoed all around me along with an evil cackle until I opened my eyes.

"Well if it isn't the dead princess", Andromeda spoke but she sounded angry.

I twisted my head up at her, venom fuelled my emotions and I spat at her, "I am not dead, I am very much alive…Soon it will be you who will be the one to be dead".

She cackled again, "Such fire in your heart, such a shame as you would have made such a great Queen".

"I will defeat you", I hissed.

"How? You have no magic, no power, no element soul".

I lifted up my sceptre and almost laughed as she winced back, "I do now".

"How? Impossible? Only those of royal blood have that sort of magic in their veins", she howled, "How? Tell me!"

"Magic", I smiled taunting her.

This angered her more and she rose up a few feet off the ground, she lifted her arms and I watched as a murder of crows left her soul and made their way to me. Their dry wings rustling like leaves in autumn. I lifted my sceptre and raised it high, "Make my light, take this blight".

BOOM!

A shockwave of light burst out from the sceptre and collided into the wave of crows, their strangled cries only crying out for a moment before they fell dead to the ground.

"LUMI!" Andromeda commanded and in a pink flash Lumi appeared, "Take care of her".

Lumi looked me dead in the eye, "Yes my Queen", she put her hand to her hip bag and pulled out a shiny round orb, "Obsidian wake from your slumber". Lumi crushed it then tossed the orb to the ground and it burst open. A scraping of rock on rock sounded as a swirl of dark orbs spiralled from where the orb broke, as they cleared a woman stood tall and waiting. She looked to be made of a shiny rock like substance, some lighter patches flashed out from her body but most of it was jet black.

"Kill the princess", Andromeda shrieked.

Obsidian the monster of rock turned, "I only see two Queens".

Andromeda's face slumped, "Two Queens? There is only one Queen and that is me…Kill the other one". There was such a bitter under current I could almost taste it in the air around me.

Obsidian put her arms to her back and pulled, a shrieking noise like nails on a chalkboard sounded as she pulled herself apart and revealed two long razor sharp daggers. I lifted my sceptre in response feeling determined, my light still glowing strong and I felt the heat of it beneath my fingers.

"ARGH", she shouted as she charged but I was already moving and running to the right. She launched an assault by swinging her arms wildly and sending the daggers towards me, I lifted the sceptre and went to say my words but I didn't need to the sceptre knew and shot out two beams of light which evaporated the daggers in mid-air, inches from my head. Obsidian glared at me, her cool stone eyes not blinking. This time I attacked and sent out a blast of light, she ripped another dagger from her back and threw it at my light to prevent it from reaching her.

"Take her down Obsidian", Lumi commanded, "Or I will take you down instead".

Obsidian looked at Lumi, the threat very real on Lumi's cold stone face but Obsidian wore it better. Turning back to me she moved, too quickly for me to dodge out of the way and I felt the lick of pain as her new dagger swiped at my arm. Looking down I found a trickle of crimson running down to the ground, it dripped steadily but it didn't faze me, I needed to win this fight. To show Junia I was going to fight to the end, somehow.

Obsidian was moving again and she swiped the dagger so close to my left ear I heard the whoosh of air but I too was moving and smashed my sceptre into the side of her face.

SMASH!

It was like trickling glass, half of her face disappeared from the impact but like a professional she didn't lift her hands up to worry, she didn't cradle her broken skull, she just whipped up another dagger and launched at me. I moved but too quickly and tripped, stumbling to the ground just as she brought the dagger down.

'Whoosh', the noise of souls was immediately recognisable now as I watched as a flurry of them ate away into the dagger and smashed it to pieces, the shards falling over my body in a harmless fashion. I looked up to see Thane commanding his soul power.

"Thane", I whispered.

"Thought you might need a hand", he smiled and then sent another wave at Obsidian who was trying to cut away at all the souls.

I stood up and lifted my sceptre and pointed it at Obsidian, I now had my chance. I felt the power vibrate through the sceptre, it was about to cascade out until a figure knocked me flying off my feet. A flash of dark and pink hair and I knew it was Lumi. I sent my sceptre round and smashed her in the face with it but unlike Obsidians hers didn't smash but she did scream out in pain. She grabbed a handful of my hair and pulled, my hand automatically went up to stop her but I knew it was useless so I smacked her with the sceptre again. She let out a cry of pain as it connected with her nose and she pulled away, blood poured from it and her hands went up and came away covered.

"You will pay for that", she howled.

I said nothing and just lifted my weapon and pointed it at her, she lifted her hands up in a defensive stance as a bright light appeared at the end of the sceptre. A screech of crows sounded and swarmed over Lumi like a shield, there was only one part of her left that I could see that could maybe turn the tables in our favour. I sent out the light and it hit her hip bag in a blast, tearing it from her side and sending out all the orb like marbles in it on the floor. I had thought she only had so many in there, five, one for each of the temples but she had collected more.

She pushed the crows away and fell to the floor grasping at her bag and the tumbling orbs, acting quickly I sent out quick flashes of light in quick successions blasting each one into oblivion.

"Noooo!" she screamed fumbling on the ground, I spotted that she managed to grab one orb before Andromeda swooped down and picked her up and they both vanished in a swirl of crows feathers.

BOOM!

Turning at the noise I found Thane still battling Obsidian, his souls had eaten away at her but she was still coming for him. Lifting my sceptre I sent a final blast at her and she shattered into millions of shards.

"Thanks...I..." Thane began but stopped, his eyes widening at something behind me.

I slowly turned to look and found Andromeda there, she had reappeared without Lumi, she no longer looked concerned, she looked angry. "How dare you destroy my minions little princess. You have upset my little Lumi and now I am not happy".

She lifted her hand and a dark mist whooshed out towards me, I lifted the sceptre and expected it to blast but...my power was out! The mist hit me square on and I flew into the air and back down landing hard on my leg screaming out as it snapped loudly. I looked into Andromeda's eyes and saw something familiar, a flash of young innocent eyes calling out to me before they clouded back over and were fuelled by the pure anger inside. Just like me she was fuelling her power on emotions but hers had grown, mine had just run out. She marched towards me and I tried to stand but my leg gave out and I cried out in pain. She lifted her hand and blasted some more of the dark mist at me.

Thane appeared and cradled his arms around me, "Time to go", he said and I felt a coldness wash over me as a flurry of his soul power showered over us and swallowed us both up.

Before I had time to breathe I blinked and we were back at the castle in Emerald Valley.

~ The Temple of Earth ~

I was fixed up fairly quickly, Stormra made sure I used one of the potions the shop keeper had given me made from the siren scale and it had worked a treat, my broken leg healed within the hour.

Thane sat by my side the whole time, his eyes never leaving mine, "I still don't get that power, your power. It was so strong and then…Nothing".

"That's because she used all that she had gathered", the armoured man said walking back in, I'd found out his name was Nate, "She had only accumulated that much through anger and it ran out, she could only hold the anger for so long".

"So her power is controlled by anger?" Thane questioned Nate.

Nate shrugged, "For now her emotions play a part yes but maybe not always, not if she learns to truly control it".

"And how do I learn to control it?" I asked.

"Time…It takes time".

"But we don't have time", I sighed feeling useless again.

"Maybe not but if you keep using it, you will gain some control over it", Nate told me.

I sat there thinking, Andromeda had been almost afraid of my powers at first until she too became angry then she was stronger than me. *Was there a specific time that both our powers would be stronger and weaker? Or was it simply the shock of the un-real-royal princess baring a power? And her eyes, something just hadn't been right about them…but what?* Before I could ask either of them anything the door burst open and all the others flooded in to see me, Fira was asking me all sorts of questions and gave me no time to answer either one of them, "How did you teleport like that? What was it like using your power? How scared were you facing Andromeda? Lumi will be mad at you for destroying her orbs. She will most definitely try to kill you for sure now. Did your sceptre get so hot it burnt?"

"Fira give her some space", Brooklyn sniggered. As I looked at them all I noticed how they were all dressed up, like really dressed up all in ball gowns other than Kenton who wore the smartest suit I had ever seen, even the palace suits didn't hold the edge this suit had. His shirt was emerald green but the actual suit itself was a soft grey but what made it have style was the gem stones that had replaced the buttons and the cuff links, they lit up and glistened with his every movement.

"Why are you all dressed up so nice?"

Fira twirled in front of me, her dress was a burnt crisp orange that held like a glittering sequin type corset at the top, then puffed out in the skirt still in a shimmering sequin design blocking out her shoes from view. Her dark skin had been littered with burning orange and fire red tiny like pebbles and glitter. She shone with the heat of Lavara, her hair was a billowing mass of dark brown curls at the top and burnt orange curls at the bottom with the slight yellow tinge in between. "We have been invited to the Emerald Valley harvest dance, tonight. We will get to meet the Earth Converter there".

"We are guests of honour", Kenton added excitedly.

"Oh", I sighed, "But I have nothing to wear".

"Not everyone is as talented as Fira at making dresses appear out of puffs of smoke and fire", Brooklyn teased, "But we all do have something to wear, even you".

I looked Brooklyn over again her long yellow hair had been let loose and it spiralled down over her shoulders and down her back. Her dress was simpler than Fira's but just as glamourous, it was cut away at the back and high at the front but had no sleeves, it didn't tuck in at the waist it just flowed right down to her feet. The fabric flowed like moving water but I could see it was made from a fine silk and in a shade of ocean blue, matching her piercing eyes. Isaura was also dressed up but not in a dress like the other two girls, she wore a suit similar to Kenton's but hers was ice white with a stormy coloured shirt underneath. The only thing that made her outfit look at all feminine was her earring that leant on her shoulder as it hung down. Her hair was tied back out of her face, her dark black hues framing her hard features but she also had a gentleness to her face.

Her mother Stormra stood just behind, she wore a dress which had an ice white corset and a fur lined skirt that had come all the way from Skye, Stormra told me it was enemy fur.

Everyone looked so nice, I turned to Thane, "What am I wearing?"

He lifted up a dress that had been hidden behind a chair and my heart sank, it was beautiful of course in its own accord but it was in royal red, dripping blood red. He saw the expression on my face, "Do you not like it?"

"Royal red", I said, "Is the colour my bloodline are cursed with for the deaths of the real royal family. The true royal colour is like a midnight black…It's hard to describe".

"Midnight black? Like the heavens at night, the colour of the universe?" Isaura spoke up.

I smiled at her and nodded, "Yes, I guess like that".

"I'm sure we can find something", Nate said and ushered me to follow him, "We have a large dressing room with hundreds of dresses, all chosen of course by the Earth Converter".

The hallways led on twisting and turning around the whole castle until we stopped at a room with a small door. *Did he really mean large dressing room? The door was too small.* Then as he opened it my jaw hit the floor, the room was at least the same size as my mother's own private rooms at the palace. The walls had been fitted floor to ceiling with mirrors and all around we strategically placed wardrobes full of beautiful garments and clothes.

"Please take a look, find what you like and wear it", Nate offered.

"Um, which was is the Earth Converters? Just so I don't take the wrong one".

"She has hers in her own private rooms", he smiled, "No need to worry". Then he left us to it, Kenton and Thane followed him obviously wanting to give us ladies some space.

"Wow I have never seen so many dresses", Brooklyn exclaimed.

I smiled, "I have, my mother's collection is in similar size but…" I trailed off thinking of my mother.

"Emerald Valley is rich in trade with the other countries, they have hundreds of miles of farmland and fields which grow crops, fruit and vegetables. They can afford to splash out", Isaura explained carrying on the subject so I didn't feel bad.

I trailed my hand over some of the dresses on the rails, none really sticking out or striking my eye. I lifted a few out sighed and put them back. I was about to give up and ask someone to choose me one when I realised that was why I hadn't found one. At home at the palace I had been so used to being told what to wear and when to wear it and on this journey the only clothes I had chosen were ones we could just about afford and no more but now I had free reign I had no idea. Taking a deep breath I started again and really began to look at the dresses, I found a few pretty Jet or Midnight black pieces but nothing again took my fancy, not until I came to the last rail where one dress sat on its own looking rather sorry for itself. It was Midnight black with a velvet corset type top that had long sleeves. From the waist up and over the breast plate and down the sleeves of the arms it was decorated with tiny diamond like gems that twinkled and sparked in the light as I moved it to look closer at it. The skirt sprayed out from the waist down in an inky depth that rippled like liquid, it too was made of fine silk like Brooklyn's and all around the bottom was a row of sparkling diamond like gems. Under the silk skirt were layers of mesh and lace under skirts to boost it out.

"Oh Mira that is beautiful", Fira beamed.

I lifted it up to my own body and glanced in the mirror, she was right it was beautiful, the only thing that let it down was my royal red hair. I stared at my hair in the mirror, I wanted to cut it all off, to dye it another colour but I was stuck with it for now.

Fira and Brooklyn helped me dress, Fira doing my make-up making me look like a true glittering princess and Brooklyn doing my hair. She done three French plaits one either side and one in the middle that all met at the left hand side of my head, she then tied them all together and curled the ends of my hair so they bounced with my movements, it trailed long down my side.

Once we were ready Isaura opened the door for us, she was rather more gentlemanly than girly but it made her Isaura, she was the huntress and bringer of food to her family as well as the Air Converter.

We walked along the hallway to the grand staircase, Thane, Kenton and Nate were all waiting for us. As we began the descent down the stairs Thane looked up, first his eyes glanced at Fira, Isaura and Brooklyn which made my tummy swirl but then he looked at me and his eyes lit up, his face took me all in. As I reached the bottom step he held out his hand to me, "Mira you look beautiful".

I felt the blush on my cheeks appear before I could try to tame it, I took his hand which made my belly twist in knots. He then led me outside along with the others to a large horse drawn carriage, giving me a boost up he then took his seat next to me. The others all sat down and then the horse man set off and we took off into the night through the forest. We passed many fields which had all been harvested and many more forest lined roads which had all the trees covered in lights and tree houses. The carriage took us miles away from the castle and eventually stopped at a small clearing which was loomed over by the biggest tree I had ever seen in my life, it had to be many times taller than the palace. Large wooden doors had been carved into the bark along with beautifully carved pictures of symbols of Earth, the branches had been covered with lights, gems and sparkling chains with golden leaves and flowers. A large seating area had been erected with tables full of food and drink, a canopied area had flashing lights and music blaring out, people were already inside dancing the night away. Guards also lined the place but they looked rather cheery and happy seen as they couldn't join in the party.

Thane led me down from the carriage and I couldn't help but notice how people fell silent and even the music died down. The crowd of people on the dance floor parted and out walked a rather petite girl with brown hair, she had a pretty pixie like face and her eyes were like Nate's and most of the people I could see from Emerald Valley, angled and slanted. She wore a leaf green dress which as she walked parted on the skirt bit and had actually been designed to look like two large leaves that glittered, the top too covered her assets with leaf like green velvet. Her hair was wavy and cascaded down just past her shoulders, atop her head she wore a tiara made from twisted twigs and in the centre was the seal that looked so similar to the other converters. I knew then who she was, the converter for earth.

She walked over to us, her bare feet barely touching the ground she walked on. She stopped and then bowed down to me, "Queen Mira, it is so lovely to finally meet you, I just wish the circumstances were not so saddening". Her voice was soft but strong, graceful almost.

I curtseyed to her, "And lovely to meet you...Um..."

"Willow, my name is Willow", she smiled her dark eyes eyeing up my dress, "Hmm not what I expected you to wear but none the less a perfect choice for the Queen".

I looked down at my sparkling attire, "Thank you for loaning me the dress, it is much appreciated".

"Loan? My Queen the dress is a gift from me to you, please keep it".

"Thank you", I felt my cheeks redden again.

"Please come and relax, for tonight we celebrate the harvest, tomorrow we will summon the element soul and journey on to Spirit".

I nodded, "Thank you for your invitation".

She bowed her head, "I must mingle with my people for tomorrow they know the enemy comes and I wish to reassure them but after your performance with Andromeda today I don't think that I will need to so much. They can see how determined you are to fight for Junia". She then left before I could answer.

I turned to Thane, "Everyone saw what happened?"

He nodded, "Of course, you appeared whilst the news reporter was still on air".

I felt shocked that all of Junia would have seen that, I had been so sure Andromeda would have taken care of the cameras.

"Don't worry about it", Thane smiled and held out his arm, "Will you dance with me, my Queen?"

"Dance?"

He nodded, "Yes…It might be the last time I can in this world and I would like it to be with you".

My heart hammered in my chest, he wanted his last dance to be with me. I took his offer and gave him my arm. He led me to the dancefloor where people automatically moved aside to let us in, the band who were playing saw that we had entered the dance floor and changed the tempo of the song, Thane put his arm around my waist and his other hand in mine, he then twisted my body in time with the tempo of the song. My legs felt like jelly but I forced them to move with his but with him leading it wasn't too difficult. I looked into his moon lit eyes and wanted to just melt into them, his eyes looked into mine and I knew then he only had eyes for me. His arms rocked me from side to side and swayed my body around the dance floor the skirts of my dress swishing with the movement making the diamonds twinkle in the moonlight. I felt so safe with him then, in his strong arms that let me go and twirled me round so my dress spiralled elegantly before pulling me back in closer, my hands landing on his chest to steady myself. I couldn't help it then as I looked up at his moonlit gaze, his eyes twinkled and flashed before me and I knew I could love him and spend my life forever with him. Then it came to me, how we could be together forever! The phoenix feather! *That's what Fira had meant but I had to figure it out on my own, how could I have been so daft as to forget about it?*

"Thane I don't want you to leave me", I whispered as I rested my head on his chest as the tempo slowed and he held me closer.

"I don't want to leave you Mira but what can we do, I have no choice once my duty to you has been done I will be taken to Spirit and to the heavens".

"The phoenix feather, it can be used to bring back a soul, a person no longer alive. I could use it to bring you back", I said arching my neck so I could look up at him.

"You would do that for me?" I could see tears welling up in his eyes.

I nodded, "I would give anything to have you by my side, to have you with me, to lo…to…to love you!" He stopped dancing and he moved so his hands held my shoulders, tears flowed down my cheeks and I couldn't stop them, "You have always been with me, I know that now, looking over me. You cared for me when you knew what my family had done to you. You have been my only friend for such a long time…I can't imagine life without you Thane".

"Mira, I love you too", he whispered and he leant his head down and kissed me. His lips brushed over mine so delicately almost like a butterfly kiss, then he pulled away, "If you so wish to bring me back then I will be honoured to be by your side for eternity".

I couldn't help myself and I flung my arms around him, he kissed the top of my hair. The music changed again and he swayed me in his arms, just holding me tightly, almost like he would never let me go.

"Mira? Are you ok?" he asked.

I looked up at him, "Yes why?"

"Your hair, it's changing", he told me.

I pulled away from him and turned to see if there was anything I could see my reflection in, on one of the tables was a silver platter with most of the food from it eaten, I rushed to it and brushed of the remains of the food and lifted it up to see my hair. Sure enough it was changing, my roots had turned dark and it was gradually bleeding its way down the strands of my hair. I turned back to Thane, "What's happening?"

He shrugged, "Maybe we should go to Nate and try and find the others, one of them might know".

Agreeing I followed him out of the dance floor, both Nate and Willow stood by the great tree talking but it was clear to see from here that Nate and Willow were an item, he had his hands clasped around hers, looking into her eyes pleading. As we neared I could hear their conversation. "Don't go Willow, stay here with me".

"I must go it's my duty to the Queen and to Junia".

"Why?"

"Because I am the element converter for earth, that's why. It's written in the stars that this is my destiny".

"But what if something happens to you?"

"Then you must lead Emerald Valley for me".

"How can I lead them all when you are their true leader?"

"Because you can and you will. I love you and trust you to do this. Don't you think that I am worried for your safety too, that when I take the element soul the enemy will come for you all?"

"I can fight".

"So can I", she said sternly, "We are both strong and we will both make it through this".

"Please don't go…I…"

"Lady Mira how can I help you?" Willow asked spotting me from the corner of her eye.

Thane answered, "Something is happening to Mira, her hair is changing colour".

Both Nate and Willow came to check my hair, "Could it be the magic that has awoken in her?" Nate said to Willow.

"Maybe", she replied.

"Not Andromeda?" I said fearfully.

"I doubt it, I think this is something else but I'm not sure what", she shrugged, "Maybe the converter in Spirit might know more".

Just as she spoke those words the ground shook all around us and a high pitched cackled rocked the atmosphere…Andromeda!

Nate looked angry, "She couldn't even just give us tonight".

"Maybe it's because of me, because I went to her earlier", I admitted.

Willow shook her hand at me to excuse my voice, "Andromeda would have come anyway. We need to gather our people ready to fight the enemy, I think I will need to call the element soul now".

"No", Nate cried out, "Our people will be too drunk and merry, we need to wait".

She turned to him, "Andromeda won't wait and our people are not overly intoxicated as they were warned this might happen, it will be fine. We have to do it now or risk her getting to the element soul before I do". She stroked his cheek in a loving way.

He held her hand for a second before nodding, "Yes you are right as always, go, get the element soul and save Junia. All of you". His eyes burned into mine for a moment with a slight anger until they softened, "Please keep her safe my Queen".

My voice got stuck in my throat, "I will try".

He nodded and then ran to the dancefloor but already the music had stopped and people had weapons at the ready, "Fighters of Emerald Valley, be at the ready, Andromeda is here, Willow needs to extract the element soul now, the enemy will be close behind. Stay strong, stay safe and stay alive". His voice was strong and commanding, not like the voice he had just used on Willow.

Willow took my arm, "My Queen if you and your friends will please follow me to the soul chamber I would much appreciate the help".

"Of course", I answered and spotted Brooklyn, Fira and Isaura rushing to us from the dancefloor.

With no need to explain to them what was happening as they had experienced this many times before we set off to the grand tree where Willow used her Tiara to unlock the seal. Inside the smell of the wood hit me, it was earthy and actually quite a comforting smell. The main hall was dark with small fairy lights lining the walls, guiding us through. A huge wooden statue stood tall of a strange half woman half tree person which we all quickly prayed to, except Brooklyn of course.

"Should we wait for Stormra and Kenton?" I asked as I finished my prayer.

"No time, I'm sure they will be safe with my guards", Willow told me standing and walking off.

I looked around as I walked, soft and plush looking cushions scattered the floor along with fragrant flower petals. Willow took us to the back of the hall where a carved out archway led to a spiral staircase which led down into the ground, more fairy lights led the way the deeper we went they looked like little fairies dancing as we moved. Soon we came to a large door like all the other temples, tree roots and vines held the door locked together until Willow used the Tiara seal to unlock it. The doors swung open revealing a room full of lush greenery, flowers and even a small underground stream that ran right through, small waterlilies sat floating atop the water with insects happily playing and floating around.

Willow wasted no time and set to work praying to the element soul which was encased in the solidified liquid, within in minutes the liquid smashed and the element soul stood free. She was slender and tall, half woman half tree nymph, her dress was made of twisted vines, flowers and leaves and her eyes glowed an emerald green. They settled on me and like the other element souls she came to me, "Dear Queen we hear your call, we will fight for Junia and we will fight beside you".

"Thank you", I said bowing to her and she bowed back and handed me a small seed. I turned it over in my hands and waited for an explanation as to how to use it but I didn't get one, she just walked to Willow and accepted that she had to go into the seal. She had just vanished from sight when I heard a familiar voice.

"Well, well, well, if it isn't the false Queen of Junia and her stupid little minions", Lumi stood by the door, a vibrant bruise covered one side of her face where my sceptre had smashed into it.

"What do you want Lumi?" I hissed.

"To end your life here, in revenge for my orbs you took from me, my poor innocent children of evil", she spat pure hatred and venom in her tone.

"Innocent? Being evil doesn't make them innocent", I told her.

"I don't care how you see it Queenie, I will destroy you".

"Bring it", I said and lifted my sceptre, I felt the anger inside me grow again and the sceptre began to glow.

"Oh not me, I'm not going to fight you but I know someone who is looking forward to it, she wants revenge for her murdered brothers and sisters", she replied and held up the last orb she had, she crushed it before she threw it to the floor and whispered, "Chaos awaken and take down this heathen, for she does not deserve the respect of our heaven". The orb exploded into pieces and a grey swirling mist shot up and out, first out from the mist appeared a large sword and an armoured hand and then the arm holding it, then came Chaos, the last of Lumi's minions. She was as wide as she was tall, long grey and mousy hair trailed smoothly down her face and sides until she shook it out of view and her face looked out at us all. She looked similar to Willow and her people, the same eyes but unlike them who were dainty and petite she was a human giant. Her whole body was covered in a strong looking metal armour which chinked as she took a step forward.

Brooklyn stepped forward and threw a huge tsunami like wave of water at her but Chaos just held up her sword and cut the water in half like it was not a pure liquid but more of a solid, the water stopped and dropped to the ground with a loud splash.

"Ha, ha, ha, ha, ha", Lumi giggled from the doorway, "Chaos, I certainly saved the best till last. Good luck defeating the undefeatable", and with that Lumi left.

I watched as Isaura and Fira both directed a joint attack at Chaos, a swirling breeze filled with hot flesh melting flames but Chaos put her sword in front of her face, the blade wide enough to cover her, the rest of her armour protected her and the flames done nothing but heat up the air of the chamber.

Fira sounded defeated already, "How are we meant to beat her?"

"Let me try", Thane said and summoned a large wail of souls which charged at her but she just smiled and spun her sword in front of her, the souls hit the blade and disintegrated. He too now looked defeated.

I looked at my sceptre the light fully flared now but I had a feeling mine would not touch her either so I lowered it back down. Suddenly a large rose thorn appeared out of Chaos's chest plate, Willow stood with her summoned element soul who had a wooden doll of Chaos in her hands and had stabbed a rose thorn into her back. Chaos huffed unamused and snapped the thorn right out of her chest.

"What now?" Fira asked looking at us all.

"A joint attack", Willow suggested, "We all combine our powers together".

"I'm in", Brooklyn called out and she swirled her hands to create a huge water ball.

"Me too", said Fira and Isaura together both of them creating huge balls of their own elements.

Thane also lifted his hands and made a soul ball and Willow and ball full of sharp vines and thorns.

Lastly I lifted up my sceptre, "And me", I spoke up.

We all aimed at her as she lifted her sword to charge, we didn't even give her a chance to make her attack on us because we could all see if she had a chance with that sword we would die in an instant. I could feel the charge of energy in the air as all our powers shot out from where we all stood and combined together in the air of the temple, a thunderous crackling sound like lighting flashed and boomed and then collided with Chaos head on. Within those moments she exploded and fell to the floor as dust, her sword thrown into the air and fell down next to her dusted soul which embedded itself into the ground and stood tall.

"Well", Brooklyn sniggered, "Undefeatable was she…She was the easiest yet".

"WHAT!" a shriek echoed through the room, "HOW CAN THIS BE…SHE WAS UNDEFEATABLE! SHE WAS MY BEST SOLDIER!"

I spotted Lumi back by the door her eyes full of pure hatred, her whole body shaking. She was about to open her mouth again when another voice broke out through the room and in charged Kenton not noticing the angry Lumi hiding by the door, "Brooklyn, we did it we scared off Andromeda, she's left…She's go…n…e". Kenton's voice trailed off as he coughed up blood.

"NOOOOO!" Brooklyn screamed and ran forward to her brother, just managing to catch him in her arms as he fell just as Lumi let go of something behind him. A small pink dagger was embedded in his spine and most probably through a lung, he wheezed painfully as Brooklyn held him tightly and sobbed, "No, no, no…No…Kenton why? Why did I let you come with us".

Lumi smiled wickedly, her pink lips pursed into a harsh grin, "Well, looks like we all have lost someone we care about huh? Enjoy this new pain and I will see you in Spirit I'm sure!" And she blinked out.

Seconds later Stormra appeared out of breath, her face flushed red then she spotted Kenton dying in Brooklyn's arms, "No…" she gasped dropping to her knees, "Andromeda stole my bag with the last potion in it before she vanished, like she knew it was there…I'll run to the Emerald guard they might have one we can…

"There's no time", Brooklyn whispered tears staining her voice, "Stay here with us".

Stormra knelt down by his side, "He didn't pray to the temple statue, I shouted after him but he refused. Said he only needed to pray to the water soul…I'm so sorry I should have stopped him and made him pray…Kenton I'm so sorry".

Brooklyn's face looked depressed and guilty, she had been the one to not pray at any other temple and Kenton had followed her lead and now he was leaving us.

Kenton's breathing becoming soft and shallow, his eyes glossing over as he took his last look at us all, "Go…on…beat them…for…me…"

"Shh don't talk baby", Brooklyn sobbed, "Just rest, it will be ok".

He peered at me, "Look…after…my…Sister".

I took his hand in mine, "I will". I then turned to Thane my heart shattering, his eyes told me in waves that he knew what it was I was thinking.

"Do it", he said strongly, "Tell them".

"Tell us what?" Brooklyn gasped through the pain.

My voice came out as a squeak, "The phoenix feather I was given by the fire element soul can bring back someone from the dead".

"In Spirit we can use it", Thane added.

"So you mean that…"

"We can bring your brother back, we have to let him go now but we will meet him there, it won't be for long".

Brooklyn's eyes lit up, "Did you hear that Kenton we can…" she stopped as she looked at his unbreathing body. Tears flooded down her cheeks, I felt tears roll down mine and as I looked at everyone else they too were crying.

Fira took my hand, "I know".

I looked at her, "What?" I whispered.

"What it's taken from you to do that for her, for Kenton…What you will lose".

I side glanced at Thane who lifted Kenton's motionless body in his strong arms, his own face full of sadness, "I will meet you all at Spirit, I need to warn the Soul Converter of what is coming", and with a swirl of souls and orbs Thane and Kenton vanished before my eyes.

The journey back up to Emerald Valley was a silent one as we all trailed back through the spiral staircase, the only noise that could be heard was Brooklyn's sobs. I guess the fact that we were going to revive his soul and body hadn't fully set in yet.

Once outside we could see the extent to what Andromeda had done. Kenton had explained that they had chased her off but not without a fight, not without a tonne of lost lives. I looked at Willow who scanned the landscape for Nate, her eyes full of worry and fear, then suddenly pulling a cart full of bodies she spotted him.

"Nate!" she called out and ran to him, she flung her arms around his shoulders and cried into him.

He cradled her and stroked her hair, "Its ok I'm fine...Where's some of your team?" he looked at me.

"They have gone to warn the Soul Converter of what is coming", I said my voice cracking.

He turned back to Willow, "I can't stay here, I need to come with you". She went to say something but he cut her off, "You mean the whole of Junia to me and if that means that this journey is the last time I will see you then I want us to journey together".

"I was going to say I want you to come with me", she sobbed, "Someone was taken in the chamber and it made me realise that I want you to fight with me by my side".

"Then that is what I shall do".

A while later Nate had gathered all his soldiers together to explain why their commander was leaving.

"As you all know Willow must leave with the future Queen of Junia to save us all, without her part of the puzzle they cannot defeat Andromeda. I have decided to go with her".

There were a few gasps and sighs at this but he continued on.

"Willow and her team were attacked in the soul chamber, in the temple, the one place they should be allowed to be safe and they weren't. One of them was killed. I need to make sure that doesn't happen to Willow because if it does then no one will be able to command the earth element soul. I need to be with her to make sure she survives and to make sure all the other converters are safe".

A teenage boy stepped forward, he must have been around fourteen. He bowed to Nate, "Then we accept your reasons, we live for Junia, Willow lives for Junia and you live for Willow...Go and win this fight for us...We will defend Emerald Valley for as long as we can".

Nate bowed to the boy and took out his sword, "Take this and command my army".

The boy's eyes widened, "With my honour sir".

All of the troops bowed, once to Nate and then to the teenage boy. Nate bowed back and then turned to us, "I need to get some things from the castle then we can leave for Spirit".

Using one of the carriages we all set off to the castle, once there Nate didn't take long and whilst we all changed back into our clothes that were more suitable for the journey ahead Willow approached me.

"I think you know why your hair is changing my Queen but you will not accept it yet. I think royal red is not really you", She lifted up some fresh clothes, "I think Royal Black is more to your suiting".

I stood there stunned and took the bundle of clothes from her, "You know about the royal colour really being black…"

She nodded, "The true colour of Cosima is of course that of the universe, black but also sprinkled with the magic of the stars".

"I wonder why?" I asked.

She shrugged, "Maybe only Junia knows, I guess it is just for us to wonder upon like so many of us do when we glance up to the heavens themselves", She then turned and left me to change.

I stood for a moment confused, wondering about the universe, the stars and Cosima and what it all meant but I couldn't conclude an answer so I hung up the ball gown on a hanger and quickly changed into the new clothes. I went to look in the mirror at myself and gasped in shock, the roots of my hair were so dark now and had bled so far down all the other strands there was only a small red line at the bottom showing what it had been before. I tied it back out of my face into a high ponytail then immediately took it down leaving it to wave over my shoulders, with it up I looked too much like Andromeda. I glanced down at the clothes Willow had given me and twirled, I now wore a dark pair of a strong leather like trousers which housed a belt which I could holster my sceptre in, I retrieved my small belt bag with the Phoenix feather in and the seed which the earth element had given me and the solidified tear from Isaura's element soul. The top half of my body was now covered with a white under top which shimmered with a pearlescent affect under a tight fighting wrap around black Kimono type thing which was held into place by a rather strong and stiff held bow which sparkled with gems and diamantes. Over the shoulders of the Kimono were leather like patches which I touched, they felt strong and coarse.

"That is the leather of an Emerald Hide Cow, it is the strongest leather known to Junia and many places use it as armour. Back in the day the royal family used to own many pieces of this leather to protect the family members when they went on their travels but after the great war we stopped letting them have it but now I want to give you some, it might help protect you in battle".

I looked down at myself, "Thank you Willow".

"It will be me thanking you if we win this", she replied, "Come the others are waiting".

I followed her down the stairs to the awaiting carriage. Nate was in the driving seat with the ropes to guide the horses. He had changed too into a similar leather attire armour as mine but his covered most of his body unlike the specially placed patches of mine. At his waist he now had two pistols holstered and a large sword across his back. I also spotted a small wand like device, just like the one I had seen the guards use.

I climbed aboard with Willow behind me, the others all gasped at how different I now looked, "You look ready for battle Mira", Isaura smiled, I think she liked how I wasn't wearing a girly dress now and that I looked like her, ready for a fight.

"I am, now let's get to Spirit, bring back Kenton and call the Spirit element soul so we can summon the final one and defeat Andromeda for good".

"Yeah!" the others all cheered.

Nate heard the cheer and set the horses on their path.

"We will be using the carriage to get us to Spirit faster, the trains will be a no go zone and even the roads will be dangerous but an Emerald Valley horse is fast and hard to kill. So hopefully we should get there with no problems using the old dirt tracks", Willow said hopefully.

"Fingers crossed", I commented and looked out as the carriage began to cross the bridge over the gap of the Abyss. As we reached the other side Nate lifted his wand and sent out a large firework spark to let the army know we were now at the border and they were on their own. I just hoped when Willow and Nate returned in the future that there was still an Emerald Valley and an army to come home too, then I realised that actually I really hoped everyone still had a home to go back to. All the countries would be fighting hard to keep the enemy at bay, I prayed to Junia for them and for me, that no matter what, that I could defeat Andromeda and bring peace and life back once again to our world.

~ The Country of Spirit ~

The journey to Spirit had been fast and without any fights but I knew that it was just the calm before the darkening storm. As we passed through the edge of Cosima I could tell that the storm was going to be heavy, the skies above had a darkened atmosphere to them with the main centre of the capital being the hardest hit. I could see buildings burning in the distance and the thick plumes of smoke shrouding everything. Andromeda had not only hit the homes in the actual capital but even on the outskirts, if we all survived this Cosima was going to take a long time to heal.

As the carriage pulled up at the gate of Spirit I could see how eerie and strange this country looked, the force field was strong but a cool light purple glow shone out casting us and all the near landscape in it.

I stepped off the carriage and took to the gate, I examined it trying to find the handle but there was none. I looked at the others, "How do we get in?"

Nate answered untying the horses from the carriage and walking them with him to the gate, "The gate of Spirit can only be opened from the inside, it stops the wrong people from being able to get in unnoticed".

"The wrong people?"

"Long ago there were a few thefts from Spirit, when there was more than one grand dark witch. They liked to use souls in their spells but the Soul Converter became angered by this and transformed the gate so only the guardians of Spirit could open it".

"That's not all of it though", Isaura added, "Is it?"

"What do you mean?" I asked.

"The Soul Converter was so angry about all those who entered trying to steal souls that she caught most of them and she took their life right from them. She made them into new guardians of Spirit, rumour has it that those people are now a mere zombie like form of their former selves".

Looking at the others they all looked a little fearful of entering this place, "Are you all scared of her?"

Isaura shrugged, "She can take life away with a click of a finger, wouldn't you be scared?"

I shrugged, "Not really. She was only trying to protect her country just like all of you".

Nate looked at me with questioning eyes, "Funny how you see it like that but most people don't. Yet you're the least religious one here".

"I guess after all I have seen and witnessed that I have adjusted to seeing things differently now".

"You might just be my favourite Queen of Junia", he smiled and then lifted his wand, he tapped it six times on the gate and we all waited.

"Why do people tap things six times in Junia to gain access to places?" I asked.

"Because of the six countries", Nate answered like I should have known but before I could comment back the gate opened and revealed a rather strangely beautiful young woman. She had a rather squared jawline and high cheek bones, she had deep grey eyes which twinkled in the light almost how Thanes eyes twinkled. Her hair was a shimmering silver which she had tied into a plait down one side, it was so long it trailed down past her waist. She wore a light purple crushed velvet looking robe and a long cloak in the same coloured material that trailed behind her.

"How can I help you?" she asked her voice sounded much older than she looked.

"I am Mira, Princess of Junia and I am here to ask the Soul Converter for help. I do believe my friend Thane might already be here with…"

"The boy", she answered.

I nodded.

"Come in all of you", she stepped aside from the gate letting us all pass, then she locked it behind us, "And why you still call yourself princess I don't understand, my Queen?"

I looked at the woman, her youthful skin glowing in the light of Spirit. "I have not had my coronation to make me Queen as of yet so my status is I guess still princess".

She shrugged, "The true Queen does not need a coronation for her people to know who she is".

I bit my lip, this girl seemed very to the point, "Um are you…the…?"

"The Soul Converter? Yes", she answered bluntly but politely, "My name is Nuelle".

"Then Thane is here with Kenton, you know what it is I wish to ask you?"

She nodded, "Yes you wish for me to help with my element soul".

"Yes and…"

"The boy?"

I nodded.

"I can only perform a resurrection with a Phoenix feather", she told me.

I riffled through my bag and took it out handing it to her.

"Very well, follow me", she said and turned, we all followed her down a cobblestone pathway which at first arrived into a small village. The village consisted of around ten or so houses and that was it, in the centre was a small water fountain which didn't spray water but souls, souls that danced out and then floated around it before shooting off into the sky which looked to be made solidly of souls in itself, it whooshed, wavered and almost sang as they moved. Past the village was a fence which showed us where the land ended. I stopped and looked out at the most mesmerising view I had seen yet. Floating in a large sea of colourful and glittering souls was an island, the island was made of rock and had whole sections melted away where souls poured out like a river, dripping and diving into the soul like ocean beneath. On top of the floating island was a huge grand temple, bigger than all of the others I had seen. The outside was a wash of light purple hues and dark purple tones, huge arches made the giant structure and within each arch was a large stained glass window.

"How do we get up there?" Brooklyn asked, her impatience showing.

"Be patient Water Converter", Nuelle said softly, "Your brother will be back soon".

Brooklyn glanced at Nuelle but said nothing, she only watched as Nuelle lifted her hands onto the fence and sang. On her left wrist sat a silver bracelet which glowed with the eerie purple light that Spirit consisted of and as she sang a sweet and delicate hymn it glowed brighter and brighter until it shook on her wrist, she lowered it to the fence and we all stood there awestruck as the light showed a hidden path all made up of souls.

"Please go ahead of me", she said, "As the path vanishes behind me".

We all took off ahead of her, Brooklyn first followed by Nate and Willow. Stormra and Isaura just behind them, then myself and Fira with Nuelle last. Once we had all reached the temple I turned to see that Nuelle was right, the pathway did disappear behind her and when her feet touched the temple grounds it had gone completely.

From here my breath was taken away from me once again, I thought the view from the village had been mesmerising but from up here it was unimaginably awestriking. From the temple gushed the waterfall of souls all singing and humming as they fell, a delicate chorus of song that was beautiful yet soul destroying at the same time. I could see for miles, Spirit was a huge country filled entirely by souls and vast carved landscape where the souls danced and swam.

Nuelle came and stood beside me, her presence was cool and calming, "Most royals never see Spirit, either too afraid of what they might see or what might be revealed to them by the souls of the past but you don't feel afraid, you feel awed".

"I have never seen anything so beautiful but also so sad", I replied, "My whole life I have been cooped up in the palace with no idea of what the world I would one day rule over was really like. Lavara so warm but dangerous for its people with the mining, Beach Haven so perfect with its soft sands but dangerous too with water all around and no real land to live from and hide when the almighty Tsunamis hit. Skye, treacherous with the animals that roam it but beautiful with its vast cool skies and high snowy mountains, Emerald Valley so green and full of fresh crops and life but cut off from Cosima with the Abyss. Then Spirit, a large country with so few people to occupy it but then it is kept safe and beautiful with the guardians that do occupy it".

"A true Queen can see the beauty in everything, even the things she doesn't fully understand...That was where you're so called ancestors failed, they had no vision", she said.

"But they were not my true ancestors though were they? I've been to the lost city and seen the truth".

"No they were not but they had no vision to see Junia for what it was. They wanted to control it and feared the magical side but soon that will change one way or another".

"Is Thane still here?" I asked gingerly feeling scared.

She nodded, "For now, his quest is nearly over, his soul orb is nearly full when it is he will disappear".

"Is there not anything you can do to stop it?" I asked.

She shook her head, "The only way was the Phoenix feather which it seems you have chosen for someone else".

I dipped my head, "We did chose it for him, I told him I would use it for him then Kenton he...He was so young I had to fix it somehow. He fought for Junia and saved my life a few times too how could I not return the favour?"

"You are already seeing as Queen that you will have to make some difficult choices", she said softly.

I nodded, "Yes I am". I felt something deep inside my chest shatter, a sudden grief flooded through me, "I wish I could save them all, Thane, Kenton and my parents".

"Why did you not choose to save one of your parents instead of Kenton or Thane?" she asked.

I looked down at my feet, studying my boots, "How can I choose between my mother and father, which one to bring back and which one to leave in Spirit, I thought it better they be together", suddenly a thought dawned on me, "Are they here?"

She looked up to the sky, "Your mother is, she managed to drift away before Andromeda could take her soul but your father is not here yet".

"Take her soul?" I gasped, "Has she taken his? Where? Why?"

"To use him against you, she has powerful dark magic Mira and to make you weak she planned on using them both against you but your mother was wise to it but your father being the king didn't understand her magic and stayed".

"Use him against me? How exactly?"

"I do not know the exact way she wishes to do this but I know it will come and you must prepare yourself for it".

"Can I see her?"

"Your mother?"

I nodded.

"Come", she said and took off into the temple, the others followed until Nuelle nodded at a rather unusual looking man. He was grey all over, his skin, his hair, his clothes and his eyes. He spoke to them all stating that Nuelle and me needed to be alone for a moment in a dull monotone sounding voice which lacked any sort of life or emotion. *Was he one of the Soul Converters Zombies?* Brooklyn was about to argue the point for Kenton but he reassured her that Kenton was the next priority on the agenda.

Nuelle led me through a funnel of walkways and my eyes took in the grandeur of the Temple of Spirit, in many ways it was much grander than my palace had been. The floor below my feet was a glittering polished marble, a mixture of purples, blacks and light blues with specs of light like stars, almost matching the colour of the souls that danced outside. Large columns of the same marble rose up from the floor and held up the huge grand ceiling which as I looked I couldn't see the top, magic had been cast here making the ceiling look like the heavens, the whole universe above Junia and beyond. The main temple room was more like a museum than a temple, special ancient artefacts and ornaments had been placed on pillars with glass casing protecting them all. Peering into one I saw a peculiar necklace which made me stop walking at once, it was as if it was calling to me,

"Mira...Save...Junia...Mira". Shaking myself mentally I took the whole piece of jewellery in, a large multi-coloured stone sat in the centre, all the colours of Junia represented, Flame red, Ocean blue, Sky white, Emerald green, Soul purple and black...*For what? Why black? Why Royal Black! The necklace looked to be of thousands of years old, why would it have the royal colour in it if the royals hadn't been around for that long?* Around the stone was a delicate detailed design in a platinum surround, leaves for earth,

flames for fire, drops for water, clouds for air, a soul for Spirit and something else, a moon and star together.

"Lady Mira?" Nuelle said standing beside me, "Are you coming?"

I turned to her and asked, "Nuelle if Cosima had an element what would it have been?"

"No one knows", she replied. "How could they? It never appeared".

I looked back at the necklace, as I did I could have sworn that a swirl of a galaxy twirled inside the stone. I shook my head.

"Mira?" She questioned, "Is everything ok?"

"I'm fine, let's go".

She led me through some more of the temple to a long corridor that held many doors and many rooms. She stopped at one door which was fairly plain compared to the others, she lifted her bracelet to the seal on the door and it clicked open. Ushering me in she then locked the door behind us, "Lady Mira what I'm about to show you could be dangerous, please do not do anything unless I tell you to".

"Ok".

She walked to the end of the small room and lifted off a cover which covered a mirror, a mirror just like my mother's back at the palace.

"I've seen one of these before, it's how I found Thane", I told her.

She nodded and smiled, "I know I put him there".

I felt cold all over, goose bumps covered my arms "You put him there?"

"Yes", she answered plainly her eyes holding no emotion, "Thane was not originally your soul guardian".

"I don't understand".

"Thane was meant to be your mother's soul guardian but with the King looking over her shoulder every five minutes Thane couldn't help as much as she needed so your mother chose to let him become yours. She knew he would be able to serve you better and help you when the time came and then eventually be able to move on. She didn't want him to not fill up his soul orb and not move on she wanted him to be able to go to the heavens, she understood your journey would be bigger and would fill it quicker". She paused for a moment touching the mirror she had just revealed, "The mirror was a gift to your mother from Spirit when she married the King. No one suspected any magic or any form of the religion from an inconspicuous mirror so she hung it in the throne room. When Thane appeared she had to make sure he stayed hidden and moved it into her own personal chamber. When he befriended you at a young age she was happy, everyone knows the palace is a lonely place for a child, that was until the King became suspicious and she had to move it for Thane's and your safety".

"The palace has a few mirrors doesn't it that can hold souls or transport people. Freya my maid took me through one".

Nuelle nodded, "Long ago the royal family would only accept mirrors from Spirit because of their gift of portals. Many I guess still work".

"What's in this one?" I asked.

"Your mother".

"Why is she in a mirror? And not outside", I moved my hand to where I imagine the outside souls to dwell from here.

"It's not safe for her to be out there. When I take the element soul from Spirit the whole place will become unstable, many souls will turn from good to bad, some will perish and others will escape out into Junia. I do not want to lose your mother's soul and when this is all done I will come and release her out and let her move on but for now, she must stay here".

I walked up to the mirror and looked in, "Can I talk to her?"

She nodded, "Call her".

"Mum, Queen Espinosia?"

The reflection in the mirror of myself warped and changed like it had when I first met Thane and it soon became my mother before me. Her long dark hair looked untouched, the royal gown she had been wearing the night things went wrong looked neat and brand new. She looked alive and well and it confused me for a moment, I went to reach out until Nuelle grabbed my hand, "You can't touch this one Mira".

I took my hand back and held it close to me, "Mum...Mum I'm sorry I didn't save you or dad! Kenton died and...And he..."

"Mira please don't apologise for deciding to bring back a friend".

"You don't understand, even before Kenton, I was going to bring back Thane...I was selfish, I was thinking about me and not you or dad or my family", tears welled up in my eyes and burst down my cheeks, "I'm sorry".

"Thane is your family too Mira, he has been with you since you were a child. I knew once you saw him again you two would grow close...I just wish..."

"Don't", I cried, "I know, I wished it too, I wished it all. To bring back all of you...To bring back him".

"But me and your father we have lived our destiny, yours is to become Queen of Junia with one of us back here you could not do that and you need to, Junia needs to be healed by your hand".

"I'm only fifteen", I sobbed, "How can I be Queen? And on my own?"

"You are nearly sixteen, the age a Queen or King can have a coronation. And you are not alone Mira, you have many friends I can tell, I can tell by your aura you are loved now by many and you care for them too", she also looked at Nuelle, Nuelle bowed her head. "All the element converters are your friends now Mira and they will stand by you when you are Queen".

"That's if I defeat Andromeda", I whispered.

"You have to believe in yourself or you won't win against her", she then gestured to the sceptre, "Your magic grows when you believe".

I looked down and saw that it was glowing, then a tingle flowed through my whole body followed by a cold shiver, I turned to Nuelle, "Lumi, she's here". *I had no idea how I knew Lumi was here but it was if the Sceptre knew of her presence and filtered it into my subconscious.*

Nuelle nodded and closed her eyes, communicating with her people.

"Mum I have to go, I love you".

"I love you to Mira, fight on and be strong".

Nuelle opened her eyes, "Thane knows and will protect Kenton's body until after the fight".

"Do we need the element soul now?" I asked.

"I can't, not yet. It would destroy Spirit if I do it now, we have to do it at the right time".

"And when is the right time?"

"Tomorrow", she answered, "On your birthday, the day of the fight for Junia".

I stood there dumbstruck, I knew it was coming, I knew it was nearly here but I hadn't thought it as tomorrow. "Why on that day?"

"Because it's written in the stars that that's the day we fight", Nuelle answered covering the mirror back up, "That's the day things change forever in Junia". She then opened the door and we rushed out, she locked it tight and then ran off in the direction of the main hall her robes and cloak billowing behind her. I ran after her trying to keep up but she was just that bit too fast for me, then I heard it, the playful tune of Lumi's voice.

"Well hello Queenie, all alone now are we?"

I spun to see her float down from the high ceiling, I was still in the hallway and Nuelle was gone. I took my sceptre from my belt and lifted it up ready to fight.

"Oh look at you, think you're a fighter now? Loving the new clothes by the way, shame, I just know it will suit your dead body better", she howled with laughter.

"Go to hell Lumi", I spat.

"It's you who will be the one going to hell my dear, destroying all my minions and orbs but it's ok, I am the greatest of all Andromeda's warriors and I will be the one to take you down", She jumped down from where she floated and clicked her fingers and two pink orbs appeared, "Fancy a game?"

"What game?"

"Not another riddle game as you clearly cheat but a game of whit, survival of the fittest. Only the greatest will win".

"What's the prize?" I asked.

She grinned, "You lose I win your sceptre and your life", she mused at it, "You win and I will give you my soul to use at your discretion".

"Your soul? How is that a prize?"

"Because you can absorb my power into the sceptre and make it even more powerful...But that ain't going to happen anyhow".

I stood there for a moment then she came before me. Her hand slit open, a small flow of blood trickling down her palm as she dragged one of her small bright pink daggers across it. The two pinks orbs danced in the air around her as she spoke, "Shake on it and swear to the deal...A blood oath can 'Never' be broken Mira".

I gingerly held out my hand and shook hers but not before she sliced my hand to match hers, the deal had been bound by blood. Then she lifted one of the pink orbs and crushed it in her hand, "Follow me".

The world before me warped and shook and within a cloud of pink smoke we had disappeared from the hallway of the Spirit temple and were now on a platform in a void of space. Lumi lifted up a long pink sword, "How's your swordsmanship?"

"My what?" I gasped as an identical black sword appeared before me. I gingerly took it from the air then Lumi howled like an enraged beast.

"ARGH", she screamed and ran at me with the sword, I froze in horror as the razor sharp blade made its way towards me.

Out of the corner of my eye I saw him, my soul guardian, Thane. He shimmered in but it was only a mere shadow of him not his whole person. He ducked and moved which confused me for a split second until Lumi was upon me, I followed his moves and ducked and moved barely out of the way as she sliced her sword down in one quick slick motion. I had no time to worry or to catch my breath as Lumi swung the blade and ran at me once more. Glancing at Thane I watched him move his arms, swinging them like he was wielding an invisible sword, he swung it in an upward motion. My vision came back to Lumi who was once again nearly upon me and I swung the sword up just like he done, the metal clanged together as both our blades smashed into one another.

"I didn't think they taught princesses the art of swordplay", Lumi sneered at me from over the top of her blade that was still pressed down on mine.

I sneered back, "They don't but my friends do".

"Let's hope they taught you good then".

So do I, I thought to myself as Lumi snatched back her blade and launched herself away from me.

We both stood there for a moment watching each other, both not knowing what the other one was going to do. Lumi cracked first tired of waiting and she ran at me once more, Thane came into view behind her dropped to his knees and arched his body backwards and brought his invisible sword up, just as she reached me I done the same, adrenaline pumping through my body my hands shaking but I held on tightly as I dropped and swung the blade up. Again the swords clashed together a small spark simmering off them.

Lumi huffed angered by the fact that I was giving her a fight, just as I thought I might have a chance she howled and swung her arm around quickly, I moved but not far enough, the tip of her blade slicing just below my elbow drawing a thin line of blood. I let out a startled cry which made her howl again but with laughter, "You cannot beat me Mira…It is in the stars that Andromeda will win".

"Then your stars are wrong", I snapped and slashed my own blade out, it connected with her cheek and a long line filled out with red, a few drips running down her face.

She lifted her hand to her face and came away with a line of blood, "You will pay for that".

She swung the sword again at me and I moved my arms in succession trying to knock her blows away from me but she was fast and angry, her arms whipping wildly around me until she connected with my shoulder hard but to both our astonishment her sword bounced off without causing my shoulder any harm.

"Emerald Valley armour!" She hissed into my face, "They would never give it to a fake royal, you must have stolen it".

"They gave it to me as a gift to help me win, they know I am the real Queen".

"It doesn't matter because once you are dead that armour will be buried with your rotting corpse".

"It won't be my corpse rotting Lumi", I sniffed, "I will win the fight for Junia, we all will".

"What? You think you and your little converters will win? Ha, not a chance", she smiled, "We are the all-powerful and Junia will be ours to rule".

"You honestly think Andromeda will share the rule over the lands she has had her eye on since a child?"

Her eyes flickered with doubt but she took the bait, "She wouldn't abandon me, I stood by her since the beginning, we will rule together…It is her birth right".

"Yes but not yours".

She clicked her tongue at me and her lip raised up in a snarl, "And not yours either, you are from the fake bloodline". And with that she launched at me, I couldn't see Thane in her blur of movement so I swung the sword whichever way I could, the metal of the blades chinked and clanged many times over until she finally gave a blow which knocked the blade from my very hands.

"Give it up princess", she cooed.

I looked at my sword which was a sprint away from me, she saw me looking at it and just as my feet began to move so did hers. We both charged at the same time but I was just that little bit closer, I dropped to my knees again and grasped the sword and spun round, she tried to stop but her feet didn't do it quick enough, her face contorted in horror as my blade pierced through her body.

"You win this round", she hissed through bloodied teeth and the void warped around us and I was thrown back to the marble floor of the temple. I stood up quickly to find Lumi was already back on her feet, the blood she had been covered in was gone as was the cut on my arm. She lifted up the other pink orb, "Ready for round two?" and she crushed it in her palm before I could answer.

The world around us warped again in a pink mist, blurring out into a clear blue as we both landed in a cool flood of water. I tried my hardest to tread the water but I had to admit I wasn't the strongest swimmer and the unexpected attack in Beach Haven by Andromeda had still left me weary. I turned to try and locate Lumi to see what this new game was.

"Junia", I heard her whisper from a distance. I had no idea what that meant so I said nothing. "Junia", she repeated sounding a little closer than before. "You were meant to say…SOUL!" she shouted right in my ear. I jumped out of my skin and screamed as she slashed my arm with a small knife, "That is your first life gone Mira, once you hit three you lose and I win…Your 'IT' now". Then she swam off and vanished in the water.

"Junia", I called out not really knowing what I was doing.

"Soul", Lumi giggled from a distance behind me.

I began to swim to where I thought I had heard her call out but as I neared I called out, "Junia", again only to hear that her voice had moved. I stopped in the water and turned trying to locate her, "Junia".

"Soul", she whispered right next to me and I cried out as she slashed my arm again, "Life number two down, one more to go".

I blinked and she had gone again I only knew she was still there as she called out, "Junia".

"Soul", I whispered feeling terrified, *she might not have died after I won the first game but what if this killed me?* I didn't have long to find out as she already knew where I was as I hadn't swam off to move and I felt the stab of pain as the third strike hit my arm. Then she grabbed my head and forced it under the water, I panicked not knowing what to do, I thrashed my arms and legs about trying to kick or punch her but they fell on emptiness.

A whooshing noise sounded in my ears as all the water cleared out from them, I thought she had let me go but she hadn't intentionally, the void of water had gone and we were back in the hallway in the temple.

"Bad luck Mira I won that means you are going to have to die and give me your sceptre", she smiled, "You swore it remember".

"I did yes, but I won game one and you won game two which means we are even, we tie, it is a draw. You haven't won completely", I told her, "We need one more game". I kept my voice strong as I said it even though I felt scared at what might happen next.

"So you did", she sneered at me, her eyes annoyed at this, "So one more game you say?" she placed her hand inside her pocket and pulled out a larger pink orb, she rolled it between her fingers her eyes focused on it, deciding whether to use it or not.

"Mira!" Thane called from down the end of the hall, his face full of fear and worry.

"Say goodbye to your little princess", Lumi barked and grabbed my shoulder and crushed the larger pink orb in her hand. The pink mist that came out from the other two had been minimal compared to what came out of this one, the smoke was chokingly strong as it whipped around us taking us both to where ever it was we were going. I just had time to see Thane running for us before we vanished from view and landed in another void in time.

As we landed Lumi let me go harshly throwing me down to the ground knocking the wind from my lungs.

"You think you are so clever don't you princess, telling me to command one more game to even the score but to tell you the truth both of us will be lucky to survive this one".

I looked over at her, "What do you mean?"

"The orb I crushed was one I found in a dark temple, on the dark realm of Junia".

"Dark realm of Junia? You mean the dark pentacle Andromeda found?"

She shook her head, "Everything in life Mira has a good and a bad side, a mirror image. There is a place where you can see the other side to Junia, what Junia would look like if it had been evil from the start...What Andromeda plans for this Junia".

"I don't understand".

"We are not just in a void Mira, we are in the middle of the two Junia's. The opposite Junia where the enemy is stronger and more terrifying will come here too, where both you and I will be opposites. I will have a good side and you a bad one".

I just stood there stunned, *Lumi a good side and me a bad one? A void? Like the one Thane mentioned before that people claim goes to another world that people never return from?* A light appeared from the edge of the void, a flickering and sharp light which split the seams of the mist and a snap of thunder crashed making me close my eyes in fear, when I opened them I was shocked to see Lumi had been right. Standing before me was myself but it wasn't me, not really. She had dark hair like how mine had become and it was short and stuck up at all angles, tattoos lined her arms and she wore a tight leather dress with strong leather boots. Lumi's opposite was shocking, she had long pink hair curled around her slim body. She wore a short pink dress and held her bag of orbs at her waist shaking, looking pure and innocent.

"Now it's time to fight ourselves", Lumi said, "And to see who wins". Lumi clicked her fingers and summoned the sword from before, the good Lumi also done the same and they both took defensive stances.

I turned to face myself and found she had a sceptre just like mine but it swirled with a darkness, whereas when I took mine from my belt and lifted it to her it shone bright. "Let the light defeat the darkness", I said to it, just as I did I heard her say the same words just in a different order, "Let the darkness defeat the light".

The two Lumi's took flight and ran at each other, their swords clashing in the pink mist that swirled around us all. My eyes found the evil me and she too was studying me, both of us trying to work out which move each of us would try first, then at the same split second we both lifted our sceptres and let our powers snap out towards each other. The beam of light from mine and the swirl of darkness from hers collided in the middle of the void and like a shimmering wave of lightning they crashed loudly, sending out sparks and small flares of power outwards, large chunks of the void floor began to melt away under the heat of the magic in the air.

The sceptre vibrated violently in my hands making it hard to keep focused, I could feel her power trying to eat away at mine. I wished so hard for help, for someone to come to my aid to help me defeat her and then Lumi. Then I gasped as a hand reached out from behind me and grasped hold of the sceptre's wand, my eyes glanced to the side and I found the ghostly image of Thane at my side, he smiled and nodded, willing me to keep strong and focused. As I felt the stronger wave of power rocket from my sceptre so did it too from the evil me standing opposite. Through the mess of our powers colliding I could just make out an evil looking Thane holding onto the dark sceptre too. I felt my power lax at the view until more hands appeared, Fira's, Brooklyn's, Isaura's, Willow's and Nuelle's, all their individual powers charging into mine and sending the sceptre into overdrive, the magic screaming and charging in the air. But as I stood there keeping the power flooding out I noticed more hands appear to help me, Kenton's he winked at me, *had Nuelle brought him back already? Or was he here in soul?* Then my breath caught in my throat, I felt numb as I spotted the King's hand with his royal seal ring take hold of the sceptre along with my mothers, they both nodded and smiled at me, their eyes glowing with pride which spurred me on more to do this. Stormra and Nate also appeared, their hands just managing to join in but their magic flowed through making the sceptre kick and butt in my hands, the power was like nothing any of us had experienced before.

Out of the corner of my eye I could just make out the two Lumi's stop fighting, they both turned to watch me and myself but they also saw that we were both equally matched just like they had been with the sword fight, I saw the evil me noticed this too and we both knew what we had to do, fighting each other wasn't the way to go but as we came to this conclusion so did they.

The two Lumi's ran for us hoping to reach us before we figured it out but we had and just as they approached we both spun our sceptres away from one another and turned it on the true enemy, Lumi!

Lumi screamed and howled in pain as my pure power boomed into her body and tore away at the evil that resided inside. I could also see across the now broken void that the good version of Lumi was also screaming in pain as the evil flushed through her and ate away at the good inside her. It seemed a shame that on one side the evil had to win and that not both sides could have the good to win but somehow we had to keep the balance. My power fizzled out just as Lumi fell to her knees, choking and shaking, her confused eyes looked up at me.

"You win little princess", she wheezed, "I am now forever in your debt...To help you on your quest to defeat Andromeda". Her eyes fluttered closed and then her body melted away from around her leaving just a small pink orb of her soul. It glowed with a strange light and at first I was scared to pick it up until Thane held my shoulder.

"Take her, she has to help you now...It's the way of the blood oath she cannot break it".

I knelt down and lifted up the pink soul orb which shimmered in the mist, my sceptre shook in my hands reacting with the orb and within a flash it had taken Lumi's soul into it. I felt a heat of power flood through it before it then went back to normal, a cool metal in my hands.

My eyes wondered over to where evil me stood also accepting the good Lumi's soul orb, we both nodded to one another before the swirl of the pink mist roared in my ears and took me away, back to the Temple of Spirit. I landed on the floor still standing, all the others sat around where I stood holding hands and chanting. It was Thane who opened his eyes first and broke the circle running to me, he went to cuddle me and to lift me up but instead his hands fell right through me.

"Huh", gasps littered the air around us as they all watched as Thane stumbled to the floor.

"What's happening to him", I stammered looking at Nuelle.

She looked saddened, her eyes welling up, "He has neared the completion of his destiny, his soul orb is nearly full".

"What does that mean?" I cried out.

"It means I won't be around for much longer", he whispered, his voice full of hurt.

Nuelle stood and came to us, "I'm sorry Mira but it is his destiny now to move on…"

"Wait…Fira…Can't the Phoenix grant us another feather?" I asked hopeful but her eyes told me it all as she looked away from me. "There has to be a way, I love him". I felt a shiver filter through my spine as I said it, declaring it to everyone around me.

"You sacrificed him for me didn't you?" Kenton said from the broken circle, I saw now that he was in fact alive and well again. Nuelle had brought him back.

I felt pain rocket through my chest, "We both chose to bring you back Kenton, me and Thane, together".

"But you lost each other in the process", he sniffed.

"Maybe so", Thane admitted, "But it doesn't change anything Kenton, we would both do the same over again to save you".

"Why?" he sobbed, crying into Brooklyn's chest.

"Because you are my friend", I told him, "And I love my friends as much as I love Thane".

"I think we could all do with some rest", Nuelle stated trying to calm the situation down, "We have another long day ahead of us tomorrow".

Tomorrow, my birthday…And most probably the day I will lose Thane…I didn't want tomorrow to come.

~ The Temple of Spirit ~

I didn't sleep that night, *how could I?* It was most probably the last night I would ever see Thane almost alive. We both sat in the main hall of the temple, talking and watching the souls sing as they floated past us. Nuelle had thought it best we all stayed in the temple as it was the safest place to be, even though Lumi had managed to get in and attack me.

I wondered how Andromeda was feeling now, knowing that I had defeated her main warrior. My mother had warned me that she might use my father to make me weaker and I was guessing she would do something horrific to make me weaker now I had taken out Lumi but I hoped that seeing my father in the void meant he had managed to get away from her and settle into Spirit.

Morning soon arrived and all the others looked just as tired as I felt, no one really wanted to talk or eat but Nuelle forced food down us all but the strange thing was we all noticed how Nuelle herself wasn't eating.

"Um Nuelle you are telling us all to eat but will you not come and eat something for yourself?" Nate asked as him and Willow ate some bread and cheese.

She glanced at Thane then back at all of us, "I have no need to eat".

Then just like that it all dawned on us, "Nuelle, are you a soul? Like Thane?" I asked, "And that's how...How you were the one to put him in the mirror? I did think how because you are so young but you're not are you?"

"I was born when spirit itself was born, I was born for the purpose of being the soul converter and nothing else. I will reside here for eternity, protecting the temple, protecting the souls and keeping the element soul safe".

Everyone looked in shock, "So you are like thousands of years old?" Kenton asked.

"Give or take a few thousand", she smiled but it didn't reach her eyes.

I suddenly felt guilty, I was feeling sorry for myself because of Thane and him leaving me but Nuelle had been a soul her whole life, she had never lived like we had, she had been born to do one thing and one thing only.

"Did you have parents?" Brooklyn asked her intrigued.

Nuelle shook her head, "No, no one in Spirit is born alive like that and we don't die. We just...Appeared when the element soul made Spirit...Me and my people have always just been...here...like this".

I could see Brooklyn wanted to ask more questions but Nuelle looked uncomfortable so I changed the subject. "So when are we going to get the element soul?"

"Once we are ready to leave", she answered, "But first I must make preparations for Spirit, I will be back soon". She left the main hall and headed down the long hallway. Pretty soon everyone was ablaze with chatter about Nuelle but I felt so guilty that I stood and left and went outside the main doors. I sat on the edge of the island letting my legs dangle freely and looked out over all the souls that swam around, my hand holding on tightly to a post in the ground just so I didn't fall.

The door behind me opened and then closed, I felt Thane sit beside me, "I'm sorry Mira, I never meant for this to happen, I never meant for you to fall for me, I never planned on…Falling for you".

"It's not your fault, it just happened", I said lifting my head towards the sky to try and stop the tears I had inside from falling out.

He nodded his head, his dark hair moved slowly not how it had before when he seemed more alive. I noticed now it had lost its shine, it looked dulled out by the fact that he was slowly vanishing in front of me, "I should have just…been…I don't know? Maybe distant with you instead of…"

"A friend? Which was what I needed…right? I was a lonely princess who knew absolutely nothing about my home, my world…Junia. You", I paused, "You have opened my eyes to all of this, to the magic, the element souls, the religions which are basically all one and the same but different in their own right. You have given me a chance to make a difference to Junia, to make it better and whole again…Maybe…That's if we succeed today".

"We will, I know it", he sounded determined, "I know you can do it".

"How?"

He shrugged, "I just have a feeling…Plus I taught you well, I hope".

I smiled and looked into his hazel eyes, "I'm going to miss you Thane".

"I'm going to miss you to Mira but I will always be with you, somehow".

"I hope so".

The door opened again and our time was cut short, it was Fira, "Nuelle said it's time".

Nuelle led us all down to the Chamber of Spirit which was actually not that well-hidden but unlike the other converters she had no other life commitments so she could keep an eye on it at all times, along with her people.

The chamber was behind a solid door which was held closed by shimmering souls, she lifted her bracelet with the seal and it popped open revealing another room full of the grand marble flooring and pillars. Set in the centre of the room was the solidified liquid with the soul set inside it. Nuelle went to the element soul and bowed, she hummed the same tune the souls outside all sang and I watched as the liquid slowly melted away from the beast inside. The beast stretched its legs and howled into the chamber making the whole room echo with it, then it turned its attention to me.

I took the whole element soul in, it was a wolf and a full on furry wolf with silver fur the same colour as Nuelle's hair. As it approached I curtseyed to it, it stopped in front of me and bowed its head down to me.

"Queen Mira, I hope you are ready for the fight ahead", it spoke in a voice that was neither male or female.

I shifted on my feet, "I hope I am ready and with my friends all by my side I think we have a chance to win this".

The wolf nodded, "I have a gift for you, for your birthday".

I stayed still as it closed its eyes and hummed the same tune Nuelle had hummed moments before. Before my eyes a lone hair fell from its fur, a soul entered the chamber and collided with the fur strand and in a flash a long flowing cloak floated in the air. It was fully silver but not furry like I had expected, it was like a fine silk and velvet mixed as one. At the neck it had two silver clips one was a moon and the other was star. Nuelle took the cloak from the air and placed it around my shoulders, clicking the two clips together.

The wolf spoke once more before Nuelle summoned him to her bracelet, "The cloak is a shield Mira use it wisely and it will protect you when you truly need it". The wolf evaporated in the air and was gone, the only sign he was still with us was the glow on Nuelle's wrist.

"We must leave now", Nuelle said and ushered us out of the chamber just as the walls shook.

"What's that?" Kenton asked.

"Spirit is unstable now", Nuelle told him, "And it will be until I command the element soul to return. We must leave now before we have to fight the souls".

"Fight the souls?" I asked shocked.

She nodded, "They will try to prevent us from leaving as they know we have the element soul. Once we have crossed the bridge to the ground they will come for us, we must run and never look back".

I felt my heart race, *Why shouldn't we look back?* I thought to myself. As if she heard me she answered, "The souls will try to enter yours if you look in their eyes, especially the evil ones. If that happens I cannot help you until the element soul has returned".

We all nodded in agreement and kept silent watching Nuelle command the bridge to appear once again to take us from the temple to the grounds. It came and we all rushed across it, Nuelle last again as it vanished behind her. Just as her foot touched the ground the screams began in the air behind us.

"Go, run!" She commanded and we all sprinted, our legs pounding into the cobblestone pathway that led through the tiny village and onto the grand gate. We could all see it looming in the not so distance. My heart was screaming in my ears for me to run faster, for us all to run faster.

"Argh, help!" Stormra cried out from behind.

"Don't look keep running", Nuelle shouted, she turned to look and cursed under her breath but she too kept running.

Another scream echoed behind us and I recognised that one as Willow's but it wasn't her that had been caught, "NATE!" she screamed.

"Willow move…" Nuelle shouted from beside me.

I took a chance glance and saw Willow had stopped and I knew she was going to run back to him. I could see and feel the souls behind us looming but what shocked me were the souls holding onto them, we knew them…Chaos had Stormra, holding her tight and soaking her soul into Stormra's, Nate had been caught by Salem who was trying to force his soul into Nate's eyes.

Lowering my sight I ran to Willow lifting my cloak around us both as I reached her hoping it would stop any souls from stealing us. "Move…Now…We need to go Willow. Nuelle can help them once we defeat Andromeda".

She sobbed and didn't budge.

"Please Willow", I begged.

Then another scream belonging to Kenton pierced the air, I didn't look to see who had him just in case they took me. I grasped my hand around Willow's and pulled.

Unwillingly she took one step, then another and then we were running for the gate again.

We just made it as Nuelle unlocked it and threw it open literally shoving us out as we made it then she slammed it tightly shut behind us and locked it tightly with the seal.

"No one can enter Spirit till my return…That also means anyone who dies, their soul cannot access Spirit till I unlock the gate which could mean Andromeda might be able to possess and use them", Nuelle told us, securing her bracelet back into place.

I looked at all the others, Brooklyn, Fira, Isaura, Nuelle, Willow, myself and Thane. We had been the only ones to make it out, all the others had been caught.

"We can't just leave them", Willow said pushing her arms into Nuelle.

Nuelle held her ground and stayed still, "I can help them when we return, they are safer in Spirit than out here, out here we could lose them and I don't want that".

"Lose them?" Brooklyn asked, "But I only just got Kenton back".

"He is not dead just possessed", she told them, "But if they managed to get out here they could wander off and I wouldn't know where".

Isaura spoke up, her face hard set and determined although I could see the fear for her mother bubbling below the surface, "We will defeat Andromeda and get them back Brooklyn, we will get all three of them back".

Brooklyn and Willow nodded.

"We need to go now", Nuelle said and she waved her hand in the air and a portal opened.

"What is that?" Fira said peering into it.

"That is what the mirrors of Spirit are made of, souls who can open pathways around Junia", Thane told us all, "We need to get to Cosima and quickly and a mirror portal is the only way".

As we all turned to face him I could see that he was fading more and more with each passing minute.

"Thane", I whispered.

"It will be fine", he grinned that cool boyish smile. I wanted to rush to him to hold his hand in mine, just one last time before the fight but I knew my hand would just fall straight through his.

Nuelle spoke to me casting my attention away from him, "My Queen, you need to go first, you have the shield of souls it will keep you safe if you need to return if this spot is not safe. I have to go last or the portal will close behind me".

I nodded, "Ok". I took a deep breath trying to be strong and looked at all my friends, "Wish me luck", and I vanished into the portal.

~ Junia Rising ~

I stepped out of the portal and found myself coming out from the very same mirror Thane had come from, secluded in the soul chamber deep under the palace. My heart raced as I tiptoed out to make sure it was safe for the others but other than me no one else was in this room. *I had to wonder why Andromeda hadn't come and smashed the mirror already, unless she had no idea it was down here.*

I took a small step back into the mirror and signalled for the others to come through. One by one they all passed and huddled into the small chamber, until finally Thane and then Nuelle passed through and the mirror closed behind us.

"Back to where we started then", Thane smiled at me, I smiled back but I knew it didn't reach my eyes. He came over to me, "I wish I could comfort you and make this easier but I can't and I'm sorry".

"Don't be sorry, you should never be sorry, you made this possible and now we have to finish this", I said trying to be strong even though my hands were shaking and my heart racing in my chest.

Nuelle stood by the chamber door, her silver hair flashing in the dim firestone light, "Shall we?"

I nodded, "Let's do this".

She opened the door and we followed her through the tunnel and back to my own private security chamber. She pushed on the trap door but couldn't get through, "It's blocked on the other side".

Thane nodded, "I'll check it out".

"But how will you move anything?" Fira asked.

"I still have my soul powers even if I cannot physically lift anything", and he swirled out of focus. A few moments later the trap door opened with a swirl of orbs and his face smiled, "Looks like Andromeda trashed your room and in doing so hid the trap door from herself".

I climbed out with the others and looked around the room, it was unrecognisable, all the walls either smashed, crumbling or no longer standing. The old painting where the hidden door used the hang was blown to nothing, just chips of wood.

"Where to now?" Brooklyn said peering out of the hole in the wall.

"The throne room", I said, "That is where she will be waiting for us, she will sit upon my mother's throne just to prove a point that she thinks she is winning".

"Then lead the way my Queen", Brooklyn said playfully.

I gave her a side glance and she nudged my rips with her elbow, giving me a frightened smile. I nodded to her, "Then follow me".

Taking point I led them out of the broken wall. I wasn't really surprised to see that there weren't any guards patrolling the palace but then she would want us to go straight to her, she would want the pleasure of killing us herself, by her own hand not by one of her guards, not now. She would know Spirit was unstable and would know we were coming.

The old corridors and long hallways looked nothing like how they did before, paintings were torn, shredded and broken where they had been searching for secret tunnels. Doors locked or destroyed, dark symbols painted on the floors and walls, evil magic coursing through the veins of the once 'half good' palace. I couldn't say it was a pure good palace since what had happened years ago. That was partly why Andromeda was the way she was, because of them and the maid. *Who hasn't made an appearance to us yet?* I thought it strange as the maid all those years ago had been after the throne herself, *surely she had to still be around, surely she would want the throne for herself with Andromeda.*

We reached the door to the throne room and I led them all in and we were greeted by the cackle of laughter that howled out from Andromeda.

"My, my, little princess Mira and her little friends made it all this way", she clapped her hands together and stood from my mother's throne. She wore a long dark silk gown which flowed like ink over the floor as she moved, around her chest area the dress burst into crows feathers making her pale skin look deathly pale, her dark hair tied up high into a sharp ponytail with braids either side. She made it to where we stood and lifted her long pale fingers with long dark polished nails, "Now hand over the element souls".

All the others took defensive stances behind me.

"Oh I see, you all still want to fight to keep them", she nodded to herself, "Well I did see that one coming, how could I not? Especially after what you 'all' did to my little Lumi". Her voice thundered through the room, the guards she did have all bowed their heads in submission to her shout but we all kept our heads up not showing her any weakness.

"We won't let you have them", I said lifting my sceptre.

She turned to me her eyes narrowing, "Why isn't your hair traitor red anymore? Why isn't it the colour of the blood of all my ancestors that yours murdered?"

"Because I'm like you", I said with a matter of fact tone to my voice, "Me and you are not so different Andromeda".

"I am of royal blood that is why it was so easy for me to take the palace and the throne. My hair is the true colour of the royal bloodline, not yours. You dyed it with sorcery, with trickery, you are a liar".

"I am of royal blood like you...My mother was your niece...Your sister was my mother's mum...She was alive Andromeda, all those years you thought your sister was dead she was alive and living only a few feet away from you in the hidden city".

"No, you lie?"

I shook my head, "The lost city of true Cosima, she had lived there with you. Adopted by a maid, a maid scared to reveal the truth until her own death bed where it was revealed but by then you had already gone. She had a daughter, Espinosia, who they trained to live and fight for the throne, she went on to catch the kings eye and revived the true bloodline into the fake by having me. I have fake royal blood but also the true royal blood in my veins, which is why my hair has changed…Because I can be the true Queen of Cosima, of Junia".

She howled with laughter, "Strong words, very strong words", but I could see in her eyes it had hit her, right where I wanted it to, in her ice cold heart. "But you see just because Espinosia had you doesn't mean you are the true Queen. I am first in line to the throne not you, by age and birth right I am the Queen".

"Maybe for now", I mused, "But once we defeat you, the throne will be mine". I lifted my sceptre higher and watched as it started to glow.

Andromeda's eyes narrowed, "Very well, have it your way. So we fight to the finish". She lifted her hands and commanded her murder of crows to appear, they filtered out through the cracks in the walls, in the ceiling and through the floor.

All of us launched into an attack, I zapped the crows with the light of my family's power, my power, which burst out through the sceptre more powerful than before. Lumi had been right, her soul did charge the sceptre. Thane and Nuelle sent out hordes of their soul power who took hold of the crows and crushed them into puffs of feathers and squawks. Fira sent out fire balls, tearing into the many who tried to shield Andromeda from us. Brooklyn made the waters rise through the floor, drowning the ones who fell stopping them from rising again. Isaura let the winds roll freely through the room sending waves of crows to the end of the room where Willow waited and sent out vines rising from the tiles and tying themselves around the crows, either killing them off or just holding them in place.

"ENOUGH!" Andromeda screamed out. The crows that remained went to her, a sight I had never dreamt of seeing happened before me. The crows plunged into her, tearing their beaks into her flesh and burrowing inside of her body. Her skin moved and contorted with the movement of the birds inside her, their feathers breaking the surface and turning her whole soul dark. With them inside her and their power combining with hers she grew taller reaching ten feet tall. Her eyes bored into mine, hers fully black now with the power of the crow. "I will kill you all and take the element souls, then Junia will bow down to me".

I lifted the sceptre about to fight her but Nuelle took my arm, "Step back my Queen, it is our turn to fight her".

I done as she said and went to Thane who stood by the door. Fira approached Andromeda first, she sang and summoned the Fire Element Soul, the Phoenix who burst out from her necklace and screamed out a howl of fire from its beak. It flew up into the air and screeched, beating its wings faster and faster until a wall of fire shot out and collided with Andromeda. She screamed in pain and a flock of crows fell from her body, in amazement I watched as she shrank back down a tiny bit. We had to extract all the crows from her.

Next up Brooklyn called her Element Soul the male siren, he boomed from her ring in a wave of water and swam in the air. He stopped in one spot and looked over Andromeda, then he cupped his hands together and commanded a huge ball of water to erupt out from them. The mass of water engulfed Andromeda and another flock of crows fell from her drowning in the water. She shrank back down some more, the look in her eyes getting angrier with every passing minute. *I had no idea what she was waiting for, why she wasn't attacking back?* But the others didn't care, they just stood up to keep fighting her but I had a feeling this wasn't it, this wasn't the end battle, the final fight.

Isaura stood up and commanded the Air Element Soul to appear from her earring, the Pegasus immerged in a gust of powerful wind that made all of us shiver. The Pegasus bowed it's head and tilted it's wings above it's body, it made a strange 'o' shape with its mouth and using its wings to propel more power into it the Pegasus blew a huge current of air which then collided with Andromeda and more crows fell from her body.

Then Willow appeared and summoned her Earth Element Soul from her Tiara, the half woman half tree nymph landed gracefully and studied the being before her. She then danced, tapping her feet loudly on the ground sending shockwaves to where Andromeda stood, from the ground shot out roots and vines which stabbed repeatedly in to the Grand Dark Witch and tore the birds from her very flesh. Her grand armour falling away from her.

I turned to Nuelle, "She won't die from this will she? That's just her armour, we will have to fight her again".

Nuelle nodded, "You my Queen will fight her again", and then she walked over to take her turn, to summon her Spirit Element Soul.

"No wait what do you mean", I said but Thane sent out a wave of souls to stop me running to her.

"They all must fight her this way, they will weaken her then you can finish her off", he told me.

"But how?"

He nodded at my sceptre, "Your power".

I nodded and held it tight, hoping that I had enough left to help them, to stop her once Nuelle had finished her part of the fight.

Nuelle summoned her Spirit Element Soul from her bracelet, Andromeda's eyes looking ready. The Wolf pounced from where Nuelle stood and unlike the others it didn't wait to command its power it just charged at the witch and bore its strong teeth into her body and tore at her over and over again, tearing out all the crows sending them flying off into the air screeching and howling after their owner. Andromeda screamed holding her body as the wolf backed off, it almost looked as if she was melting, all the feathers and birds dropping from her flesh as she shrank back down to her normal size.

I looked at all my friends, they all stood next to their element souls, waiting for what would happen next.

"Your turn", Thane whispered and I nodded to him.

I raised my sceptre and summoned into it all the power I could muster up, I could feel it flowing out through me and into the solid metal before me, conducting its way through and then spilling out and smashing into Andromeda in a quick spiral of magic. I held my breath as the light took her over and I could no longer see her, I summoned more, as much as I could, almost willing as much as when I had defeated Lumi, when all the others had helped me but now they all stood with their element souls, guarding them.

The light began to subside as my power flickered off and I lowered the sceptre to see…To see that Andromeda was still standing there alive. Her inky black dress had not a mark on it.

"How?" I stammered.

"Because you are not the true Queen, that power of yours is weak, you cannot defeat me", and she lifted her hand and threw it to the side, my sceptre was snatched right out from my hands and smashed against the wall. The top half crunched and dropped to the floor revealing that the powerful orb at the top had been broken. *My only form of power, taken from my grasp.*

I turned to Thane confusion over his fading face. Then I looked at the others, they too all looked confused, *we had this is the bag, it was meant to be, what went wrong?*

"Mira", a voice I recognised filled the room. I turned to see my father sitting at his throne, his eyes full of anger, resentment and hatred.

"Dad", I said taking a step towards him before saying, "Your dead, I saw you in Spirit".

"No you didn't, I am here, I have always been here, with the rightful Queen", he motioned his hand to Andromeda who smirked at me.

"No you and mum, you both helped me defeat Lumi", I told him.

"That was your mother, she made it look like I was there so you would fight on but she cannot leave Spirit to help you now can she".

I stopped, no, this couldn't be right, I had seen his ring and his hand, it was him, "No it was you, you aren't real".

"I am real", he commanded.

"No…Mum said she would use you to hurt me, you are just a soul now, a soul a grand dark witch can possess".

"Your mum used him to lie to you", Andromeda hissed, "He's been here all along remember".

"I…I will save you and send you to Spirit dad", I called out, I went to run to him, to them but before I could move another muscle Andromeda lifted her hand at me and I felt my feet leave the floor, I rose up higher and higher off the floor, my hair nearly touching the ceiling.

"Say goodbye to your father Mira", Andromeda sniggered and threw her arm down hard and me with it. As I fell the cloak from the Spirit Element soul wrapped itself around me, the force of the air lifting it around my body.

SMASH!!!

I felt the full force of my body hit the ground, the wind taken out right from my lungs but that wasn't all. I was still falling. A huge hole had opened out right beneath me as I hit the floor, sending me down into a never forgiving darkness. No scream could escape my lungs as I fell, my breath not quite come back to me yet.

BANG!!!

This time I stopped, my body aching slightly from the hit. Looking up I could see that I had fallen miles and miles below Cosima. I sat up slowly, preparing myself to feel broken bones or a punctured lung but as I stood I felt no pain, just a murmuring ache. *But how? I had just fallen from up there, I should be dead?* My hand lifted the cloak I had received from the Spirit Element Soul, I smiled. It really was the strongest shield I could have.

Looking back up and around I knew I had to try and find a way back up there, to help them all. They needed me but then I remembered my Sceptre being smashed, "Well I will just have to find another way", I whispered to myself.

A swirl of orbs danced in my vision, I shook them away, *maybe I had hurt my head after all?* They didn't leave, they entered my mind and sang, opening something and revealing something I had forgotten, something I needed to know. A memory but it was still foggy and faded at the back of my mind.

I stood and began to walk, trying to find a way out. As I reached a small hill like mound I stopped as something called out to me, "Mira", it sang my name so gracefully, calling me, telling me its location. I carried on walking following its voice. The wind was whipping wildly at my hair making it hard to see through the solid now dark mass of strands, it kept calling to me deep in my mind like a shy vibration. It called so dreamily to me that even though I was aching I felt myself move my aching feet taking off in the direction the vibrations were coming from.

My movements were a blur as everything around me faded, I knew I was in the lost city of Cosima but everything milked together into browns, reds, greys, blacks and oranges as buildings, ruins, bricks, rubble and soil all passed me by.

I headed towards and into the old palace pushing the old rusted doors open, I didn't bother to see if it was safe or not I just walked right in, cobwebs clawed at my face and spiders hurried away from my presence. The dust was thick and heavy in the air but it too vibrated along with whatever was calling me, deeper into the palace I went not caring about the dark gloom or the strange silvery glow that gave my eyes some light to focus on. Deeper in I went until I came to an old picture of a past King and his family, I knew it wasn't the ones I had seen in the memories these ones were even older, maybe even the first royals to ever rule over Junia. The picture was painted in oils and hung heavy in a dented and dusty old golden frame, I placed my hand over the King's Sceptre and the picture swung forward revealing a hidden passage way that wouldn't lead up to the new palace but downwards, further into True Cosima's core.

I followed the passage down, flames sparking up as ancient fire stones hung in torches but this wasn't the only element present, all of them were here somehow. Small trees had been planted in small recesses, they glowed with earthly power but didn't grow out of control they just stayed small, above them hanging along the walls were glittering chains with what I thought were diamonds but they were droplets of water that didn't move, I only knew this as I brushed my finger over one and it came away wet, the droplet I had taken away was instantly replaced by another, they glowed like rain drop necklaces dancing over the walls. As I looked up I noticed souls creeping and whispering past, they circled around as I walked but never came low enough to reach me. The floor as I walked lower down in the passageway became a foggy mist, it chilled my feet but not enough to freeze me. That was it all the elements were here, Earth, Water, Spirit, Fire and Air, all of them working together to protect whatever it was that was hidden down here.

I came to the end of the tunnel and approached a large wooden door, it wasn't fancy or appealing in any way it was just a door, a door that vibrated with the feeling that I needed to go inside and see what was there, I needed to help and let lose what was inside. I reached my fingers up and stroked the handle, I clasped my hands tightly round it and pulled…

I held the handle tightly in my hands as the door creaked open, dust fell over my shoulder as it then opened to a full view of what lay in wait inside. My eyes couldn't believe themselves, hidden deep in the depths of the old palace was…Another Element Soul, the one that burnt out and gave Cosima no power of its own. It lay half hidden in a mound of dirt and half covered in the same crystallised liquid as all the other element souls. *But how was it here? How had no one known about it being here before?*

I approached it with caution, gently kneeling down to it and wiping some of the dirt from it. I jumped back with a yelp, as a bright light sparked from it, from my touch. As I let go the light disappeared.

"What is this?" I said to myself.

"It's the final element soul", Thane answered.

I spun round and came face to face with him, he flickered in and out of focus, "Thane your still here? Are the element souls still fighting her?"

He shook his head, "Andromeda has all the element souls and she is going to call the final one".

"And the others? The Converters?"

"Imprisoned for now but she plans to execute them soon", he whispered, his voice cracking with sadness. I couldn't help it, I reached out to hold him, I wanted to make his sadness go away but as my hand glided through his faded and hollowed chest I felt dizzy.

WHOOSH!!!

I was gone from the Cosiman element soul, the world around me had been taken out from under my feet, a swirling mass of orbs and souls until...BOOM...I landed in the Temple of Spirit. My mind raced in confusion, *if I was here...was I dead?* I could hear the howling wind of souls outside of the temple as they lost control. The ground shaking below me with the force of their cries.

I went to run *but where could I run to?* Then a glowing aura called to me, it wasn't dark or light, but a mixture of all the colours of the elements together. I approached the lights and stopped beside the glass case that held the necklace I had seen when I had first come here, the one Nuelle had kept safe all this time, The Universal necklace.

I lifted my hand up and the glass evaporated from around it and the coolness of the necklace embedded itself into my palm. The necklace glowed brighter and engulfed me in it… ZAP … I opened my eyes to see I was now back with Thane in the Final Element Souls Chamber.

"What just happened?" he asked. I held up the necklace and his eyes widened, "Mira is that?"

"The universal necklace, Andromeda cannot summon the final element soul with the other element souls only the Converter of the final soul can do that", I smiled.

"What is the final element?" he asked me.

"Universe and Time…This element controls everything about Junia", I said and knelt back down to where the element soul lay in waiting.

I placed the necklace over solidified liquid and prayed, "The Element Soul of Cosima, hear my plea, I wish to save my Kingdom and everybody, dark forces have arisen and cannot be defeated by my hand, I need your help, please grant me your help". I placed my hand over the gem stone in the necklace and felt it grow warm, my power flowing through my hands and smothering the gemstone. The gemstone let out a burst of light and a small vibration and that was it, I knew the final element soul was with me.

"Nothing happened", Thane said walking beside me.

I looked into the now empty void of crystallised liquid, "I wouldn't be so sure", I smiled at him.

"How are you going to get back up there?" He asked, "I don't have much power left, I cannot take you".

"You don't need to", I said and tied the chain of the necklace around my neck, I then hovered my hand over the gemstone and hummed, hummed the tune that all the others sang to their element souls, the song of Junia.

The ground beneath our feet began to shiver and shake, then I heard a loud splitting and crunching sound as solid rock and granite lifted up with us. The power of the element soul and my own power lifting us up in the air with the ground beneath us.

"Mira, the ceiling, it will crush you, stop it!" Thane exclaimed, I could feel a cool sensation as he tried to shake my arm but his hand just fell through mine.

"Don't worry", I whispered closing my eyes and humming louder, the song gathering more voices as memory orbs and other souls joined us. The souls of the people who could not yet reach Spirit. Even the people above the ground heard it and began to sing, even the people who resided in True Cosima couldn't help but sing and hum along with us. I heard Thane gasp and I felt something pass through my body as we rose higher and higher. The song now so loud I could no longer hear the blood rushing in my veins as my heart beat loudly with fear and also excitement at what could potentially happen now we had the final element soul.

"It's Mira", I heard Fira's voice exclaim from somewhere.

It was then I opened my eyes and stared out in wonderment.

"What has she done? What is happening to the ground? Where did all these old buildings come from? Is that the old palace?" Loads of voices asked questions from all around me but I too wondered what it was I had done, I only wanted a platform to bring me back up to the surface but what I found shocked me, I had raised True Cosima from its slumber and brought it back up to the light of day.

The two Cosima's were coming together, the old and new palace somehow merging as one, the buildings fitting in together.

I could see Koal and his people coming out from their makeshift homes, bewildered looks on their faces and shielding their eyes from the atmosphere up here, no longer underground.

"You!" It was such an accusing tone from Andromeda, "Why aren't you dead, that fall should have killed you".

"I had some help from my friends", I said and looked at Nuelle who was being held by some palace guards, as was everyone else but she knew I meant the cloak.

"Well your just in time to witness their demise", she announced with a cruel snarl in her throat.

"I don't think so", I announced back to her, "It is you who will witness your own demise".

"And how do you plan on doing that? I have all the element souls and I can command the final one".

"Try it", I said crossing my arms over my chest, "Call it and see what happens".

"Mira?" Brooklyn and the others gasped.

But I stood my ground, "Go on".

Andromeda sniggered, "Very well princess". I watched as she lifted her hands, all the element souls where there only in coloured orb form, small spheres of pure magic. She raised them higher and called out, "Combine and create, bring me the final element soul".

Nothing happened.

"Combine and create!" she commanded the souls but they did nothing, "You, what have you done?" she howled at me.

"It's what you done Andromeda, not me…" I said, "Or should I say The Maid who brainwashed Andromeda".

Andromeda's face contorted with pain, her eyes rolled back into her skull showing just the bare whites. Then with a shimmer of dark magic the familiar mousey coloured hair and face of the maid appeared before us, a cruel and twisted hiss left her lips, "My name child is Luciferia and I'm not just a palace maid, I am the most powerful grand dark witch to ever live".

"But you're not alive now are you?" I told her, "You died the day you hid Andromeda in the tunnels but instead of moving onto Spirit you made sure that your soul would go to a new host. The darkness I saw going into Andromeda as a child wasn't magic but a part of your soul to make sure that you could come back to finish what you started and when you died you possessed Andromeda's body and mind, just like I saw the souls of Lumi's puppets do to my friends in Spirit".

"How do you know this? No one knows of what I have done and achieved", Luciferia snapped.

"No but the good version of you does, she knows and she showed me in the tunnels in True Cosima, she wanted me to know that it was you that caused all this and not Andromeda, she is truly innocent in all of this".

"She might be innocent child but there is nothing you can do to help her now, I am a part of her in soul, body and mind. To kill me would be to kill her", she taunted.

"Maybe so but if that is the only way to free her then so be it, I will defeat you".

"And how do you plan on doing that? You haven't succeeded so far".

"With what you helped me find of course", I smiled lifting the necklace up in my hand to show her.

"The Universal necklace!" she cried out, "But how…Only the last element converter can touch it…But you…No…No…Not you".

I took the necklace from my neck and lifted it into the air and called out, "Element Soul for the Universe and Time please I need your help".

A swirl of colours released themselves from the gemstone in the centre of the necklace and danced around the air, the other element souls in Luciferia's hands blinked out and vanished from her grasp and blinked back into view above the necklace. They all shimmered and glided around until the final colour of the Universe, the dark inky black with the glimmering stars released itself from the gemstone and all the elements collided together. A small planetary boom shook the ground we all stood on and then the necklace let out a burst of shimmering star light engulfing all the elements until the loudest roar I had ever heard echoed all around Cosima.

I looked up to see a black dragon with glittering scales swoop down and land beside me, its wings were as wide as it was long and they glowed with gems lining them in all the colours of the elements. It bowed its head to me, "Queen Mira of Junia, the Final Element Converter of Junia I grant you my help". It then turned to Andromeda and Luciferia, "And the Dark Witch Luciferia, you will no longer wreak havoc over my lands, the stars forbid you to do so. And my royal blood tie Andromeda I'm saddened to have to fight one of my own, one of the royal family but needs must and I must save Junia".

"You will never defeat me", she cackled and spun on the spot lifting a darkened cloak behind her which was in fact a pure carpet of crows. They grew all around her as she grew and absorbed themselves back into her like before but this time it was different. BOOM! The ground shook and a new beast screeched before us, a giant flying Crow that was as big as the Dragon before me.

The dragon turned to me, "Free your friends and take this". It blew out a small flame of colourful fire and a clink of metal hit the ground. I leant down to find the sceptre, my sceptre and it was healed.

I nodded, "I will, thank you". I stepped back from it as it lifted its huge wings and took off, a large gust of wind almost pushing me over but I stood strong. The fight between beasts erupted in the air as the Dragon and the Crow took to thrashing each other.

I took this as my chance and ran to the others, the palace guards all looked at me in fear as I raised my sceptre, "Release them now". They all done as they were told and let my friends go.

Fira was the first one to hug me, "Mira...You're a Converter too...How?"

"Cosima always had an element soul and a hidden converter but we never needed them before because they are only needed when Junia is in the greatest peril. The soul sleeps for eternity to build up its strength for when it is needed and the converter is awakened when required".

Brooklyn came up to me and took my shoulder in her hand, "I'm sorry I doubted you Mira, you are one of us and I knew it but I just didn't want to see it".

"That water was washed under the bridge ages ago", I smiled and hugged her too then all the others came over and held us. "The fight isn't over yet though".

"We will stand by you no matter what Mira", Willow said and Isaura nodded with her. Nuelle just stood back and smiled a pure knowing look in her eyes, she knew this was how things were really meant to be, us all as a team fighting the dark witch.

"My element soul still may need our help, I think it gave me my sceptre back for a reason and I might need you guys like when I did with Lumi".

"Well let's go help", Isaura grinned, "Let's take down this bird crazy witch".

I couldn't help but smile, these girls really were my friends and they really were with me all the way, "Let's go".

We all ran back to where I had raised the ground in the palace gardens, the dragon and crow were fighting hard in the skies, chunks of feathers and dragon scales littered the earth below and around us. I could see the crow tiring as its attacks weren't as strong as they had been but my dragon too was slowing down, its wings damaged by the crows claws.

"Ready?" I asked.

"READY!" Everyone else shouted behind me.

I lifted my sceptre and aimed it at my element soul, the sceptre lit up in my hands flooding the area with a light so powerful and bright, "I Call upon the stars of ancestors passed, they will guide the shining light, take me down the narrow path, to kill the unsightly blight". One by one all my element converters placed their hands on the wand of the sceptre, their power fuelling it more, giving it the strength it needed. Then totally unexpected was a wave of souls but not Thane's souls as these were different, the newly fallen by Luciferia's own hand, they too collided into the sceptre.

"What's happening?" I shouted to Nuelle.

"They wish to help, let them", she replied.

I nodded and held the sceptre tighter, the light emitting out was so bright and powerful that I couldn't bear to look at it. As I winced away from the light I felt Thane's presence stand beside me, I opened my eyes and watched him, his whole body was weaving in and out of focus, his time so nearly up.

"Thane I wish I could save you and I wish I could save Andromeda to…Tell her won't you, on the other side that I forgive her, that I know none of this was her fault!" I had to shout it out to him over the noise of the magic in the air.

He leant in towards me and tried to brush a kiss on my cheek but all I felt was the cool chill of air, like a butterfly wing brushing over me, "I might be able to help grant one of those wishes Mira, I just wish that I could grant both", his voice sounded far away even though he was so close to me. Then raising his arms he summoned the last of his soul power aiming it at the bag placed around my hip. The lip of the bag opened and out floated the solidified tear of the Pegasus from Skye and the Seed from Emerald Valley, the two gifts from the element souls that I had yet to use. He lifted them up and forced them into the light of the Sceptre and winked at me before noise took over all my senses.

BOOM! CRASH! WHOOSH!

The light exploded out and whooshed up into the air and merged with the final element soul, the dragon absorbed all our power and regenerated the wounds on its wings. It spun it the air around the crow making a vacuum effect around it, the crow so tired it gave in to the vacuum and drifted around the air like a rag doll. The dragon stopped suddenly and opened its mouth and I watched as the biggest ball of colourful flame burst out and smashed into the crow. The crow screeched in pain, all its feathers melting off from its torso, its eyes alive with pure pain and anguish.

"NOOOO! This cannot be happening to meeeee!" Luciferia's voice screamed as all the crows powers left her. We all watched as her and her wicked power exploded in the sky leaving a swirl of feathers gliding down from the heavens, like autumnal leaves falling from the trees. Cosima fell silent as everyone watched the rain of feathers but there was something else falling.

I stepped away from my friends and walked over to where the thing was falling, the shower of feathers covered my whole body as I reached her. I gently lifted my arms out and took hold of the baby that fell from the sky.

"From death comes new life", Nuelle spoke softly from beside me, I hadn't heard or seen her glide over to join me.

"I don't understand?"

"Thane granted your wish, the Pegasus tear can cleanse away evil poisons from ones soul and the seed from the Tree Nymph can regenerate new life into the old...He allowed her to be reborn".

"So this is Andromeda, she has been reborn?"

Nuelle nodded slowly, "Andromeda wasn't born evil, Luciferia cursed Andromeda's mind with the darkness and you have just freed her. You have given her the chance to grow up and live her life how it should have been".

"So what happens now?" I asked, the air still dancing with the dead wings of the crow.

"You raise her to become what she should have been", Nuelle smiled and touched the babies hand who in turn let out a happy gurgle, "A good Queen, a good true Queen".

"You mean, I have to raise her?"

She nodded, "Yes, strange birthday present for a sixteen year old I know but you will have all your friends to help you".

I turned to look at them all, Fira who was sobbing with happiness, Brooklyn who just looked confused and Isaura who held Willow as they both worried over their loved ones.

I looked down at the baby I held in my arms, the glow of the darkest royal black hair, her cute small features and her gurgling smile, "I don't want her to know of her past, of what she done", I said approaching the others, "I don't want Junia to know that I am raising the witch who nearly destroyed it all, even if in reality it wasn't really her. I don't think the people of Junia would fully understand".

"Then don't tell them, just tell them she is your child now", Nuelle said.

"I want to change her name, I want her to have a real fresh start…"

Nuelle nodded, "Then change it".

"Will she? Will she grow up to be evil again?" Fira asked a slight worried look on her face.

Nuelle shook her head, "No, that was a different part of her which you all banished, she is a baby again, a pure and innocent soul. She is good as long as you all teach her to be good".

I stared into those dark eyes, "Then I will rename her…Topaz…"

Suddenly all the element converters before me bowed and recalled her name, "Princess Topaz of Junia".

But there was one person missing, one person who wasn't bowing and rejoicing in the rebirth of the princess. The one person I named her for as he had shown me the crystal Topaz plant in Skye…Thane.

I spun on the spot and looked around, "Thane?" I called out.

Nuelle came and took my face gently in her hands, "He has gone now".

"But I didn't get to say goodbye", I choked.

She lowered her head, "I am sorry, my Queen".

I held the baby, Topaz close to my chest as I felt my heart shatter into a million pieces and cried a million tears for the love of my life.

~ Light Paradise ~

I sat on the throne waiting for Mr Phillipe to stop faffing around, I was due to go on the air in just a few moments to address my Kingdom and he was so excited it was driving me insane.

I was nowhere near as nervous as I was the first time I went on air, I mean I had stopped Junia from falling and I was now raising the child who had nearly caused it all as my own. I wore one of my own dresses this time, not one of my mother's, I guess it just felt too disrespectful of me to do so now. After all I had been through I wanted people to see me for me. My dress was a delicate cream with pure Beach Haven pearls all sewn into the corset of the fabric and a shimmer of mother of pearl combined into the material of the skirt. A new tiara had been made for me from platinum and a gem to represent every country of

Junia, Aquamarine for Beach Haven, Celestite for Spirit, Emerald for Emerald Valley, Ruby for Lavara, Topaz for Skye and Jet for Cosima. A few diamonds were also scattered across it for that expensive and regal look.

Next to me on the throne was Topaz who I had dressed in a similar dress to mine, a small cream and pearl embroidered headband settled across her dark hair. And all around me were the converters, all dressed in their countries colours, all their clothing shimmering and regal looking. I had made them my ladies in waiting, my protectors and my friends.

Mr Phillipe bowed to me, "Queen Mira, are you ready to address your Kingdom?"

I nodded, "I am".

He counted me down, "5,4,3,2,1…" The Junia anthem played in the background and I heard him announce my name, Mira the Queen of Junia.

I sat on my throne, my head held high, "My people of Junia, the war has been won, the ground we stand on is slowly healing, the religions have been accepted back onto Cosiman soil and we now know there was indeed a sixth element…The element of Cosima to control the Universe and Time…The final element soul who saved us all".

I could hear cheers outside of the grand throne room and I knew it was the maids and servants watching the screens out there, cheering me on. It made me feel warm and loved and I knew it shone over my face.

"Cosima would also like to thank the element converters who left their temples and their homes to help save the world we live in. Without their help none of this would have been possible. I also want to thank everyone in Junia for fighting for your countries and for never giving up hope. I also send praise to the countries of Junia whose temples were destroyed by the attacks, aid will be sent along with money to rebuild them all. I would also like to get everyone to remember all those who fell, all those precious souls who were lost to the dark times. I declare that each year on this day we will celebrate them by having it as a remembrance day, Fallen Souls Day".

I then went on to explain about who Topaz was but a slightly unauthenticated version made up by all of us converters together. We had decided to tell Junia that Topaz was indeed actually my own child, that Thane had been my long term boyfriend and father to my child and would have been the King for my Queen's throne but he had died in battle saving us and that I had gone into labour shortly after the final battle from shock. The people of Junia rejoiced at the news of a new-born princess, after all the bloodshed, death and sadness that had become Junia over the past few weeks was now blossoming into something happier, with Topaz being the new bud to blossom.

Another cheer sounded and I felt bad for lying to my people, lying like so many generations of my family had done but I had to protect her innocence. If anyone found out they may try to revive the evil that had once been and I couldn't allow that. She was to be protected by me.

Mr Phillipe soon wrapped things up and it was back to normal palace duties for everyone else.

Once I was allowed to leave I took Topaz into the palace gardens which was now in full bloom. The smell of the fresh flowers reminded me of my childhood playing hide and seek from Freya in all the shrubbery and as I clung to Topaz I wished all that happiness for her. I glided through all the gardens until I found the palace cemetery, two new and shiny graves sat polished in the Cosiman high sun. *Queen Espinosia and King Jacobious.* There was also a plush marble statue to represent all the lives lost of the citizens of Junia, I lent down and placed a wreath of crystal Topaz flowers in the hope that they might be able to be reborn just like my own Topaz had. I then wondered over to my parents graves and placed one on each of theirs before letting Topaz down to crawl around on the soft grass, then I spoke to them.

"Mum…Dad…I hope wherever you are that you can be proud of me? I'm sorry I couldn't save you both or bring you both back. I miss you so much and wish that I could see you again to tell you how much I love you but I know you have always known my love for you. I wish you could have met Topaz, she's beautiful you know, a true royal princess with the most amazing smile. I think one day she will make a great Queen for Junia, a good Queen".

I sat there for a while in the warm sun, watching my adoptive daughter play with the petals of a daisy. I was in a world of my own and didn't hear Nuelle approached from the palace, "Mira?"

"Yes Nuelle?"

"If you could have one thing, one thing only what would it be?"

"Nuelle you're not making sense?" I replied letting out a small laugh and picking up my child from the grass and snuggling her into my arms.

All the others came and stood beside us, I noticed how Nate had snuck out to see Willow. I had asked him to be in charge of my palace guard and he had promoted Kenton to his second in command. Stormra too had decided to stay at the palace as one of the maids, said she liked the warmth here.

"What is the one thing your heart would ask for?" She said.

I looked down at the hem of my dress but I couldn't see my shoes, "To see him, one last time, to say…Goodbye".

"Then come with me", she exclaimed and made me pass Topaz to Fira who took the little princess to play. She took my hand and led me along the grand halls which were still being redecorated and fixed up. Although the merge of the two Cosima's had been almost plain sailing some fixtures needed to be fixed and there was the fact that I wanted all the fake royal red to be eliminated from our home.

She took me to the Queen's chambers which had now become my own, "I have a gift", she beamed swishing the doors open. The rooms had been decorated for me, in delicate silvers, greys and royal black hues. The carpet looked almost like the shimmering velvet of Nuelle's cloak, my huge four poster bed adorned with sheets of silk and curtains made from the finest crushed velvet. Topaz's cot sat to one side also decorated with pretty silver baby blankets, I didn't want her out of my sight now she was my responsibility. She stopped at the large centre piece wall which had a grand fireplace built in and above it, a mirror. A special mirror from Spirit I could tell by the graceful design.

"For me?" I smiled and touched it, my fingers shaking with anticipation.

She nodded, "Yes. A rather late coronation present but still a great gift don't you think?"

"Nuelle I love it, thank you".

"Glad you like it, I will leave you to look it over".

"Oh no you don't have to…Go", but she had already left the room and closed the door quietly behind her.

I walked around the room, my heart a little deflated, I thought she had meant something else that I might see him, to say goodbye. He was the one thing my heart desired…Nothing else…Well other than my parents but that was a different need altogether, he was my one true love, the one person I wanted to see just one last time.

After sitting on my bed for a while staring at my new gift I soon wondered over to the mirror and looked into it, my long dark hair trailed around my pale features in waves. I stood for a while but saw nothing, only me. I turned away but stopped when I heard it.

"Mira?"

"Thane?" I glanced into the mirror and saw him, his charming face looking back out at me, his boyish grin and his dark brown hair. "THANE".

"Er yeah it's me", he laughed.

"But how?"

"I refused to leave for the heavens, I'm a lost soul now…So Nuelle put me in here, to keep me safe and so I could be with you".

Tears ran down my cheeks as I placed my hand to the cool glass, "Forever?"

He lifted his hand to mine, "Forever".

~ The End ~

Thank you for taking the time to read my book 'Junia', can I ask a favour? I can? Why thank you. If you enjoyed this book would you please leave me a review on Amazon and Goodreads. Reviews help independently published authors like myself and would mean so much to me. Thanks again and I pray to Junia for you.

.x.x.x.x.